Aaron's War

a novel of war and devotion

Richard McMaster

Aaron's War by Richard McMaster

ISBN: 979-8-218-40702-5

Praise for Aarons War

Barnes and Nobel review and selection for catalog

An unglamorous and comprehensive look at WWII through the life of Aaron Vanko. This composite begins with Aaron, an Iowa farm boy, a senior in high school. He is caught up in war fever, and, despite the objections of his parents, and he joins his two friends, Tony and Fritz, as they enlist. He marries his best girl, Mary, before he leaves, despite the disapproval of both sets of parents.

Unlike many war stories, this novel in three parts, follows Aaron through enlistment, marriage and boot camp; then the horrors of the march through France, freezing cold, subsistence rations and the Battle of the Bulge, when only Mary's letters sustain him; and, finally, the readjustment from military back to civilian life.

This remarkable book offers a most realistic look at the effects of war on the soldier, but also on his family, friends, and fellow recruits.

• *USA TODAY Best-Selling Author Holly S. Roberts* - **A coming of age story** that grips your soul and takes you on a thought-provoking journey.

• *Judge's Commentary, Writers Digest* - **The premise behind this wartime tale,** that a boy signs up to fight the enemy only to find out that he has a bigger stake in things than he realized, is one I haven't really encountered and it worked out well. Watching Aaron struggle not only with how to be a soldier in the middle of a war, but a Jew, was fascinating. And on top of that, he fell in love, married, and while away at war, found out that he was going to be a father. Any of those identity crises would be enough to break a person, so it's no surprise that by the time he returns to the United States, he is a changed man and doesn't know how to readjust to civilian life. This book offers a pretty realistic take on the war and doesn't glorify or romanticize things, which I greatly appreciated. When he had the meal at the end with Bernhard, I enjoyed the simplicity that the German (who was actually French) laid things out for him: they were both Jewish and that's why he couldn't kill him. Talking things through, he encouraged Aaron to go home to his wife and let her help him, and I honestly feel that in that scene, he was my favorite character of the book. I felt that things flowed smoothly, honestly, and realistically through the book and was so glad to see a glimpse of hope reappear in Aaron by the ending.

• *Cindi Reise, President of Phoenix Writers Club* - **Extremely well written story** that kept you on its path with characters that are real and relatable and brought you along on their ride with ease. It touches on a problem that has been ignored for too long telling of the PTSD that our fathers and grandfathers covered with alcohol. Many accolades to you, and you are a poet!

• *Tom Porter, author of All I Need to Know About Business I Learned from A Duck* - **An engaging,** informative and thought-provoking tale of survival, love and faith. Make room for Richard McMaster on your list of up-and-coming authors."

• *Pam Robertson* - **There is no end of stories** dealing with WWII. Richard McMaster has written a story of a farm boy from Iowa who joins up for this war, then falls in love. "Aaron's War" takes what might seem like a predictable story and surprises the reader to the last page. You would expect PTSD to be an issue, but there are lots of other interesting characters and twists in this book. Aaron's return to 'life' won't disappoint. I look forward to more from this author!

• *Unknown* - **Richard McMaster's newest work, Aaron's War,** is the author's third and best, fictional novel. Both the title and cover provide possible hints as to the book's contents. The military helmet signals a war, the fencepost, fencing and long grasses imply a rural setting and the title suggests that Aaron may be fighting more than just a military war. All are correct, but the author shares so much more in the pages that follow.

In 1943, at the height of US involvement in WWII, Aaron Vanko is a high school student living on an Iowa farm with his immigrant parents. He is a quiet and gentle teen whose childhood has been relatively simple. After enlisting in the army, Aaron begins to wonder if he even has the ability to kill the enemy. He also learns he is Jewish, but knows little of the Jewish faith, what it means to be a Jew, or how it might affect the Christian woman he plans to marry. *As he fights the enemy overseas, he continues to struggle with questions regarding Judaism and his responsibilities as a soldier. Now, surrounded by death and destruction, Aaron is haunted by the nightmares that rob him of sleep. He is fighting a new battle...a personal war. Rifles and guns won't win this this one because ultimately, it is a war between his heart and his head.

• *Lynn M Safris* - **Aaron's War is the story of Aaron** and his struggles to understand and resolve the conflicts he experiences as a teenager and as a young man living and serving his country in the war years of the '40's. The novel presents an intimate journey through the hell of "growing up" while fighting on the battlefields of WWII. It reveals the nightmarish effects the war leaves on one soldier and his loved ones and the personal war he is left with to fight alone. The descriptions and details given throughout this author's writing draw the reader into each page, making Aaron's journey feel like their own. I believe this book would appeal to a wide audience of readers. I truly enjoyed reading Aaron's War and I highly recommend this book.

• *Pamela Coulter, Phoenix Writers Club* - **This book starts out making you care** about the characters. They are well-drawn and sympathetic, with some unusual characteristics. I can see that this is a finely researched book, with authentic depictions of battles in WWII. Having laid the foundation of the protagonist so carefully, his movements through the battles, external and internal are realistic and gut-wrenching. This is something you want to keep reading. I would highly recommend this book.

• *JRLHTM* - **What seems to be just one more love story during WWII,** Richard McMaster's book "Aaron's War" has taken his main character and painted him with unpredictable twists and turns to keep the reader intrigued to the very last page. A recommended read for. You can tend to go on a bit explaining feelings, places, events etc., but some things are just hard to be brief about. Not once did I think, " just get on with it "!!! Or "why didn't you just say" .... Truth. It was really good. I invited my husband to read it...we'll see if he does. He's currently without a book to read. I panic without a read in the wings

• *Elizabeth Price* - **An unglamorous and comprehensive look at WWII** through the life of Aaron Vanko. This composite begins with Aaron, an Iowa farm boy, a senior in high school. He is caught up in war fever, and, despite the objections of his parents, and he joins his two friends, Tony and Fritz, as they enlist. He marries his best girl, Mary, before he leaves, despite the disapproval of both sets of parents.

Unlike many war stories, this novel in three parts, follows Aaron through enlistment, marriage and boot camp; then the horrors of the march through France, freezing cold, subsistence rations and the Battle of the Bulge, when only Mary's letters sustain him; and, finally, the readjustment from military back to civilian life.

This remarkable book offers a most realistic look at the effects of war on the soldier, but also on his family, friends, and fellow recruits.

• *Tim Asper* - **Our book club read this book** - we were initially drawn to it as we live in Iowa and the book is set in Iowa. It made for a great discussion. The story centers around a WWII vet who endures the terrible effects of PTSD and it was very insightful. This is one man's fictional journey, but it could describe so many soldiers in so many wars.

• - *Helpful* - **I enjoyed this book because it held my attention.** Aaron's mother revealed a deep family secret to him on the night before he left home to fight in world war II. I was never quite sure what was going to come next, to me, always the sign of a good book.. I did not realize what Aaron's issues were going to be, nor did I imagine anything about his big issue with the German soldier who would become a part of his life. This book is not a cut and dried story.

• *John R Risinger* - **Couldn't put it down** once I started reading. So good our book club read it, providing much thought-provoking discussion about our family members in WW II. Wonderful word pictures about patriotism, romantic love, anti-Semitism, the horrors of war and PTSD, and finally HOPE. Would recommend Aarons War as an excellent read!

Dedication

For Paula
From the Lucky One

Other Books by Richard McMaster

Voyage of Life. The Voyage of Life story is told as the Robert Cole *Voyage of Life* paintings are described: Childhood, Youth, Manhood, and Old Age. The paintings are a metaphor for Sean's life. In early manhood he thinks MADDY, his one true love, has left him for another man and spends his life wondering what happened.

Shadow in the Night. Twelve days before Christmas LUKE loses his job and his wife is called away to care for her dying mother. Left alone at Christmas time, of the major traumatic life events—being fired from a job, fearing divorce, plotting murder, the death of a family member and jail time, any one of which can threaten your very existence—he faces them all.

A Love Divided by Time. FORREST AND ALLIE believed they found love in a previous life and being born again was a game of hide and seek to find each other in plain sight, seeking their better halves, united and whole. When tragedy strikes, Forrest makes a pact to find her killer, raise their daughter, and find peace by joining her in the ever after.

2019 finalist unpublished book of the year of the Arizona Author's Association.

The Attic. The attic is an emotional story about facing adversity and overcoming loss. When BYRON KELLY's wife dies, he faces assault charges and a lawsuit, and flees to Chicago and assumes a new identity. When Byron Kelly becomes a whistleblower on the run from the FBI he hides out in the attic of a dying old man, HENRY STEELE. Byron cares for the old man and learns he is estranged from his daughter over the death of her mother, his wife, because of family secrets he has kept from her.

For information on other novels go to www.Richard-McMaster.com

Author's Note

World War II was a romantic time for my mother and father. They were in love. They needed each other. Mom said that after the war, Dad came back a different man. I remember one Christmas Eve when I was a young man, sitting around the tree with my grandparents waiting for Dad to come home so we could open presents. That Christmas, my sister got four sticks of butter and I a quarter pound of cashews. That is what we both wanted. When Dad came in the back door, Mom took him downstairs and I followed. He was lying on the dirty cold concrete basement floor. Mom gave him a blanket and told him to stay there. He was drunk. He died of liver cancer when I was young man, many said the result of years of alcoholic abuse.

I always thought Dad wasn't the tough guy he appeared to be. Hollywood perpetuates this kind of false imagery. It makes war seem so simple and straightforward. Soldiers kill or are killed. And it makes the watcher believe that people kill each other because they are told to and the enemy is evil. Rarely do moviemakers expose the underbelly of killing, the damage done to those who pull the trigger. Hollywood tries to make us believe that all soldiers engage in combat and fire at each other. Yet, according to research cited in the book *On Killing: The Psychological Cost of Learning to Kill in War and Society*, by Dave Grossman, only 15–20 percent of the soldiers fired at the enemy in

WWII. For soldiers who have an aversion to killing or engage in closeup killing, the PTSD effects are more profound.

Studies have shown that the more time soldiers are in combat, the more likely they are to become a psychiatric casualty.

Aaron, the gentle soldier, is the son of Jewish immigrant parents. As his platoon fights their way into the heart of Germany, his religious conflicts grow. The cities he passes through feature magnificent churches and synagogues, German soldiers carry Bibles and even wear belts engraved with the words *Gott Mit Un* (God with us). Melding with Aaron's aversion to killing are thoughts of destroying men who worship the same God. Aaron searches for answers as to who his God is, and why his marriage to a Christian woman is forbidden.

Aaron was given his name by his Jewish father and mother. Biblically, Aaron (*Ahron*) was the brother of Moses and the first high priest. *The Pentateuch*, the first five books of the Hebrew Bible, lays out the laws of Moses, and fifteen times the Lord speaks to Moses and Aaron. Aaron was known for loving and pursuing peace. He is also an Islamic patriarch, and the Quran refers to him as a prophet. The story of Biblical Aaron resonates today as man overwhelms religion with interpretations or casts it aside.

I thought the character name was appropriate for one of the messages of the story about my Aaron, the gentle soldier who was confused about his own religion in a war where Christians were killing Christians and Germans were attempting to eradicate the Jewish race.

Part 1

THE JOURNEY FROM HOME

Maybe is suspended by a thin thread high up between yes and no,
the arbitrator of the two.
Yes knows and no knows. Both can be wrong.
Maybe sees beyond the end of the stream,
knowing it does not end, is always seeking its way home.
Maybe knows beyond the dark night that the sun can rise,
And beyond the sunset a restful night.

Voyage of Life
—Richard McMaster

1

AARON VANKO WAS a quiet, wavy-haired farm boy who lived with his Ukrainian parents near Ankeny, Saylor Township, an unincorporated area north of Des Moines, Iowa. His parents sold chickens and eggs to townsfolk and nearby restaurants. He helped the family eke out a living growing beans and corn and raising cows and chickens, which made him strong. Well over six feet, he was the tallest and strongest boy in his school. Like his Woodside High classmates, totaling only seven boys and eight girls, he longed to leave his youth and step boldly into manhood.

Fritz, his best friend, was voted the most likely to succeed and Aaron, everyone teased, was destined for the priesthood. He was embarrassed by the talk, since his family never went to church. And angry that his friends didn't think he would be a good soldier.

It was 1943, and war was uppermost in everyone's mind, on the streets, in homes, in schools, at the markets, and on the job. Late at night in hushed bedroom conversations, often just a few words ended the day. Someone would say, "Our boys are givin' 'em hell!" sometimes with conviction, sometimes from fear. There was no such talk on the Vanko farm. Discussing the war was forbidden. Serious dinner conversations were strictly limited to farming and schooling.

Aaron called Samuel *Bat'ko*, which meant *father* in their Ukrainian dialect. His mother, Mary, went by *Maty*, which meant *mother*. They sometimes called him *syn*, for *son*.

Whenever Aaron brought up anything about the war, Bat'ko would always say, "War is for other people, not for us." Chewing his food as if gnawing on a grisly piece of meat, his father would grimace, "War settles nothing and is usually about nothing, except greed. Boys are just checkers in their little games."

Maty lifted her head and smiled. "And how was school today?" Asking about Aaron's schooling was always her way of changing the subject.

Whenever Aaron asked Maty where they came from, who their relatives were, why they didn't go to church, she always scrunched up her face and dismissed him with a wave of her hand. He learned at an early age that when Maty and Bat'ko waved the back of their hands in the air that was the end of the discussion. Sometimes, when she raised her open hand, she had no answers.

As Aaron matured, he appreciated Maty's gentle wisdom. To questions of religion, which Aaron often asked her, she would close her eyes and say in her broken English "*Syn*. What do we need of religion? We have God right here. Right here." She opened her eyes and gently held her hands out, palms open. "Right here in this room." Dinner conversations that veered into forbidden territory often ended abruptly, like one was falling off a cliff. Tonight was no different. Looking at his father, Aaron blurted out, "Bat'ko, Fritz and Tony are enlisting."

Bat'ko didn't look up from his plate. He waved his hand dismissively.

"Bat'ko, why can't we ever talk about anything but school and farming? Everybody is joining the fight. Even the girls at school are asking who's gonna join, and they all talk about going to work at the ordnance plant. We have to—"

Maty stopped chewing and squinted at Aaron, then cautiously back to Bat'ko, who scowled.

"That's just big talk, boy talk. You're not a man. You don't know. You do your talking out there with your friends, not at my dinner table." Bat'ko waved his hand toward the front door. "War is not good. Ever. Here, we don't talk about war."

That night after Aaron went to bed, when Samuel and Ida finished their prayers and rose up from their knees to climb into bed, Ida said, "You know Aaron will be drafted?"

Pulling the covers up tight under his neck, warming himself as the last logs he tossed on the fire were dying out, Samuel closed his eyes, and said in a hoarse whisper, "Never. I don't want to hear that."

* * *

Sleep came hard. All night, Samuel Vanko reminisced about a time he had forced from his thinking. He had fled Ukraine with his parents when he was nine years old, after the Russians destroyed Husiatyn, leaving behind his older brother, David, who had disappeared. They ran to avoid the soldiers, who conscripted able-bodied boys, killing or driving everyone else away from their land. Fire destroyed more than 600 buildings in the small town, and Jews were forcibly moved from the western borders of Russia toward the interior. About 100,000 exiles died of exposure or starvation; those who stayed were raped and murdered. Local kids, openly formed anti-Semitic gangs and joined into the sport of hunting down and killing Jews.

The three refugees fled Ukraine for Czechoslovakia, where they were taken in by a Christian family. Samuel left behind memories of horrors and loose ends, of bearded old men and soldiers and fires, and tried to forget. He was a good student, and after his family moved to New York, he became a part of a close-knit Jewish community. Three years after celebrating his Bar Mitzvah, he was married to another refugee from his country, Ida Gottstein, in a match arranged by her Aunt Batya. But he still couldn't find peace or forget what he knew. He could see how Jews were treated even in America, how they stayed to themselves, how the rabbis went along with segregation, cautious and passive. Samuel's bat'ko hated the rabbis of Husiatyn for not fighting the Russians, and now he had to deal with them in New York. Samuel wanted the promise of America, to raise a family as a family, not as persecuted Jews, not feeling as unsafe in New York as in his native Ukraine.

Samuel had studied hard, and over time, rarely spoke in his native Ukrainian tongue. He admonished Ida to learn better English and not to use Ukrainian words in front of Aaron. "Forget you were Ukrainian. Forget the past," he would say. "Aaron will be an American. Remember how the Russians hated us. Let him be free of all of that."

* * *

Sleep was hard to find in the Vanko house that night. Lying awake as the fire faded, Ida waited, silent and still, bundled against the rising Iowa cold. Aaron tossed and turned in his bed just a few feet away on the other side of the wall, while Bat'ko and Maty stared into the darkness. Ida knew Samuel wasn't asleep, because he hadn't started snoring. These days, snoring was a blessing, as welcome as summer storms in drought.

Samuel broke the silence. "We have him now."

Ida rolled over and placed her arm on his chest. "This is America. If he has to, he will serve with honor. This is not like home, where they steal fourteen-year-old boys for the army even though they hate us."

"Yes, this is America. Still, they take young boys to fight their wars," Samuel said.

"Maybe it will be different. At least they don't steal them."

"I know David's dead. I know it in my heart. I still see him at night. It would have been kinder had they shot him." Samuel always said he would rather the town fight the Russians and die than to let them take their boys. "But maybe—"

"Bat'ko, this is not Russia."

Aaron listened to them murmuring, half hearing. He wanted to tell them he was going to enlist with his friends, soon. He wanted them to be proud. Watching the cold fall sky through his window, he waited for sleep.

* * *

Friday night was unusually warm. Winter bared its teeth early in November, but Iowa weather was as well known for its extremes as it was for corn. Bitter, cold winter with wind chill temperatures fifty below zero. Sweltering over-100-degree summer days blanketed nights of hunting for sleep lying in a pool of your own sweat. Hourly swings in weather were not a surprise to Iowans when late fall days played tug-of-war with winter ones. There were even brief, occasional, surprise summer interruptions.

"Let's go fishing. It's the last time we can fish until spring," was the way Tony put it. "The catfish'll be biting." Tony always thought the fish were biting, and Fritz and Aaron usually went along because he brought the Schlitz beer.

Fritz, Tony, and Aaron had been first playground friends in grade school, teammates in sports, and classmates in high school.

When they were nine years old, they had cut their fingers with Aaron's pocket knife behind Tony's father's bakery and pressed them together, vowing to be blood brothers for life. Playmates, classmates, teammates, family—and one day, war mates.

Fritz Adele was a fourth-generation German American. His great-grandfather landed in the colonies in 1750 on the ship *Phoenix*. His Aryan blond hair and blue-eyed intensity were gifts from his Swedish schoolteacher mom. Fritz was about the same height as Aaron, a full six feet, but his broader shoulders and barrel chest gave him the look of a bear wrestler. He was muscular from head to toe; his thick neck blended into broad shoulders. Without a T-shirt, he drew second glances even from other boys. His father worked for the Enterprise Coal Company, one of the top coal producers in Iowa, employing half the Ankeny population.

Tony Stallone was more than a head shorter than his two blood brothers. He was pure Italian with a Roman nose, long, dark face, and lean, wiry body. Tony, cheerfully nicknamed "Wop" by his close friends, lived on a small farm, just a mile as the crow flies from Aaron's. His folks owned a small bakery in Highland Park, on the north side of Des Moines, delivering fresh Italian bread, dinner rolls, sweet- cream or jam-filled *cornettos*, and *panettone* to area grocery stores and homes.

War talk was hard to avoid, and Tony's bragging and Fritz's steely patriotism were logs on the fire of schoolboy pressure. The threat of the draft loomed over hero stories, anxiety and patriotism running into the rising count of boys who had already enlisted and died. Being drafted felt less patriotic than volunteering, but Aaron still felt torn.

The fish weren't biting, and the cloudless, full-moon night was turning frosty. Tony sat on the river bank covered with a blanket. "Fritz, what are you gonna do?" Tony asked.

Without hesitation, Fritz answered, "I'm in. It's the right thing to do. I ain't waiting to be drafted!"

Tony added quickly, "Me too." Looking to Fritz, he continued, "I'd better join up, or the war'll be over before I get there. If we all sign up together, I heard they'll send us to the same unit."

"Wouldn't that be wacky?" Fritz chuckled.

"Aaron?" Tony poked him. "Hey, you awake?"

Aaron was especially quiet tonight. He knew Fritz and Tony's folks were different. Tony's father liked to talk about his Army days in World War I, how they broke through the German lines in the battle of the Hindenburg Line, a hundred-day offensive. Aaron wanted to do the right thing, but Maty and Bat'ko would be so disappointed. Still, he was going to be drafted anyway, so why not? After a long silence, Aaron said, "Let's join tomorrow. You really think we could stay together?"

Tony had pulled the blanket tight and was snoring.

"I'm sure Wop's with us," Fritz said. "But I think he might sleep through the war."

"You and me better stand guard," Aaron said, laughing.

For several minutes Aaron and Fritz contemplated the commitment they'd just made as they watched the black river water lumber past to the sounds of a hoot owl and Tony's snoring.

Fritz broke the silence. "Don't feel like you have to." "What do you mean?"

"You don't have to join up, just because we're friends." "What are you saying?" Aaron huffed.

"If you want to, but if you want to wait—"

After a long silence, Fritz looked back to Aaron. "You still awake?"

Aaron huddled under a blanket staring across the water, watching a taut fishing line pulsate in the swift current. The moon trailed directly up to his feet. He grunted just enough to acknowledge the question.

"I wonder if I'll make it back," Fritz said softly.

Aaron pondered the statement, wondering what to say, or whether to say anything "What are you talking about? Don't think like that," Aaron admonished.

"Just a weird feeling."

Aaron shivered. "Nah. Not you, man."

Suddenly the wind shifted to the northwest. Iowa winters usually rode in on northwest winds. "I don't think war is all they're saying it is. Do you believe all that stuff?"

"Nah, it's all just talk."

"What do you think my chances are?" Aaron asked. "I'd bet on you, Mister Smarty Pants," Fritz laughed.

Aaron had earned all A's on his last report card, for the first time. But Fritz always got A's. Tony was the underachiever of the trio, struggling for C's.

"You know . . ." Fritz didn't finish the sentence and the moment drifted in the cool night air. "You know, I figure there are two kinds of people," Fritz said. "Those who can kill and those who can't." He looked over at Aaron. "Do you remember when Billy Hunter came after you? I heard he sucker-punched you. What was that all about?"

"Billy thought I put some chickens in the front seat of his truck. Guess they made a mess."

"Heard you walked away. You could have kicked his ass. Hell, you could kick my ass."

Aaron got the point. "Could you, you know, kill someone? Would it bother you at all?" he asked his friend.

"Sure, I can. Damn straight I could," Fritz answered proudly.

"I don't know," Aaron said. "It's hard to imagine killing someone. Seems they're just soldiers. They'd be like us, wouldn't they?"

"I can't think about that. That'd get me killed for sure." The river lapped against the bank as Tony's snoring grew louder. "Okay, if a man raped and killed your sister, you'd have to kill him, right?" Fritz asked.

"I don't have a sister."

"I would. Wouldn't everybody?"

"I'd like to kill your sister. She's always hanging around."

"Yeah," Fritz chuckled.

A few minutes later Aaron broke the silence. "You mean, if I caught him in the act, or after he was arrested?"

"Like it would make a difference!"

A few minutes later, Fritz tossed a rock in the river and laughed. "I put the chickens in Billy's truck."

Aaron laid back on his blanket and smiled. Pulling his coat tight, he folded his arms and stared into the sky, where only a few brave stars were visible under the full moon.

Aaron thought about killing and the time years earlier when his father had bought him a BB gun for Christmas. Every day he had lined up cans on the fencepost, and before long, he had become a good shot. He had even called his mom and dad from the barn to show them how he could plink one off its perch in rapid fire from twenty yards. Months later, walking in the wooded area behind their house, his BB gun slung over his shoulder, he had spotted a cardinal in a tree and slowly crept up to within a few yards. The cardinal hadn't flown away, basking in the first warm summer day, singing, calling for a mate, *purdy purdy purdy . . . whoit, whoit, whoit, whoit. Psst!* The BB hit the cardinal mid-chest and a red drop of blood appeared. The cardinal turned his head and tried to shake his feathers to rid himself of the pinch in his chest, staring at Aaron as if he were asking why.

Purdy, purdy, purdy. The bird leaned forward and fell, banging into the branches of the tree and then to the ground. His feet were stiff and pointed skyward. Aaron remembered how his heart raced and the guilty feeling as he stared at the lifeless bird.

A rustling in the woods nearby startled Aaron back to the present. A deer crept out into the open, as if attempting to tip-toe past the three boys. The buck still had a rack of antlers on one side, having shed the other. Was this Aaron's buck? Was that too long ago?

He thought of the time when he was ten, when his father had taken him hunting for the first time. They had sat at dusk in the brush, out of sight, waiting for what his dad promised the biggest buck he would ever see.

"It will be a full rack, antlers here to there. You will see, sin," Bat'ko had said, holding his hands out wide. They had held their breath, listening intently for the buck breaking through the brush. Every sound had sent off alarm bells. Just as his eyelids had begun to droop, his dad had nudged him. There, larger than he imagined, was the buck.

Holding his finger to his lips, moving in slowly, Bat'ko handed the gun to Aaron. Aaron remembered how important he felt like a grown-up. Manhood offered before its time. Shouldering the gun, just as he had so many times in target practice, he had taken careful aim. The buck turned and looked back, as if he were staring directly at Aaron, his big brown eyes locked on his. The gun had exploded and knocked Aaron back. The deer had darted into the woods.

Father's prideful smile had turned to a frown when he had looked back to Aaron. "What happened? You're a good shot. Are you blind?"

2

IT HAD BEEN two years of talk among blood brothers, two years of hard thinking about responsibility and courage. Aaron had been sixteen in 1941 when the Japanese bombed Pearl Harbor. The radio had run a news alert sometime Sunday afternoon as Aaron had been riding in Fritz's just-repaired 1932 Chevy coupe, on their way to Des Moines.

When Aaron returned home with the news, he rushed into the barn to find his father pitching straw into the horse stall. Bat'ko looked up, nodded, and kept pitching. For several minutes, the only sounds were of the airy old barn breathing in and out, the pitchfork tines scraping on the hard-packed dirt floor and Bat'ko's groans as he pitched straw, one sweep after another.

Aaron leaned his lanky frame against one of the barn supports and watched him. His father had changed. He looked older. Or maybe it was Aaron who'd changed. He now shaved daily and had a five o'clock shadow at the end of the day. He felt different, too. Did it show? Did Bat'ko notice?

Standing beside him, as if he were also waiting for Bat'ko to look up from pitching straw, was the large family dog Cubby, named because from a distance, he looked like a bear cub. He was ink- black with pearl-white teeth that flashed ominously at strangers or smiled whenever he saw Aaron. The black dog had just strolled in one day, with no invitation, and joined the family, digging into his own comfortable spot under the back porch.

The war in Europe had been underway for years, but in 1941, Pearl Harbor became a household name when 188 US aircraft were destroyed, 2,403 Americans were killed, and 1,178 others were wounded. The last vestiges of American isolationism were shredded. Enlistments would leave every neighborhood or farm community to part with their young men, many of whom would never return.

Aaron, like so many others, couldn't hold back his feelings. He finally blurted out, "The Japanese have bombed Pearl Harbor!"

Bat'ko stood erect and let out a sigh as he grabbed his lower back and grimaced. Leaning against the stall, he looked back to Aaron. "Vat is this Pearl Harbor?"

Aaron exploded with the news, despite Bat'ko's taboo about discussing the war. His father nodded and took a deep breath. From that moment on, the atmosphere in the Vanko house would change. Bat'ko would no longer sit at the kitchen table and watch him do his schoolwork. For the first time since kindergarten, there would be no more father learning from son. Maty had used to clean in circles around them, under elbows and papers, feigning disinterest, clanging pots and pans. Then out of the blue, she would ask a question. "Vat is this Mississippi?"

"It's a state, like, you know, the United States of America. And a river, too. A long and powerful river," Aaron stated proudly.

"*Vat is this Pearl Harbor?*" Were the words *Pearl Harbor* so life-changing?

Bat'ko was out the door before first light, sometimes skipping breakfast, and returning to the barn after dinner. Dinners only got more awkward. Maty did her best to keep the peace. Aaron came to feel like he was holding his breath around Bat'ko.

By 1943, when the first Doolittle bombs were dropped on Tokyo, the war was being waged in the Pacific, on the water and the islands. American forces joined the ground war in North Africa and Italy at the same time Germany was consolidating extensive European land holdings and propping up puppet governments. German submarines terrorized the seas. There were now 121 U-boats. In the first three months of 1942, 273 merchant ships were sunk. Hitler was carrying out plans to annihilate Jews, social misfits, Gypsies, homosexuals, pacifists, and criminals of any kind. The drafting of young American men was in full force.

Aaron's classmates were changing with the news. Everything seemed more urgent, more important. Two years after the Pearl Harbor attack, the talk of killing Jerries and Japs came easy.

Also, like all other generations of boys, Aaron and his classmates stood helplessly at the threshold of manhood. Exploding hormones turned their heads toward even the faintest glance from girls, the sound of giggling, the sweet scent of Chanel No.5. In the ageless dance between the sexes, boys were no match for the fandango of batting eyelashes from soft-curved, curly-haired girls. Irresistible instincts pushed them all to get on with marrying and producing children.

And why not choose a girl now? The black cloud of war sparked feelings that life had to be packed into a brief span of time. Finding that one girl could provide a partner who could share the fears a boy couldn't share with friends. And with her, you could leave an heir to continue your name and memory. War talk also added some twists to the hunt between the sexes. Some boys had unspoken fears of fighting a war without having experienced the first tingle of holding a woman naked in their arms, or of carrying the unmanly secret that they hadn't.

So, after a night of patriotic poking and probing, three blood brothers had come of age as they rounded the corner of finishing high school and watched older boys parade off to war. They committed to enlisting the next day. Thoughts of joining in the fight took on an air of setting out on a big game hunt in Africa.

Aaron knew enlisting was the right thing to do, but the boasting of friends and the silence around the dinner table was unnerving. Boys he knew had already served, and some had died or returned to face the life of a cripple or an amputee. And there was no doubt that Bat'ko would disapprove. Maty would cry.

Aaron avoided his parents the next morning, rushing out the door as soon as Fritz pulled up to the house. Bat'ko was in the barn and Maty in the kitchen. Aaron breezed by her and mumbled a goodbye as he bolted.

In Highland Park, they met with Sergeant Taggart, an Army recruiter and grizzled veteran who walked with a cane. His back- slapping, jovial enthusiasm was contagious and brought smiles to the boys' lips. His description of Army life was strategically slanted, and they ate up his stories of misery twisted toward honor. He made boredom sound like leisure time, killing the enemy like arcade shooting. With a twinkle in his eye, he nudged Fritz. "Girls love Army uniforms most. In Europe, the women fall all over themselves for Army guys."

Taggart's raspy voice boomed into the room, and he kept making them repeat themselves, both signs of his deafness, the product of too much time on the artillery range. His shouting felt like a celebration to the boys.

"American Army soldiers are the best fed and the best equipped. I just came back from Italy. Fighting the Italian army is like hunting hedgehogs: they're dumb, and they stink." He laughed. "You ever seen the Italian flag? It's all white." The recruiting sergeant guffawed, slapping his thighs. "Say now, Tony, you're not Italian, are you?

"Well, yes, sir, I am."

"Well, the Italians we're fighting aren't relatives of yours, that's for sure. They're fascists."

When the sergeant was alone with Aaron, he lowered his voice and said in a fatherly tone, "I see you're listed as a farmer?"

"Yes. I live on a farm with my folks."

"You know they grant deferments for farmers, don't you? It's an option if you have any doubts."

"It doesn't matter," Aaron stated proudly. "I want to fight."

Taggart gave them a rundown of dates and boot camp expectations. "Boot camp will probably be in Mississippi. You hear that, boys? You're gonna get a little vacation from the miserable Iowa weather. I'm a California boy. I could never live here. You'll hear from us on when to report, but not until after you graduate."

Several times, he promised them they'd be together through boot camp and said no doubt they'd serve in the same unit. He said he slept in a double bed, which resulted in giggles and rolling eyes as they planned for their own adventures, shook hands, signed the forms, and practiced saluting enthusiastically.

When they left the recruiting station, Tony wanted to show them the Basilica of St. John, a Catholic Church located just north of the Des Moines loop. "We can't leave until you see this place! It makes the church in Ankeny look like a shack! Seriously!" Dedicated sixteen years before, it resembled St. Paul's Basilica outside the walls of Rome.

Aaron had never seen a church so big. A 100-foot-high campanile housed a 600-pound bronze bell beside the main structure. Aaron had attended Catholic mass two weeks ago with Fritz in Ankeny. It had been more uncomfortable than dreaming he was naked on the first day of school. But he pretended to be as excited as Tony and hoped he wouldn't embarrass himself.

As they entered the Basilica of St. John, Fritz and Tony dipped their fingers in a bowl of holy water, kneeled, and moved their hands down from their foreheads and back and forth across their chest so fast that Aaron didn't know what to do. Bat'ko and Maty always said prayers of thanksgiving for the blessing of food on the table and good health but didn't cross themselves. He mumbled and kneeled.

Usually Tony was loud and animated, but inside these hallowed walls, he whispered and moved reverently, like a barefoot monk.

He grabbed Aaron's arm. "Hey, you don't have to do the stuff we do. I know you don't go to church here."

As they entered the classic Roman nave, Aaron crooked his neck to admire a cavernous half-moon, gold-leaf ceiling. Standing like sentries were Roman columns finished in plaster and Travertine marble. Their hushed words echoed above two long rows of pews that stretched out in waves. Below the ceiling stretched clerestory windows, reaching out to the heavens, depicting the life of Jesus: his birth, him as a young man, loaves and fishes, the crucifixion, and the resurrection. Aaron had heard his friends refer to Jesus before, casually in conversations, like when Fritz said, "Help me, Jesus" while pushing his stalled Chevy down the driveway. Why did Tony cross himself before each game?

Nudging Fritz, Tony said, "Let's light a candle. You know, before we . . . you know . . . go off."

Fritz smiled. "Can't hurt."

Looking back to Aaron, who was lagging behind, Tony said, "C'mon if you want. You don't have to be Catholic to do this part."

As they walked up the side aisle, Aaron could see a large statue of a woman wearing a simple robe holding a small baby. In the center of her chest was a brilliant red heart.

The sound of their footsteps echoed in the solemn quiet. When they reached the end, they came to a table with rows of candles, a third of them lit, casting flickering shadows off a statue of the same woman on the facing wall. Aaron kneeled beside his friends and watched as they lit candles and bowed their heads, soothed by the aroma of the melting wax of the votive candles.

Aaron wasn't clear on the purpose of lighting the candles, but he assumed it was somehow about good luck for the days ahead.

Out of the corner of his eye, he could see Fritz and Tony,

their eyes closed and their lips moving in prayer. But he couldn't concentrate, because right beside him was a grotesque statue of Jesus wearing a bloody, thorny crown, hanging from a cross, spikes driven through his wounded feet and hands. On the altar below the crucified Jesus was a large, open Bible.

"Did you light a candle? What do you think of the cathedral?" Tony asked as they rose up and turned to leave.

"I don't know. It's really big." Aaron had never seen a building as magnificent as this, let alone a church. He felt out of place. He didn't have a religion of his own. "It's pretty."

"Pretty!" whispered Tony. "You're funny, Aaron. You should see it during a mass! All lit up! I love this place."

Aaron nodded, and let his friends lead him out of the church. Why didn't he have a place like this? Bat'ko and Maty were religious, or at least they prayed, but whenever Aaron asked about their religion, Bat'ko would say, "I don't need someone telling me how to pray." When Aaron talked about his Catholic friends, Bat'ko's response was always, "God is our religion. You say your prayers, don't you? God has taken care of you, hasn't He? He has put food on our table. Look how good our crops are. What more could you want in any religion than God himself?"

Maty's disapproving frown told a different story. For the longest time, Aaron thought it was more that his Maty wanted no religion in the house, none.

As they stepped out of the cathedral into the afternoon sun, Aaron regretted not lighting a candle. He could use all the good luck and prayers he could get.

The relief and excitement he'd felt when he signed the papers had been short-lived. Anxiety now set in, the silent counting of days before graduation and then before boot camp, much like the moments when an outmatched boxer was alone in his dressing room before the fight. He still had to tell his folks. But the decision was made. He watched

Fritz and Tony whooping up ahead, and shook himself a little, running to join them.

3

DINNER WAS THE best time to break the news, Aaron reasoned. But as days passed, good intentions stuck in his throat.

The night he finally managed to tell them, the talk around the Vanko dinner table was, as usual, about farming—the price of beans, repairing the chicken coop, selling chickens and eggs, costs in general, and scheduled chores. Tension drifted in the cloud of smoke that had escaped the opening and closing of the wood- burning cook stove door.

Tonight, Bat'ko was especially silent. Maty fidgeted and picked at her food, wringing her hands as if she was expecting bad news. The oppressive silence begged for sounds to fill it.

"I enlisted in the Army," Aaron blurted out.

As Aaron had expected, Bat'ko didn't immediately react. And as irritating as that was, Aaron had come to admire Bat'ko's thoughtful silences. He wasn't one to say the first thing that came to his mind. If he had been a poker player and drawn four aces, no one in the game would have suspected. Reaching across the table, he scooped a serving spoon of mashed potatoes onto his plate and a ladle of gravy. Maty stopped wringing her hands and stared at Bat'ko, waiting for his response.

"Bat'ko, did you hear me?" Aaron questioned, forcefully.

Looking up from his plate, Bat'ko—Samuel—furrowed his brows and studied Aaron. Was this the little boy who used to ride on Digger, the family workhorse? The boy who had sat at the kitchen table and learned his ABC's under Samuel's watchful eye? The boy who had taught him new words and lessons in American geography, civics, and read him poetry?

When had he stopped being a little boy? Could Samuel recall the day, the moment, that the boy had grown up? Was he really no longer a boy? Was Samuel willing to let his son become a man, to face a cruel world? When had been the last time Aaron had crawled up onto his lap? How could Samuel have known then that Aaron would never be that young again?

"Okay," was Batko's muffled response.

"Okay? That's all you have to say?" Aaron heard Maty's sigh, and out of the corner of his eye saw her stiffen.

"Okay, you told us. What else is there? You're a man, yes? You ask what I have to say after you enlist. You're a man, but such a boy. That is what I have to say. Politicians use boys to fight wars. I have nothing to say to you. Nothing. You could have not joined in. Stayed on the farm. No, you're such a man you want to fight." Samuel looked over to Ida. "So just like that, he is gone."

Maty was wringing her hands again, and tears began to flow. "Maty, don't do that," Aaron said.

As his father pushed back from the table, the chair scraped angrily against the floor. "Syn, don't tell your maty what to do. She has the right. You break her heart. That is on you."

The only sounds after that were the wind whistling through a thousand unseen cracks and Aaron's maty sniffling. Outside, the dog barked. Bat'ko pulled his coat on and rushed from the house.

* * *

Away from home, life felt different too, as if the manhood switch had been flipped. A small voice was reminding Aaron to pay attention, to waste no time. One night, he surprised Fritz and Tony by announcing he wasn't going with them to Miller's Bend. Instead, he went roller skating alone, feeling the push and pull of invisible forces that move men's lives.

The Ankeny Roller Rink was just south of the railroad tracks, near the new ordnance plant where they made thirty- and fifty-caliber bullets. When he arrived, he quickly laced up his skates and wasted no time launching into the flow. The floor sparkled like diamonds under the strobe light and mirrored silver globe suspended above the oval rink. The sounds of the ball-bearing wheels were meditative and mesmerizing as Aaron glided loop after loop after loop, slipping between and around the other skaters.

Not far ahead was a fallen female. Without hesitation, Aaron swooped in, lifted her up off the floor, and set her on her skates. He held her for a moment as they skated in unison. Her thin waist was warm and soft. Embarrassment struck them both, and he gently let her go and glided away. She smiled as he turned again and skated on, wondering about the tall, graceful boy who had just swept her onto her feet and made her heart race.

One time around the rink and Aaron was behind her and then beside her. "Are you okay?"

As she looked to her right, he darted behind to her left, and once again, Aaron twirled and began to skate backward facing her.

"I'm okay. I'm a better skater than that," Mary blushed and smiled.

"You are good. I watched you skating." His dark wavy hair was parted and combed to one side.

"Thanks. I'm Mary. Mary Woodruff," she said, extending her hand. He held it as they skated together, feeling electricity in his fingertips.

He gracefully pulled her in a circle around him, inhaling her scent. Under the strobe, she moved in still frames, like snapshots. Her curled, auburn hair was first in her face, then flipping back and forth. Her white teeth, her giggle, and her more serious and pondering looks all became pictures he would file away forever.

"I'm Aaron. Aaron Vanko. Where do you go to school?" "Right here in Ankeny."

"City girl?" he teased.

"Kind of. Dad's a pastor. But we live on the edge of town."

"I go to Woodside," Aaron declared, as he looked directly into her eyes. Suddenly, he felt warm. The inevitable, unpredictable moment had arrived. Some boys might have passed up such a rare occasion, but not Aaron. It was just the two of them alone, in a blurry sea of muffled skate wheels whirling around them singing out *alleluia*.

Mary fanned herself. "God, it's hot in here."

Taking her by the hand, he guided her to the end of the rink floor. "Let's get some air."

In this moment, he almost forgot boot camp, almost forgot that life was going to change. Now he had something better to do with his life. This moment would stretch into hours and days of clinging to each other, as if love could be lost by looking away. And then, just like that, there would be boot camp and then some far-off land, and more regrets as well.

* * *

The attraction grew strong. Mary and Aaron were meant to be together, inseparably, but his work and her church, and the lack of transportation made it difficult. Bat'ko was stingy with the use of his truck, so Aaron relied on Fritz, who had his own car, and Tony, who sometimes drove his father's bread delivery truck. But good luck for Aaron came in the form of Lloyd Claywell's misfortune.

Lloyd was a widower who lived a mile and a half to the northeast, about a half-mile from Ankeny and a quarter-mile from Mary. An Englishman who still spoke with a proud British clip, Mister Claywell had fallen off his horse and broken his leg. Aaron was hired to be his other leg, to carry out daily chores and run errands, to do pretty much everything but cook. Although Aaron had to keep up with chores at home too, he suddenly had new freedom.

The thirty cents an hour of spending money was welcomed, but especially the freedom of using an auto and his farmer's gas ration card. Gas was twenty-one cents a gallon, cheaper than milk, which was sixty-two cents. Bread was nine cents a loaf. The preferred gas ration card was what Mary's father had. As a minister, he had a red *C* gas ration sticker that allowed unlimited use, like that of a politician and other VIPs.

Mister Claywell's son Martin had served on the aircraft carrier *Enterprise*, and Aaron listened attentively as Mister Claywell told stories about how the Japanese had defeated the Navy the previous summer and how revenge was exacted in the Battle of Midway. Four great Japanese carriers were sunk, 275 aircraft were destroyed, and 3,500 Japanese warriors died. Two months later, in the Battle of the Eastern Solomons, the *Enterprise* was seriously damaged and had to withdraw from the battle. Martin, a first-class Boatswain mate, was then transferred to a new destroyer, the USS *Fiske* (DE-143), an Edsall class built primarily for ocean escort service, with equipment to hunt for submarines.

* * *

Spring arrived with April showers after a drier-than-normal winter as the calendar checked off days until graduation and then boot camp. Home was all stiff smiles and suppressed groans. Any day, he expected to get his orders. Every day after school, he rushed to check off evening chores for Mister Claywell, then home to assist his dad, enduring his silence and cold stares. Then after dinner, he drove to town to see Mary, to stand near the doorway and talk for a few restless minutes and with flirting eyes and nervous giggles, sneaking a touch of her hand. Inside, over her shoulder, he could see her parents moving from room to room and their sideways glances toward the open door. Until at last Pastor Woodruff would say, "Mary, it's time to come inside. Tell your friend good night."

After weeks of his showing up on her doorstep, Mary finally asked him in to meet her parents. When Aaron entered the living room, Pastor Woodruff was sitting on a cushion in his oversized, maple rocking chair, resting his hands on his stomach, twiddling his thumbs. Mary's mother, Sarah, sat adjacent from him in a plain wood rocker. Mary stood beside her as Aaron was invited to sit on the sofa, facing their serious, staring faces.

"Mary tells us you've enlisted in the Army. Proud of you, boy." Pastor Geoffrey Woodruff was bald on the top of his head, with white hair springing wildly over his ears, like white weeds.

Aaron tried not to appear nervous. He quickly figured out there could be no secrets before pastor's gray, penetrating eyes. He reassured himself with a glance at Mary, and then at her mother. When he looked back, the pastor's gaze was intense, as if he were digging down into his soul. "Thank you, sir."

"Daddy's brother is coach of the Iowa Seahawks, you know, the football team," Mary proudly stated. Mary knew both her father and Aaron were sports fans.

Pastor Woodruff turned his head and looked at her. "He's not really a coach. He's a physician at the university. He's friends with Bud Wilkinson, one of the coaches. He helps out."

"Aaron is a sports fan," Mary said enthusiastically.

Smiling, Pastor Woodruff said, "So you're a sports fan? You're not a Yankee fan, are you?"

"No," Aaron grinned. "The Cardinals, I guess."

"Good answer," Pastor Woodruff looked to his daughter approvingly. Looking back to Aaron, he said, "A lot of their good players are in the military now. Musial's still playing."

"Aaron plays baseball too," Mary interjected.

"You listen to the World Series?" Pastor Woodruff reached for his pipe and a package of Red Man. Dipping it deeply into the pouch with his index finger packed the tobacco tightly into his pipe.

Holding the match over the bowl and sucking madly, he lit it. Aaron watched as the match burned to the edge of the pastor's fingers. With a start, Pastor Woodruff jerked the match away and shook it.

"Some of it," Aaron said. "We have a radio, but it only works once in a while."

The conversation stopped as the pastor puffed hard, releasing plumes of smoke. Mary's mother seized the opportunity to change the subject. With an angelic smile, she asked, "Have I seen you in our church?"

Mary's mother wore her white hair in a bun on top of her head, covered by a hairnet, held in place with a long hat pin that could as easily have been a weapon as a knitting needle. Pastor and Mrs. Woodruff seemed older than Aaron's parents.

Swallowing hard, he answered weakly, "No. I haven't been to your church."

"Aaron is a fine name," Pastor Woodruff said. "Aaron," he repeated admiringly. Looking over to Mary, he added, "If you'd been a boy, you might have been named Aaron, or maybe Joseph. Your father is Samuel? Right? Your mother Ida? We've bought eggs from them."

Looking to the pastor, Mrs. Woodruff folded her hands in her lap and ventured, "I'm not sure I've come across the name Ida in my readings."

Pastor Woodruff continued. "Aaron, brother of Moses. Some scholars say he was with Moses when he heard the voice of God."

"Oh, Father, not now," Mary tried to hide her embarrassment. "Aaron doesn't want to hear about the Old Testament."

Everyone's gaze fell on Pastor Woodruff as he alternated between chewing on the stem of his pipe and puffing smoke. Taking it out of his mouth, he banged it against the side of the rusty Folgers coffee tin sitting on his lap. He pulled the can up under his chin to spit out a string of brown tobacco juice.

"We live on a farm not too far from here," Aaron said. "West. Maybe four miles. As the crow flies."

Mary leaned forward. "Aaron's been rebuilding the fence around the pasture there. You know, Aaron, my father's a carpenter, too. He built this house. I remember watching him when I was a little girl."

Pastor Woodruff had two talents, saving souls and carpentry, and sometimes the carpentry was his toolbox for saving souls. He was always first to help a member of his congregation build a chicken coop, fix a door, or raise a barn. He was always interested in lending a helping hand and especially interested in finding souls to save.

She had been five years old when he built their house on the outskirts of Ankeny, a time filled with special memories of sitting on the ground for hours, watching in fascination how adeptly he slid boards off his shoulder and dropped them onto the sawhorses. And how he retrieved his folding wood tape measure from his carpenter's apron, flipped it open to the required length, pulled a pencil from behind his ear and scratched it sharply across the board, then, in one circular motion, returned it to the spot behind his ear.

When it came time for nailing, she would lean forward, as if watching a magician perform a trick, she had seen many times before, hoping to discover the magic. The pastor would withdraw a rusty, straightened, number-eight common nail from his apron pocket. Next, he would tap it into place. Mary would then silently count the number of strikes required to pound it in. Gripping the hammer at the far end of the ash handle, he would drive it home with two mighty blows and, knowing she was watching, look back and wink before he lightly tapped the nail head.

Her mother, Sarah, had talents to sketch landscape pictures and tend their ever-expanding vegetable and flower garden. Each fall, Sarah would gather up seeds and cuts of plants. Through proper soil and the right amount of watering and care, flowers flourished. They added color and variety to Sunday church services and brightened the bedsides of the sick and the graves of the departed.

"That's fine. Fine," the pastor nodded. "But I'm more a pastor than a carpenter."

Aaron sat uncomfortably in silence until the pastor suddenly rose up out of his chair. As the pastor was walking out of the living room, pipe smoke followed him like a storm cloud hanging over his head. Without looking back, he said, "I have a sermon to write, so I'd better get to work." Pausing and looking back to Aaron, he added, "I think my sermon will be about growing up and how God's spirit takes on new meanings. You know, I was your age once. Imagine that. I was about your age when I had an epiphany about God. I'll share that story with the congregation Sunday."

After a brief silence, Aaron asked sheepishly, "What happened?"

"Well, you'll have to come to church and find out. But I learned that God is there for us, wherever we are and at times we don't expect."

* * *

In the days ahead, Mary's leash was lengthened.

On the weekends, as daylight stretched with the advancing spring season, so did her time sitting with Aaron on the front porch swing. The aroma of blooming lilacs in Sarah's flower garden sweetened their time together. They were allowed to take short country drives, they could see occasional movies, and sometimes they joined friends for midday ice cream or sodas. The first film they saw together, in late April, was *The Road to Morocco*, starring Bob Hope and Bing Crosby. Accompanying it was a newsreel about sailors on leave in Hattiesburg, Mississippi, and the war in Europe. Aaron and Mary tried not to talk about the war, though. They preferred comedies to the newsreels. The newsreels reminded them that time was short.

As the weather warmed in May, Aaron's farm chores brought agonizing weekdays when he wasn't able to call on Mary. Gradually, though, Mister Claywell recovered enough to take over again, and Aaron had more time for Mary. Farmer Claywell let Aaron continue driving his son's car, aware he would be leaving for boot camp after graduation.

Aaron spent his nervous energy on farm chores, silently working alongside Claywell or his father, while thoughts of Mary never left his mind. The times apart and together were like the spring rain and sunny days, the fuel for summer vegetables and fresh flowers.

Cruelly, time passed slowly when they weren't together and quickly when they were, gobbling up minutes and hours. The urgency to be together heightened as their time for his departure drew near. Staying together as long as possible became the only thing that mattered on each desperate May afternoon, as the month raced toward the finish line.

One of those May afternoons, as time was drawing down, Aaron picked Mary up to see the Saturday matinee, *Casablanca*. She was wearing his favorite over-the-knee blue print dress, and he watched her apply red lipstick when they were out of sight of the house. When Rick (played by Aaron's favorite actor, Humphrey Bogart) showed his undying love for Ilsa Lund (played by the beautiful Ingrid Bergman) by kissing her goodbye and letting her go, he peeked at Mary, only to see tears streaming. Aaron took her hand and quickly looked away.

After the movie, they detoured to Miller's Bend, in the backwaters on the lee side where the river curved to cross Doc Miller's farm. As boys, he, Fritz, and Tony had made it their favorite hot summer day spot for catfish, carp, and dreaming of the future. As weather and chores allowed, they could be found there leaning back on the riverbank, watching their bobbers dip and curl in the current. Whenever Mary was there, Fritz and Tony would act like young school kids, not seniors in high school about to be men, going off to war. They showed off, giggled, skipped stones, and tried to wrestle each other into the water.

Neither Fritz nor Tony had girlfriends: there were only eight girls in their graduating class, so choices were limited. The first time Tony had met Mary, all he had said to Aaron was, "Where'd you find that dreamboat?" Nudging Fritz, who had been staring at his bobber as if the intensity of his gaze would cause a fish to bite.

Tony added, "What a dish, huh?"

Always the serious one, Fritz had looked back and grunted his response, then returned his gaze to his fishing line as it stretched tight, tugging against the current.

That month of May was the wettest anyone remembered. Aaron and Mary had often driven to Miller's Bend on rainy days, along the shoulder to avoid deep muddy ruts, his arm around her as naturally as if they were swinging on the porch. Privately, Aaron hoped the rainy days would drive off his friends so that he and Mary could be alone.

Parking as closely as possible to the trunk of a large cottonwood tree, Aaron turned off the car engine. It sputtered and coughed before it popped and went silent. He rolled the window down, and for several minutes, they listened to the sounds of the gentle rain and the water lapping at the shoreline.

Graduation was two weeks away, and still there was no word on where and when he was supposed to report to the Army. At the time he enlisted, love had been a stranger, just a glowing ember waiting to flare up. Now being with Mary was like pouring gasoline over simmering coals, and thinking about leaving her was the wind to fuel the fire.

"Do you think about the Army?" Mary's question was quiet and cautious.

There was no safe place to hide from the ebb and flow of war reports, nor was the inside of the car a haven from thoughts of the future that followed them everywhere. Now, close to the end of their time together, difficult questions trickled out. Aaron held his breath.

In the dimming daylight, Mary's eyes were like deep pools of midnight.

"I think more about having to leave you than anything," Aaron said. Reaching over, he pulled her toward him. As Mary slid across the seat and nestled in beside him, he moved the floor shifter into first gear, out of the way, and set the emergency brake. Their hearts raced as they turned and faced each other. Their lips met ever so slowly, lightly at first, then devoured each other. A crescendo of feverish passion brought them to discover a secret passageway to being one, a marriage of souls. She reached under his shirt and placed her hand on his chest.

She gasped and held him tight. "Oh, Aaron." Their lips met again.

Then, reeling, gasping for air, she pushed back. "No! What are we doing? We can't do this."

Sighing, Aaron released his hand and melted back. "Let's get some air."

It had stopped raining. Easing back, he opened the car door, took her by the hand and helped her out of the car. She stumbled awkwardly but regained her balance in his arms. Breathing the rain- cleansed evening air, they leaned against the front fender, wrapped in each other's arms, gazing longingly to the early evening heavens, their lips separated by a whisper.

"We're so lucky to have found each other," Mary reflected. "I never go to that skating rink."

"Me neither," Aaron said. "And I was alone. I'm always with my friends. I'm so lucky."

"No, I'm the lucky one."

"I guess that makes me *Lucky Two*," Aaron joked, holding two fingers up.

"Okay, *Lucky Two*," Mary giggled.

After a silent moment, Aaron asked, "Remember when I first met the pastor and he began to tell a story? Said he was going to use it in a sermon. What was the story?"

Mary giggled again. "He loves that story. When Father was a boy, he watched a friend drown, and he nearly drowned himself. They were swimming in the river and got caught in a whirlpool. Gasping for air, Father cried out for God's help. Suddenly, as if the whirlpool had spit him out, he found himself in calm waters. He talks about Joseph and how, when tested, he put his trust in God."

Mary's voice deepened to imitate her father. "'Imagine your wife is pregnant but not by you. You want to believe her. You know it must be true, she couldn't have been with another man. But it was impossible to understand. I guess when logic fails, faith steps in.'" Then she looked at Aaron seriously. "He was a man of the greatest faith, so he let go and trusted. Let go and let God. Just as my father did in the middle of that whirlpool. Daddy likes you. He thinks you're a good person with a good heart. But—"

"But what?"

"He wonders about your religion, whether you'll steer me away from mine."

"What religion does he think I have?" "What church do you go to?"

"My parents don't go to church. But they pray," Aaron added quickly. "Does that frighten you?"

"Kinda. My faith is important to me, to my family. I was raised in the church. The congregation is my family."

"I'd never steal you away from that. I think faith is a personal thing, and maybe it doesn't matter where you go to pray." He pulled back and placed his hands on her shoulders, his gaze demanding her attention.

"Mary, I want you to marry me. That's the road we're on. It's as clear as a sunny day. I hope you feel the same. We've had so little time; it's like our life is being pushed through the eye of a needle. Do you feel the same way? What do I have to do?" He hadn't planned this, but the idea of marrying her felt as natural as the next day's rain.

Mary laid her head on his chest. "Of course, we'll marry. I believe that. It feels so right." Mary looked up at him dreamily.

"I mean now!"

Mary appeared confused. "How can we marry now?" "I'll find a way. I'll go to your father and ask him." "No. He'll never approve."

"Then he needs to tell me that. Tell me why we can't." Shaking her head, "I'm only seventeen. He won't—" "We will."

"What if he never approves?"

Aaron held her close. "We'll find a way."

4

BUT THE WAY forward together wasn't clear, not really. Mary tried to reassure him, saying her father really liked him, that religion wouldn't be an issue. But the more she talked, the more Aaron doubted. Something was troubling about Pastor Woodruff's inquisitive gaze and probing questions about where his family came from, about where his relatives lived, and, in roundabout ways, about his religion. Aaron always remained vague, saying he didn't belong to a local church. The pastor's scowl and disapproving sideway glances showed he knew. Were they the stares of a father protecting his daughter? Was Aaron unworthy, or a soul to save, a project?

The weather alternated two rainy days with one sunny one. Spring storms brought the riverbank to the brink of overflowing and turned the Iowa black soil into mud. Aaron and Mary fell into a routine, working and playing. On sunny days, there were make-up chores and field work as much as the soil allowed, and on rainy days, there were occasional movies in Ankeny or Highland Park, and on the way home, stop-offs at Miller's Bend. In May, Mary cried through her pick, *The Song of Bernadette*, back for a second run after its release at the end of December. Aaron kept his arms around her, her head nestled in the crook of his neck. Aaron picked *Hands Across the Border*, starring Roy Rogers and his horse Trigger. They laughed through *Popeye* and *Donald Duck* cartoons, then *Woody Woodpecker* and *Tom and Jerry*, imitating

Woody's laugh and Donald's quacky lisp. It was as if they were holding on to being kids as long as they could.

On sunny days, in the afternoon after chores, they could count on Fritz and Tony to be fishing at Miller's Bend. Best of all, on rainy days, sometimes they were alone. In thunderstorms, they cuddled in the front seat and watched the river rise and seek out new channels. When lightning flashed, and the thunder clapped angrily, Mary burrowed her head into his farm-hardened arms. They listened to Jimmy Dorsey and his Orchestra playing "*Besame Mucho*."

"It's like this is our own private place, sweetheart." Aaron reflected on the peace that had come as suddenly as the thunder and lightning that shook the car minutes before. Rolling the window down, he breathed in the calm, fresh-washed air.

"I love it when you call me sweetheart." Mary looked up, searching for the outline of his face in the dark.

"Sweetheart, sweetheart, sweetheart." Aaron's words mirrored the smile on his face. "Keep it up, darling."

"I love it when you call me darling, pumpkin."

"Ooh," Mary responded. "I love it most when you love me." "Well, that's all the time." Aaron leaned down, his lips searched for hers, and they kissed gently, reverently.

Suddenly Aaron pushed away, his expression stony. He pounded his fist on the steering wheel.

Mary reeled back and watched as he rested his head on the steering wheel, her mouth agape. "What's wrong?" Reaching out, she placed her hand on his shoulder.

Aaron took a deep breath, lifted his head and stared out over the hood of the car. "This is so hard." Aaron stiffened and focused a stern look on Mary. "Just a year ago, I was a farm boy who spent my days in school, fishing with friends, doing chores, and now everything is so complicated."

"You mean the war?"

"Yeah. Well, a little. The worst part is leaving you. But it's something I have to do. Want to do. No, it's not the war." Banging his fist on the steering wheel again, he continued. "The other night I couldn't sleep. I was thinking about your father not approving of us getting married. I don't think he trusts me."

"Don't worry about that. We'll be married. You'll see. I know we will."

"I hope so, but it feels that life is lining up against us." "No. We can't care about all that."

"What will happen when I'm gone?"

"I'm strong. While you're fighting for the country, I'll fight for us.

Bing Crosby crooned "I Love You" on the radio. Singing along, they leaned playfully into a distracted kiss, and changed the subject, again.

* * *

The spring rain had dampened the Iowa countryside, muddying the fields and widening the river out over its banks. But with graduation a week away, that rain now yielded to bright sunny days. Mayflies gave way to June bugs and the worst infestation of mosquitoes in memory.

Now, whenever they could be together away from the prying eyes of her parents, they sat in the car at Miller's Bend and listened to the radio. Aaron's family radio worked half the time and never when he wanted it to, and his dad's truck didn't have one. Claywell's Chevy did.

When he was home, Aaron helped his bat'ko and maty with chores, as much as the mud allowed. It was hard to watch Maty work in the garden. She was forty-three when she gave birth to Aaron; now she was sixty-one, and years of hard work had curved her spine until it was difficult for her to stand erect.

As he watched her, he wondered what would happen to the garden when he wasn't there to help. Would it go to weed? Father was showing his age, too. Could he handle the farm? The recruiter said some young boys stayed home to help out on the farms. What he meant was some boys ducked the war by tending to their farms. It hadn't seemed like a real option at the time.

The beans needed a lot of weeding. Aaron was tall and sinewy, but he was still no match for his father's steady strength. They went up and down the rows in silent, machine-like fashion. Aaron helped his father as much as he would let him, but since his enlistment, the quiet had been punishing. He hadn't even mentioned Mary to his father and didn't know if Maty had.

* * *

The week before graduation, Aaron received his orders to report to the Army on July 6th. Until then, he would continue to work for Mister Claywell and on the family farm. The graduation ceremony was Saturday, and the next Wednesday, Mary started her new job among the liberated women who made up 35 percent of the wartime workforce, at the ordnance plant in Ankeny. Her salary was thirty- two dollars a week.

On the day before her first workday, she negotiated with her father to stay out until five o'clock. Her new job, Aaron's sunny workdays, and the tightening restrictions imposed by her father made their days together as precious as diamonds.

Today, they spent some time at Miller's Bend listening to the radio and skipping stones. For a while, she watched Aaron, Fritz, and Tony scurry up and down the riverbank to find the best currents where the fish would be biting. After two frustrating hours of swatting flies without even a fish nibble, Fritz and Tony left. As the sun rose higher in the sky, the mosquitos moved into the shadows. Aaron and Mary cozied up in Claywell's '32 Chevy and switched between two radio stations, listening to Bing Crosby's "I'll be Seeing You," "Swinging on a Star" by the Andrew Sisters, "Don't Fence Me In," by Lawrence Welk, and yesterday's Glenn Miller's band music. Glenn Miller had enlisted and joined the war effort.

At 10:30, the music was interrupted. Mary was leaning against the driver's side door with her feet on Aaron's lap. She sat upright and leaned in close to the radio.

We interrupt our program to bring you a special broadcast. The German news agency Trans Oceans announced today that the Allied invasion has begun. I repeat: The German news agency Trans Oceans announced today that the Allied invasion has begun. There was no Allied confirmation.

A stream of bulletins followed into the late afternoon. One announced that US submarines had sunk fifteen more Japanese cargo ships. Another warned that announcements from Germany about the invasion could be a ruse to learn of Allied plans. Still there was no announcement by the Allied forces that an invasion was underway. Aaron and Mary listened attentively. Every time a bulletin was broadcast they expected to hear from the president or some other confirmation of the latest developments.

"I'll bet it's true. I'll bet the GIs are giving 'em hell right now." Aaron's initial enthusiasm quickly abated, like clouds covering the sun. "Did you know Charlie Younger? He graduated last year and enlisted. I wonder where he is."

"He went to my church," Mary answered.

"He was in England. Bet he's still there. Wonder what's happening? Seems kind of hard to imagine storming a beach while the Germans are trying to pick you off."

Suddenly the airwaves crackled, and only static came from the radio. It was as if the river had stopped flowing, as if the gentle breeze that had helped keep the mosquitoes and flies away was holding its breath.

. . . And now we have just been informed that we can expect an important broadcast from the British capital. We take you to London for a statement from Commander General Eisenhower.

Mary snuggled against Aaron's chest.

Soldiers, sailors, and airmen of the Allied Expeditionary Forces: You are about to embark upon the Great Crusade, toward which we have striven these many months. The eyes of the world are upon you. The hopes and prayers of liberty-loving people everywhere march with you. In company with our brave Allies and brothers-in-arms on other fronts, you will bring about the destruction of the German war machine, the elimination of Nazi tyranny over the oppressed peoples of Europe, and security for ourselves in a free world.

Your task will not be an easy one. Your enemy is well trained, well equipped and battle-hardened. He will fight savagely.

But this is the year 1944, and much has happened since 1940 and 41, the years of the Nazi triumphs. The United Nations have inflicted upon the Germans great defeats, in open battle, man-to-man. Our air offensive has seriously reduced their strength in the air and their capacity to wage war on the ground. Our home fronts have given us an overwhelming superiority in weapons and munitions of war and placed at our disposal great reserves of trained fighting men. The tide has turned. The free men of the world are marching together to victory.

I have full confidence in your courage, devotion to duty, and skill in battle. We will accept nothing less than full victory.

Good luck! And let us all beseech the blessing of Almighty God upon this great and noble undertaking.

As soon as the radio announcement ended, Mary screamed, "Aaron! Look at the time. It's six o'clock! I was supposed to be home by five. Father will kill me."

The car didn't start the first time. Lately, Aaron parked on hills so when the weak battery played out he could run alongside the car and hop in when, having gained enough speed, he could jump- start it. Now they were on a narrow grassy flat path.

"Don't fail me now," Aaron pleaded. Pumping the gas pedal, he felt his spirits plummet as the motor ground over and over. Looking over to Mary, he raised his eyebrows to signal this was their last chance. Vroom, the engine came to life. Shifting into reverse, he backed up and slid in a semicircle, then slammed the car into first gear and sped away.

Mary bobbed in her seat as the '32 Chevy bounced along the dusty washboard road. When they arrived, she looked over to Aaron, smiled, and coyly reached out to touch his hand before she rushed to the door and disappeared.

Once the door shut, her father rushed to her, a switch in his hand. "How dare you. You know what time it is?" Mary backed away. He began to swing wildly.

Her mother watched from the hallway.

"Father, don't. It was a mistake. It won't happen again." Shrinking away, she began to cry. "Father, don't."

The first swings missed their mark, and he began to zero in on her exposed ankles as she turned her back. "Mistake? Out there with your soldier boy? He's bad for you. So what were you doing all day?" "Daddy, we were listening to the news. You've heard?" She pleaded as tears streamed down her face. Pastor Woodruff's switch found its mark below her hemline. She cried out in pain. "I said stop. Daddy, don't. Stop!" Turning toward him, she reached out and jerked the switch out of his hand. "I said stop!"

"You listen to your father," her mother said as Mary rushed by on her way to her room.

Her father yelled after her, "You're not seeing him again. Your soldier is leaving, and it's best you not see him. I know what happens with soldiers. And it's not going to happen to you."

* * *

The next day Aaron picked Mary up at the ordnance plant at the end of her shift. Before she even said hello, she burst into tears, slid across the seat, and burrowed her head into his arms. She stammered, "Father forbids me to see you again. He was furious when I got home late. Oh, Aaron, tell me what to do."

Aaron pushed back, his gaze narrowed. Her face was red and puffy, marked by a dried riverbed of earlier tears. "He says we're making it harder for me. Harder for you too. He says our hearts are doing all the thinking."

"Did you tell them we were getting married?"

"No," she answered sheepishly, bowing her head. "He'll never approve."

"We still have to try. I leave soon."

"I've never seen him so mad. He's worried about us . . . right before you leave, and all."

Aaron shifted the car into third gear and picked up speed, heading toward Mary's. "We're gonna be married, and we can't see each other?"

Mary began to cry. "Maybe if he knew?"

Aaron could see the red lines on her ankles. "Did he—?"

Mary was silent. She wanted Aaron to hold her. More than that, she wanted him to turn the car around and leave with her, to escape Iowa and not look back. As much as that, she wanted her parents to approve. She envisioned a church wedding with her friends and family and most of all, her father's blessings.

"Mary, your folks need to know we're serious. We're going to marry. They need to know that. Why keep us apart?"

When they arrived at the house, Aaron skidded to a stop and took a deep breath. "I'll talk to him," Aaron said angrily. "I'll make him listen."

"You won't get mad?" she pleaded.

When they got out of the car, Aaron walked past her, his footsteps thundering, his heart racing, wondering what to say, glancing back to make sure she was following him.

Pastor Woodruff opened the door and invited him in. His white hair flared out wildly over his ears. Aaron took a deep breath and saw that her mother had moved next to him.

"Pastor, I want to apologize for bringing Mary home late last night. We got caught up in listening to the invasion news and—"

Raising his hand in the air, Pastor Woodruff cut him off. Puffs of pipe smoke, like a chugging locomotive, curled up toward the ceiling.

"And we lost track of time," Aaron finished. "It won't happen again, I promise."

"Aaron. Let's walk." Taking the pipe out of his mouth, the pastor pointed it to the open front door. "Let's go outside." Gently taking Aaron's arm, he guided him off the porch and up the dirt walkway to his car. Mary watched from the front porch steps. "Mary, you go inside. We're going to have a little chat."

When they arrived, Pastor Woodruff opened the car door and calmly took the pipe out of his mouth and banged it on the sole of his shoe, then ran his finger inside the bowl, banged it into the palm of his hand and stuck it in his pocket.

"Aaron, I need to be clear about this. You're not to see her again. You're going off to war. And rest assured, I'll be praying for you. But if you return, things will be different here."

Thoughts of not returning from the war had tormented Aaron in the night. But having Pastor Woodruff raise the specter of those nightmares shocked him. Aaron stood with his mouth open, searching for something to say. "Not see her? Why?"

"Yes, I mean you won't see her. Now. And forever." Shrugging his shoulders and waving his hands dismissively, Pastor Woodruff continued. "A lot will change in the time you're gone. For you and for her. You're both young. Mary has her church."

"We want to marry. Now. Before I leave," Aaron blurted out.

Red-faced, Pastor Woodruff took the pipe out of his pocket and jammed it back into his mouth, unlit. Holding it firmly in his teeth, he chewed his words angrily. "How dare you? No. You cannot marry my daughter. Ever."

Stunned at the pastor's anger, Aaron responded meekly, "Because she's too young?"

"Of course, she's too young. Someday, you'll find a girl of your own kind and Mary will find someone in our faith." Guiding him by his arm, he opened the car door and declared, "Now you need to leave here."

Aaron could see that Mary was still standing on the front porch.

Her mother peered through the front window.

"I love Mary, and she loves me," Aaron declared boldly. Abruptly, he shifted from pleading to indignation. Bitterly, he lashed out, "We're going to marry anyway. It doesn't matter if you approve."

"She's only seventeen. You need my permission. You'll be a long way from here when she's eighteen. I'll not let you hurt my daughter. Ever." Pastor Woodruff gripped his arm tightly and nudged him to the open car door. "A lot of soldiers think they fall in love before they leave. Why are you any different? Leave now."

Aaron began to get into the car, turned and faced Pastor Woodruff. "You can't keep us apart forever." Rising back out of the car, he stood, towering over the pastor. "I guess we'll see what God wants. Maybe God won't bring me back, but I swear that if He does, I'm going to marry your daughter. We'll see what God wants."

Looking over his shoulder, he could see Mary still standing on the front porch with her hands on her face, beet-red, her mouth open and tears flowing.

5

LOVE WAS A stream that became a raging river in Saylor, Iowa. Mary and Aaron clung to each other despite her father's rage. July was nearly upon them and thoughts of boot camp turned into anxiety.

A church friend of Mary's worked the same shift at the ordnance plant and agreed to give her a ride to and from work. Mary hadn't learned to drive yet; her father discouraged her. But Aaron and Mary made a plan, driven by urgency and the daily news. Mary would tell her dad that she had a ride each day with a female co-worker but instead, Aaron would drive her home each day, dropping her off down the road from her house so her father didn't spot him.

Together, they would listen to reports on the radio, which held some optimism. Allied soldiers had begun to move across Europe, but there were ominous reports about the force of German V1 rocket planes that could fly 400 miles per hour to deliver their destructive payloads. US Forces had captured Rome, but the Germans were annihilating London. Aaron and Mary tried not to talk about the war, pretending the summer would be endless.

The first time they met after work, Mary ran to him. Aaron was leaning against the black Chevy in his white T-shirt, wearing painted-on arcuate Levi jeans with pant bottoms rolled up. "Millie, that's Aaron!" she called, and hurried toward him in her gunmetal gray coveralls. She crashed into his arms, and he lifted her and spun her around.

Mildred Armstrong, a petite brunette, waited awkwardly behind them, standing with her hands on her waist, popping her gum loudly. Several years older than Mary, she lived with two other girls in her farmhouse just outside the Ankeny city limits. Her husband, Butch, had accepted a commission into the Marines and was at war.

After a moment, Millie beamed, her white teeth glistening, and held out her hand. Aaron broke away and smiled, keeping his arm around Mary.

"Dad won't let us be together. So Aaron's going to give me a ride home. That okay with you, Millie?"

Millie chewed her gum wildly. "My God, of course. You kids need to be together. You can trust me, kid. I'll pick you up in the morning as planned, and Aaron can get you home."

The only time Aaron and Mary were together now was the drive home. He took a circuitous route, with torturous brief side road embraces. He always dropped her off a quarter mile from the house. Once, they saw her father's car approaching them as they drove, but Aaron turned quickly onto a side road. They giggled and held each other, enjoying adrenaline kisses and twenty more stolen minutes.

Summer days were growing longer, and Aaron's time shorter. June was passing in the cadence of marching soldiers stomping out the beat of war. Aaron's next step was boot camp on July 5th. Fritz and Tony planned to spend their last day of civilian life with their parents. Tony said he'd see Aaron at Camp Dodge early the next morning, and Fritz said he and his folks would pick him up at seven. Aaron had his own plans.

On July 4th, Mary accompanied her parents on an annual church picnic to Riverview Park, a popular amusement park in Des Moines. It was reopening after a flood, just in time for the Independence Day celebration.

As Aaron drove across the fresh-painted white wooden bridge into the park, he noted the river had receded, but was still higher than normal for this time of year. The scent of just-picked lilacs from his maty's garden on the seat next to him sweetened the moment.

From the parking lot Aaron, walked past the merry-go-round, past the flying scooters, past the *clang-clang* of the kiddie boat bells, through the park past the dodge cars, and into the penny arcade, where he stopped to flatten a penny and engrave it. At the far end he stopped and watched members of Pastor Woodruff's congregation gather in the picnic area. From a distance, he studied the faces, hoping to catch a glance of Mary, and took a seat in the middle of the park on a bench.

Sitting alone, Aaron watched a steady stream of young men with their girlfriends, fathers and mothers with their children holding giant puffs of cotton candy, and husbands and wives holding hands. He was facing the roller coaster and over and over watched one of two three-car trains climb through a tunnel up a 650-foot incline and fall into eight dips and turns in a one-minute ride.

A young man in an Army uniform, with his favorite girl at his side, was trying to win a teddy bear at the shooting gallery. Aaron watched him plunk his money down and shoulder the rifle time and again, until he eventually slunk away in disappointment.

The steady hum of conversation and laughter blended with amusement park sounds: The *clack, clack, clack* of the coaster as it climbed the first incline; the creaking of the wood support struts as the cars went spinning around the track; the screams of joy from the Tunnel of Love; the *clomp, clomp, clomp* of the pony ride, small, serious child voices, kids yelling in pretense that they were real cowboys; the *thump, thump, thump* of baseballs; the *zing, zing, zing* of the shooting gallery; the tooting of the horn of the train that passed by every fifteen minutes, loaded with waving children; and the organ music from the carousel as it went around and around.

Dusk was settling over the park, which was aglow under thousands of lights, as Aaron blended into the crowd of park patrons gathered in front of the bandstand on the west side of the park, awaiting the beginning of the Fourth of July celebration. Before the fireworks, the mayor of Des Moines introduced WWI Medal of Honor winner Edouard Izac. He told his incredible story of escape from a German POW camp across the mountains of southwest Germany, which involved eating only raw vegetables and swimming the Rhine River past sentries, all to deliver secret U-boat information.

Aaron moved to the back of the crowd as Pastor Woodruff took the stage. Off to the right of the platform, he saw Mary standing beside her mother. She had already seen him and was smiling, waiting for him to find her. Their gazes locked over the heads of the faithful. When Pastor

Woodruff rose to give the invocation, Aaron watched Mary slip past bowed heads and rush to the parking lot, where they had agreed to meet.

All eyes were on the stage and Pastor Woodruff. When she entered the empty parking lot, she stopped and looked in all directions. From behind, Aaron lifted her off her feet and twirled her around and around to the back of the parking lot, where he was parked. He was clutching a bouquet of lilacs.

Their eager mouths said *I love you*. When their lips parted, their chests heaved in the hot and humid summer night air. "Aaron, I can't bear to be without you." Their lips met again as he held her in an eternal embrace.

Aaron held her at arm's length and studied her, grinning. She was wearing a print blouse buttoned to her neck and penny loafers. A poodle's happy face was embroidered onto the bottom of her skirt. Her hair was pulled back in a chignon bun.

"You are one gorgeous girl," Aaron said.

"Sorry I couldn't get away sooner. Father was watching like a hawk." Mary leaned in and buried her head in his chest.

Barroom! The ground shook and the sky exploded with a thousand colorful sparkling lights, then another thousand and another thousand. Mary leaned back into his arms as they watched. "Will I ever be this happy again?" Aaron asked. He kissed her forehead, leaning against the car door, one foot on the running board, his arms around her waist.

Mary squeezed his hand. "Soon. You'll see. Then forever."

The fireworks ended as suddenly as they began, and a hush fell over the night, followed by the sounds of the park coming back to life and the low murmur of the mingling crowd. Celebrators began to file into the parking lot, car lights flashed, engines roared to life. Staring up to the heavens, clinging to the moment, dread standing at his side, looking for hope in the few brave stars above the glow of the park, Aaron tried to imagine forever. Could anything last forever? Everything he understood told him that there were beginnings and endings, but now he was staring into infinity. Going off to war felt just as everlasting.

"You're leaving tomorrow. When will we be together again?" Mary asked.

"I'll be back in September, I guess, after boot camp." "What happens then?"

"We'll be together, that's what happens. We'll tie the knot, and then I'll be sent off—somewhere."

"But before that, we'll get married. Right? Please tell me again," Mary pleaded.

"You'll be eighteen. No one can stop us. Everyone will understand in time. Love always wins, sweetheart."

Breaking away again, Mary let out a gasp. Her hair bun had come loose and was hanging wildly. She pulled at her hair and shook her head and flipped it from side to side.

Aaron watched and collected the memory. "God, I love you so. Oh, how I wish we could steal away now and forget this crazy damn world, pretend we never heard about war, find a place where love is the rule and not hate."

"Oh, I wish we could marry now. So much."

"Oh, yeah. Right now." Aaron sent his wish into the night.

Then he stiffened. In the distance he could see Mary's mother at the far end of the parking lot, searching.

Mary panicked. "I have to go."

Hoping to lock away the moment, Aaron studied the lines of her face. Looking into her eyes was like looking into a twinkling starry night. Her hair hung loosely at her shoulders and flipped to one side when she cocked her head. Her mouth formed that crooked smile, like she knew secrets, like even when things were bad there was some simple truth, beyond his understanding of how life worked.

Mary saw how troubled he was, his dark, wavy hair parted to the side, the kindness and love in his eyes. With a determined smile she said, "We won't have to wait long. Then we will have forever. Remember that. *Forever.*" She was turning away, looking back over her shoulder, a breath away.

"Nothing can keep us apart. Nothing. Don't ever forget that. I love you," Aaron said in voice that was like a whispered prayer. "Mary, I almost forgot." Digging deeply into his pocket, he retrieved the flattened penny and reached out to hand it to her.

Taking it in her hand, she read the inscription, *Lucky One.*

A brief smile, then she turned to leave.

The fragrance of lilacs reminded him he had laid them on the hood of the car. "Mary!" he called out.

She turned and saw that he was holding out a bouquet of lilacs and rushed back, smiled, rushed back and swiped them out of his hand.

He watched as she faded from sight.

* * *

That night, while in bed, Aaron kept remembering Mary's voice in the rain. "*What if he never approves?*"

After midnight he gave in to not sleeping and went outside. He was surprised to find his maty sitting in a rocking chair at the far end of the porch, her feet on the floor, gently moving back and forth, her arms folded like she was rocking a baby. He sat across from her in a straight-backed wood porch chair.

A light breeze had chased away the stars and covered the moon with clouds. Aaron stared toward the east, knowing that soon the sun would peek out from the top of the other half of the world.

The creaky rocker was the only sound in the night. She was smoking a cigarette. "It won't be long. I wish it was not true."

When she inhaled, he could see bags under her eyes and lines in her forehead, which made Maty look older than Aaron remembered. Her gray hair flared out from under her black headscarf like dry fall weeds.

"I'm getting married."

Maty shrugged her shoulders dismissively, as if she was expecting he would come home tonight with that news. "She's a nice girl, no?" "Her father won't approve. He's a pastor and she's only seventeen,"

Aaron said.

Maty began coughing. Aaron watched as she struggled to stop and catch her breath. "Neither will your bat'ko."

Aaron hadn't considered Bat'ko. Of course, he would say Aaron was too young. They'd exchanged few words since he enlisted, as if he had told an unforgiveable lie. Bat'ko had a way of reducing life to black and white, but lately Aaron saw shades of gray.

"Why would he feel that way?"

"You're too young," Maty answered curtly. "But I'm not too young to go to war?'

"You're too young for that, too!"

"Her father is asking about my religion. He thinks I'm not good enough."

Maty took a deep drag on her cigarette and flipped the ash off to the side. "All fathers think that way about their daughters."

"Why don't we go to church?" Aaron asked.

The announcement of his intent to marry hardly drew a glance, but his last question jolted Maty. She jerked her head and stopped rocking. A flash of fear crossed her face.

After a few minutes of silence, Aaron pressed on. "All my friends go to church. Why don't we? I need to know."

Snuffing out the cigarette into a cupped shard of a broken clay pot, she pulled a pouch of tobacco off the seat and slipped a sheet of cigarette paper free. Gently tapping a line of tobacco on the paper, she rolled it tightly and ran her tongue along the seam to seal it. As she lit the cigarette, he could see her red swollen eyes.

"We just don't."

"What is our religion? Are we Catholics? Are we anything? Maty, I need to know before I leave." Aaron's gaze pleaded.

After a long pause, she answered, "We aren't Catholic. We are Jewish."

Aaron's mouth dropped open. He thought she would skirt the issue, like sometimes people who don't have a church home may say something like "We don't follow any particular religion." But *Jewish*?

"What does that mean? We are Jewish? I thought we weren't anything anymore."

"We always have been. And we always will be."

Aaron jumped to his feet. "Jewish? I don't even know what that is. I don't want to be Jewish. I want to be Catholic like my friends." Turning his back to her, gripping the railing, he searched for a horizon that was still lost to the dark night. "Jewish? Are we ashamed of that? You never—"

"No, you should be proud."

Aaron whirled around. "Proud! Proud like Bat'ko who hides everything? Every time I asked, he dismissed me with a wave of his hand. I found that Bible in the barn. It was just gibberish."

"It is the Torah. It is written in Hebrew." Shaking her head, she added softly, barely loud enough for him to hear, "He hides it."

"How can I be proud? I didn't know this until now, and I don't even know what being Jewish is. I don't know any Jewish people. We don't go to church."

"Synagogue," Maty interrupted.

"Oh, my God. On the eve of going off to war, you tell me this? I hear people talk about Jews. I've talked about them, and now I find out that talk was about me."

Maty took a deep drag on her cigarette and shook her head. The rocker was now crying out at a maddening pace, back and forth and back and forth.

"Maty, stop it. Stop rocking. What's wrong?"

The quiet snapped to attention. "Your father hides it. It is difficult. Jews are wronged, always. In this country, too. He doesn't want you to know that."

"But here in Iowa?"

"Yes, everywhere. Even America is not always friendly to Jews. They don't steal our property or take our children, but they could. Your father has never trusted politicians."

"A Jew? I am a Jew." The words drifted in the sweltering night. A cricket on the porch punctuated the silence. A barn owl commented.

Thick smoke circled Maty. "Your father does not allow talk about this. But I will tell you. He is from Husiatyn, a Ukrainian city. In 1914, Russians ordered the Jews out, set fire to everything. Your bat'ko and his maty and bat'ko were the only ones from the family who made it here. His brother was taken for the army, we think. Your bat'ko and I met in New York. Borough Park. We married there. Now we are here."

Aaron cringed in stunned silence, strange words crawling on him like spiders spinning a web. Several minutes passed. "How did you meet?"

"My maty took me to meet him and his bat'ko and maty." "Your maty introduced you to Bat'ko?"

"It wasn't like that. We were matched." "You weren't in love?"

Maty packed another cigarette and lit it. "I think your father wanted to marry someone else. That's okay, we learn love. Your bat'ko is a hard man. He didn't get along with the rabbis. When we were old enough, we moved here. We are safe here."

"What are we hiding from?"

"Everything your father does is to protect the family. And then you go fight in the war. Now you know. Bat'ko will not say anything, but this is another dagger in his heart. He still wants his brother to be alive." Maty began to wring her hands. "It eats at him."

"Wait. What does it mean to be Jewish if we don t go to church or synagogue?"

"Maybe not now, but maybe we will go someday. We won't live here always. Your bat'ko wants us to be with our people. He keeps the Torah. You saw it."

"I'm going to war tomorrow. Now I learn I'm Jewish . . . because my father wants to protect me . . . and I can't marry the woman I love. Nothing makes sense."

Maty began to slowly rock again. "Religion tore your bat'ko's heart. The Russians hated Jews. Being Jewish is what took his brother. Then, he blamed the rabbis for not standing up to the soldiers. In New York, he still fought with the rabbi. Now gentiles want to take you away."

"Who wants to take me away now? Take me away from what? From a religion I don't even know? Your religion? No. I don't need anyone's permission to marry." Aaron stood suddenly, anger was rising in his voice. "Her father will never allow her to marry a Jew and you don't want me to marry a gentile, or whatever you call her. She'll be eighteen this summer." Still, his heart was sinking. *What will Mary think?*

Maty stopped rocking, stiffened, and snuffed out her cigarette. Her face hardened. "You love her?" she said in a stern voice. "So you have found your *bashert*, have you? Like Bat'ko said, you are such a boy. What do you know? Bat'ko will forbid it. This isn't about man's laws. This is God's. A Jew who marries a non-Jew goes against the Torah. It is one of the commandments from Mount Sinai. It cannot happen." Aaron sat and slumped into the chair. She looked so frail his anger died in his throat. The first light of day was now casting long shadows from the trees onto the porch.

Softly, almost in a whisper, Aaron spoke. "This is a fine time to learn all of this. A fine sendoff. Fight for your country and its freedoms, but I can't marry the woman I love. Well, we'll be married and maybe when I come back, we'll move from here. Find our own hiding place."

By the time the first shadows crossed the barnyard, Aaron was sitting in the same stiff wooden chair, his duffle bag on the porch beside him.

Maty was in the kitchen preparing breakfast: blinchiki, paprika fries, and tea.

Out in the corral, he watched Digger, a twenty-five-year-old gray workhorse with his head slung low over the top rail. Then he glanced past the rows of beans out to the bright morning sun breaking through the tops of the trees. It seemed so long ago that Claywell's Chevy was parked in the barnyard waiting for him to take Mary to Miller's Bend. Now the Chevy was gone. It was like stepping out of boyhood and into manhood, and knowing it.

Bat'ko burst through the door onto the porch, startled to see Aaron sitting there. He grunted his good morning and limped toward the barn. Aaron knew Bat'ko's back was ailing, but Bat'ko was too stubborn to let it slow him down. As he disappeared into the barn, Aaron decided he had to confront him.

He found Bat'ko leaning against the horse stall, his hand pressing on his lower back. Aaron stood in the doorway, his feet planted wide, his jaw set. "I am in the Army. That cannot be changed."

Bat'ko looked back but did not turn around. "You came to tell me that?"

"I want to go. It's my duty. Don't you have to fight for what you believe?"

"What you believe. What is that?" Bat'ko turned toward him. "This is my country, *our* country. Don't we fight for our country?"

"They can win the war without you." His voice was filled with sadness. Aaron knew by the look on his face he was on the verge of not talking any more. A wave of his hand would end all discussions.

Aaron took a deep breath. "Maty says I'm Jewish."

Bat'ko's head jerked up, his gaze narrowed. "She did, did she? Well you *should* know, And now you do. But it makes no difference. There is no synagogue here. Maybe I should have taken you to Des Moines. Someday you will understand."

"Soon I'll be going to boot camp and then . . . " Aaron, wanted to lash out, but he knew that would end the discussion and time was short. He had to keep Bat'ko talking. Not let him wave his large, unrelenting, dismissive, calloused hands. "What else do I need to know? Before I leave."

Without hesitating Bat'ko answered. "Remember you are a Jew." Aaron interrupted. "Whatever that is."

"You will learn. You can't change who you are. There are people who will hate you.

"This is America."

Bat'ko snorted. "This is America. You are such a boy, and I'm telling you Jews can be hated anywhere. Everywhere Jews are, we have had to fight. We don't have a country to fight for. We only fight for our faith."

"There is no one to fight here," Aaron said. "No one."

Bat'ko looked puzzled. Bat'ko usually had a sparkle in his eyes and was taller and the strongest man he ever met. Now his large frame was bent. Hoarsely, he spoke. "We are here because I didn't want you to have to fight. This was to be the end of fighting. But now you join the Army to fight."

Bat'ko sat on a bale of hay and stared up to Aaron. Was Bat'ko choosing what to say or going over old scenes, conjuring up the past? "When I was a boy the Russians crossed the Zabrotz River and destroyed our village. It was 1914. The soldiers and our neighbors, their pogroms, the police and government, destroyed Husiatyn, my town. Whatever was yours, your property, your home, was no longer. Almost everything, all the buildings, gone by fire. Jews scattered into the wind, and those who didn't were raped and murdered, everything gone. Even boys joined in the sport, hunting down and murdering Jews."

Bat'ko's head rested in his hands. He stared down to the dirt and scattered straw. "The Russians came into our house. They murdered my bubbee. My bat'ko's brother fought them with a shovel. He was killed by a soldier's bayonet. They burned down our home. My maty hid me in the nearby field, but I watched. They caught my older brother David and made him a Russian soldier. He was fourteen. They made a boy who couldn't kill into a soldier. He cried. I could see his tears as they took him away. You know, he would have been a rabbi. You are like him. He was a sweet boy. I did nothing but stare, unable to even cry. I never wanted that for you."

"Bat'ko, they are not making me do this. We are fighting so that does not happen." Aaron had never seen his Bat'ko like this. He wanted to reach out and comfort him, but this was not ever done in the Vanko house. "What happened to your brother?"

Without looking up, he answered. "I wonder every day. I never heard from him again." Rising and looking at Aaron, his eyes aflame, he said, "He is dead. I am sure." Staring off into the distance, he continued. "I would go fight for you, but I would fight the Russians. I wish I had fought that night. I would rather have died then to hide and live seeing that. I hate the Russians."

"This is a good fight."

"So, who are you fighting for? America? Even here has Jew haters. Especially those Americans who are holding out their hands who claim to help. I fear them most. At least I know the Jew haters. You stick to your own. I would not fight with the Russians. That is what you are doing. If there was a Jewish country, I would fight for it."

"Then why are we here? Why Iowa? Why not with Jews somewhere?"

"The people here don't care who we are or where we came from. We sell our beans, our chickens, our eggs. No one cares. Everybody is from somewhere else. They do not ask about religion. And here there are no rabbis. The rabbis in Husiatyn cowered, and the Russians took my brother. How can good people not do anything?"

"This is why I am going to fight," Aaron repeated meekly. Bat'ko's growl shattered the calm. "So you fight for America?

No! You stick to your own. Do you hear me, stick to your own! Where Christians make the laws, Jew are subservient. Germany is a country of Christians. This war starts out as Christians fighting Christians. Whoever wins, Jews lose."

Aaron bristled. "Yesterday, I was not Jewish. Today, I am. How can I stick to my own?" he argued.

Bat'ko's response came slowly and in a series of grunts, as if complaining about rough weeds. Aaron knew the grunts were for him. "You will find other Jews, and they will find you for the same reason. It's our race. Don't ever forget that. We were chosen."

"When was I to learn this?"

"You should have before now. That is true. But now you know. You have the rest of your life to learn. I never wanted to see you suffer like we did." Bat'ko held his breath, and looked around, like a dog sniffing out danger, as a gust of wind rattled loose barn boards. "God willing, you will have a lifetime to be Jewish." Bat'ko raised his hand and waved it from side to side. "Enough questions. You will learn."

Aaron could see the energy in Bat'ko return. *Now is not the time*, he thought. *But when will there be a good time? I'm running out of time.* "I am going to marry Mary," he blurted out.

Bat'ko turned his head and scowled. "You are such a man you can tell me what you will do." His steely gaze in the dim light caused Aaron to flinch. The barn was silent, except for a whistling breeze through the walls and Bat'ko's heavy breathing. The sun was finding new cracks in the boards and casting long thin streaks of light, capturing fine dust particles in their dance.

"You have not been listening. You can't marry a gentile. I know what is best for you." His voice rattled the barn. "I forbid it. I can do this. You go do your war thing. You will learn what this world is all about. There is no place for marrying outside of your religion."

"My religion. I have no religion. How can you do this to me? I won't let you."

"Go learn to be a Jew. When you come back, you'll be a good Jew. Someday we will move away and be with our kind. You will see. What I am saying is final."

Bat'ko pushed open the barn door and without even a sideways glance brushed by Aaron.

Before the barn door closed, Aaron exclaimed. "So, our God is different? Religions have different Gods?"

Bat'ko slowed and turned back to Aaron. "Prayers always go to God. Prayers go to the same God. Everyone's. Same God."

As Bat'ko was walked away, Aaron shouted, "So if all religions share the same God, why can't I marry her?"

Aaron moved back to the front porch and sat. Maty was rocking back and forth, the pillow from her bed supporting her back. Aaron watched in silence as she smoked a cigarette, smiling nervously, waiting for him to say something. He stared down into his hands folded together in his lap.

Maty broke the silence. "He is very sad you're leaving." "I'm not being stolen. I joined up."

"He knows."

After a minute, Aaron rose and moved his duffle bag to the front step. He stood looking out, glancing occasionally to the side of the barn where Bat'ko was working. The sound of a truck in the distance floated onto the porch. He looked back to Maty, who had stopped rocking and listened to the sound appear to take her son away. Together they sighed as it came to a stop

Fritz was grinning at him over the side of the truck bed. "Let's go, soldier," he said, his eyes sparkling in anticipation of the adventure ahead.

Aaron reached out to help his maty out of her rocker. She reached up to him and kissed him on the mouth, then on both cheeks, and placed her hand on the top of his head and smoothed his hair back, like when he was a small boy, and used the Ukrainian word she had used for him then. "My *syn*. Life will change. For all of us. The whole world." Her eyes were hard. Sad. She looked worn out.

Aaron threw his bag into the back of the truck and hopped in beside Fritz. As they drove away, he looked back to see Maty was still sitting on the porch. He could see Bat'ko had stepped out of the barn shadows and raised his hand to shade his eyes. Aaron thought he was waving goodbye, and so he waved. Bat'ko lowered his hand and turned away, his shoulders slumped.

Aaron looked over to Fritz, who was staring out over the tailgate to the dusty trail left by the truck, then back to his bat'ko and maty. *So, I am a Jew.*

<h1 style="text-align:center">6</h1>

AARON HAD NEVER traveled outside the state. His destination now was Camp Shelby, Mississippi, nearly a thousand miles from Camp Dodge, Iowa. All the boys on the bus, even the usually gregarious Tony, seemed subdued. They sat quietly, watching the Midwestern landscape roll past.

The first stop was Mexico, Missouri, where they lunched on ham sandwiches, potato salad, and Coca-Colas and picked up seven boys. In Poplar Bluff, Missouri, the bus made a dinner stop for an hour, then again during the night to refuel. The night's progress was marked by signposts, illuminated by the bus headlights as they passed through small sleepy towns. But sleep was difficult. The upright, hard, plastic bench seats, worn bus shocks, and the mixture of cigarette smoke and exhaust fumes drifting in through the open windows gave Aaron a headache. When the sun was just beginning to lighten the night sky, they breakfasted in Winona, Mississippi.

When they arrived at camp, a tall army drill sergeant earned instant legendary status when he stood directly in the path of the bleary-eyed boys stepping off the bus. The sergeant's uniform was as perfectly creased as his wooden demeanor. Standing only as far away from the bus door as the passage of one new soldier allowed, he instructed them to assemble in the center of the parking lot. When someone wasn't moving fast enough, the sergeant stepped into his path and locked the slacker's face in his memory. They all lined up and stood at attention, their first lesson in Army discipline. The first afternoon of boot camp was suffocating and hot, and the tension built like a rubber band stretching tighter. There would be more intimidating, physically exhausting, and mentally challenging days to come, but Aaron would always remember this day as one of the most anxious of his boot camp experience.

Left to stand for two hours in the oppressive heat, even the cockiest of boys dared only speak in whispers.

"Is he going to be our leader? God, I'll bet he's a tough son of a bitch."

"I wouldn't cross him."

"What's next?"

"Don't sit down: the D.I. will rip you a new asshole."

"Shut up, don't talk to me."

"We aren't supposed to talk."

Back and forth, the banter buzzed up and down the ranks.

In the days ahead, wearing down under the relentless glare and imposing will of the drill sergeant, the boys' whispered questions shifted.

"Why all the marching?"

"When will we get guns?"

"Does the Army know about this guy?"

"He just likes to bully people. I'd like to beat his brains in."

Boasts were always followed by a quick peek over the shoulder. A drill sergeant with a bad attitude, waiting for the Army, marching until you dropped every day, and worse. There was the loneliness, too. Sure, some found relief in the artful bitching about the Army, and others in longing gazes at pictures of sweethearts. Each recruit was required to write home. Some complained about Army life. Others penned two-liners: *Hell here. How's Dad?* And then there were the lonely ones who scrawled two-pagers and filled the bottom of the page with *Xs* and *Os*.

Aaron thought hard about what he should write to Mary. How could he explain in a letter that he was Jewish? His thoughts ran in circles. *Maybe it's better in a letter. For her. What will she think? Why say anything? I can be what I want. Bat'ko said I will always be Jewish. Maybe it's better. How can I explain?*

On the third night, Aaron wrote his first letter to Mary. As he sat on his bunk and adjusted to the dim light, pen in hand, he knew he had to tell her. But he couldn't.

Dear Mary,

Boot camp is hard, but not as hard not being with you. Our drill sergeant is a jerk. But the men in my barracks are pretty good guys. They're from all over, but mostly from the South. I don't always understand them, especially the ones from Mississippi. I'm glad Tony and Fritz are here.

Fritz made squad leader, so at least I've got that. We're holding each other up. I don't know when I'll see you again. I look at your picture every night—the one Tony took at Miller's Bend.

Sleep is hard to find and harder to keep. All the snoring and sleepwalking keeps me awake. They sound like hibernating bears. I'd hate to go to war as a sleepwalker.

Write me soon.

Aaron—Lucky Two

Two weeks into basic training, he felt he couldn't march one more step, that he was facing a wall of hot granite. He felt boredom and blisters on top of bored blisters, standing at attention at four in the morning, hoping the sun wouldn't rise and scorch the earth with another sweltering day. A good amount of the training was spent in the De Soto National Forest, setting up camps, digging in, and looking for make-believe enemies. Mosquitoes and flies hovered mercilessly and attacked without remorse in the oppressive heat; often the thermometer pierced the hundred-degree mark. The humidity clung to them like a fine, hot mist.

Aaron felt like an actor in a cheap costume in a movie without a script, learning a new language—curse words. Swearing was the jargon to describe everything, from the food to the weather. Crying was not an option, but your soul wept. Cowardice was forbidden, although at times you wanted to run and hide. He was a boy doing the manliest of things, preparing for war, learning to kill. As he watched the others, he still wondered if it was in his heart to take a life. Was it in any man's heart? Had Fritz looked into his soul? Was Aaron alone? Looking back, would he find out he was still just a boy?

Aaron had only a kid's hard times to call on, so even the worst moments in his young life now seemed mere flickers of inconvenience. He recalled a time when he had been ten and Bat'ko had sent him out to the bean field to tug and toss the worst infestation of giant ragweed; he had stood and stooped standing to battle, row after row, and the rows' end like a mirage he would never reach. Or the time he was told to bury a deer carcass that had died in the middle of the field, gut shot by a careless hunter, then rotted in the hot summer sun for days.

Boys becoming soldiers learned to march, to take orders, to salute and snap to, and to respond instantly to military rank identification. When the recruits felt they could take no more, surrendering their youth, energy, and will, the real training began—fundamentals of making war. They learned to rappel with ropes, make rope bridges, construct tent cities, dig foxholes, train with bayonets, be hygienic after hand-to-hand combat, crawl under barbed wire with machine guns firing over their heads, and march with purpose on twenty- five-mile hot-as-hell hikes into the woods, with full packs, helmets, canteens, and ammo packs to seek out a faux enemy. It was all part of learning to hate and kill.

When Aaron was issued an M1 Garand .30 caliber rifle, the drill sergeant admonished him, "Keep it with you at all times; it will become a matter of life or death. Keep it by your side. Never, never, never under any circumstances let it out of your sight."

Aaron was taught to assemble and disassemble it, in his bunk, in the field, in the dark of night, and in his dreams, and to shoot from all positions, out of foxholes, off sandbags, and on the flat ground with the gun resting on his elbow. *Take a deep breath, relax, aim, stop breathing, and squeeze the trigger.*

Pride was always lurking in the shadows, and now was whispering in Aaron's ear when the drill sergeant knelt beside him on the shooting range. His M1 rested on a sandbag, pointed at the shooting range target, a glowering Hitler-mustached cardboard man. Lying in the bright, scorching sunlight, Aaron couldn't suppress a smile when he heard, "That's good shooting. Here, keep it tight against your shoulder. Otherwise, you'll wear your shoulder out. Take a deep breath, hold it. Some guys say they can pull the trigger between heartbeats."

Had he turned a corner? Had the sergeant's horns come off, or was the devil in a white coat whispering in his ear? It was surprising and a bit disconcerting to hear that he was good with a rifle. Aaron filled with pride, not the *nationalstolz* that led Germany to this war, but nonetheless as dangerous. Being the best with a gun always got you on the front lines. And as he swelled with pride, he could hear Fritz's haunting words, *"Can you kill a man?"*

In the civilian world, pride can be a good thing, resulting in a job well done and even a promotion. But in the Army, it was just as likely to get you killed. "Follow me, men!" could be a man's final words. A more thoughtful choice for Aaron might have been to promote his ability to repair farm machinery, in the hopes of landing a job in the motor pool. The Army needed skilled mechanics. He could even end up driving for a general. All much safer than the front lines. But Aaron took up the challenge to be the best, winning a sharpshooter medal, then unit honors as the best with an M1, and in the end, a ticket straight to the front lines.

He wrote to Mary about his achievements, but once again he couldn't find the words to reveal what his maty had disclosed.

Dear Mary,
Happy Birthday! Wish I could have been there.
Did you blow out all 18 candles?
Do you know how much I love you and miss you? This is a damned lonely place. The men in my unit are good guys, but I'm sick of 'em. The drill sergeant isn't so bad after all. I did better than everyone else in rifle training. Even got a sharpshooter medal. Guys in my unit make fun of it. Say they'll make me into a sniper.
Good news, the war will end soon. The way it's going, by the time I get there, the fighting will be over. Wouldn't that be great?
I've got twenty more days of this and God knows what then. I heard we're gonna get some time off. As soon as they let me out of here, I'll race home.
I said I'd wait forever to marry you if I had to. But forever is too far off. When you say the word, let's go see the justice of the peace.
How's Bat'ko and Maty?
I love you, Aaron—Lucky Two

One week before the scheduled end of boot camp, the drill sergeant unexpectedly appeared. The minute he cleared the entrance, he announced they could go on about their business, and then, when it was quiet, he said, "At the end of training, it has been our custom that each unit volunteer men for the boxing tournament. First, I am asking for volunteers, and second—you know how it is, men: if I don't get 'em voluntarily,

I'll volunteer some of you. This is just a sport, but we are fighting men now, and I expect a good show." Uneasiness spread throughout the barracks. Sarge could have just as easily announced someone had died. Heads dipped low. Only a few bravely glanced at the others to see if anyone would volunteer.

One soldier's growling stomach broke the silence and laughter broke out. The sergeant smiled.

Most of the curious gazes fell on the obvious choices—Buster Klocko, a 200-pound block of a Chicago Polish kid, who had arrived at boot camp with a black eye and a gash over his good eye and had flunked every inspection on account of needing a shave. Carmelo Martini, a tall, thin Italian boy from St. Louis. Carmelo, known as Mello, was the first to step forward and volunteer. Buster would have been the first, but his mind didn't work that fast. As soon as Mello volunteered, so did Buster.

"Men, I need another volunteer. We need to provide four men. I'm not planning to disappoint General Carpenter." Another hand went up instantly.

"Darrell. Sure, you're up for this?"

Darrell nodded that he was. Darrell was a quiet boy, a loner who hadn't excelled in any phase of the training and was habitually last in everything. His behind-his-back nickname was "Dummy."

Sergeant Masters addressed the unit in a pleasant and friendly voice. "Men, you will be representing each member of your unit, and you'll do us all proud. We need another."

No other hands went up as he surveyed the room. "Aaron, I'll bet you'd do us proud."

Aaron was surprised to hear his name called. He was one of the larger boys, but never a fighter.

The drill sergeant made his way down the row of men and stood beside him, and once again he felt that sinking feeling, as if he was standing next to the devil himself.

"What do you think? You up for this?" The sergeant challenged him with a smile.

Aaron could taste the mix of sweet pride and bile in his throat. "Yes, sir, I'm up for it."

Even if he could have said no, he couldn't take back that Yes. He had never been in a fistfight, let alone in a boxing ring. Sure, once he got angry in a baseball game and there was pushing and shoving, but pushing and shoving on an Iowa ball diamond was different than an Army boot camp boxing tournament. Now he was a soldier, where toughness was demanded and timidity was ridiculed.

Weren't base boxing tournaments for guys who had lived on their own and had already been exposed to the blunt end of *kill or be killed?* Weren't there man-boys from all over the country to choose from, from all walks of life, the unloved, the beaten, and the banished? Why then Aaron?

There was little preparation for the tournament, little time for training or to reflect. As an untrained boxer, Aaron wondered what it was like to step out in the ring. Who would be his opponent? Fritz said not to worry. "Just keep your guard up." He held his hands high up close to his face to demonstrate. And, laughing, he added, "If you're outmatched, one punch and you won't feel a thing."

The encouragement of members of Aaron's unit filled him with pride, but he also had fears and doubts. *I can take it*, he said to himself. When he thought he couldn't, pride was always there to push him on. But pride had a second face, one that could be your worst opponent in the boxing ring.

That Saturday night, only four fights were settled by knockout. Mostly, the others featured flailing fists cutting through the air, which resulted in three-round decisions by the three judges. Two were mercifully stopped when the fighters were knocked out on their feet and still being pounded mercilessly.

Dummy Darrell's fight was the most entertaining, and he was the most pitied, going down in the first round. He ended up in the infirmary. The referee had called the two fighters to the center of the ring to begin the fight, instructed them to touch gloves and box. Immediately after touching gloves, Darrell's opponent took one step forward and brought his right hand crashing against Darrell's temple. It was doubtful Darrell ever saw the punch.

Buster Klocko wasn't victorious either, a surprise to the members of his unit, but his opponent had training. When a tough-guy fighter is pitted against the boxer, the boxer usually wins. The boxer shifted right and left past Buster's wild frustrated and angry attempts to land even one punch. The boxer deftly darted in and out, and then, with the precision of a rapier, tore away at Buster's face.

Buster, impatient as a bull in heat, stalked his opponent, strutting from side to side and lunging wildly. His opponent, ever the skilled athlete, danced away but inflicted harm with each retreat. Slow and helpless, Buster looked every bit the amateur he was. In the end, he was bloody and wobbly in the center of the ring as the judges announced his defeat.

Carmelo was a different kind of surprise to the over 1,000 men who were jammed into the gymnasium. It seemed as if cockiness alone could carry the man. Always smiling, always on the go, he moved like a ballerina with boxing gloves, presenting a frustrating and elusive target. Unable to land blows to any effect, his slower opponent awkwardly moved from side to side, throwing punches into the air, while Carmelo sent jab after jab to his opponent's face. The fight went three rounds, but the outcome was never in doubt. Aaron's fight could have ended in the second round and should have. The first round was a mismatch and the second started out when the Minnesota Swede's loaded-up right hand caught Aaron squarely on the nose, which promptly spouted blood, like a newly struck oil well.

The second most dangerous man in the ring for any fight can be the referee, though. When the blow came, Aaron immediately buckled to his knees and then slowly slumped to the floor. Rather than beginning the count, the referee stood over Aaron and encouraged him to get up and finish the fight. He took him by the arm and helped him to his feet.

The blow stung, and there was blood everywhere. Aaron couldn't see through his watery eyes or think clearly. As he stood before his opponent, he shook his head from side to side, as if to avoid being stung by swarming bees. For the remainder of the round, blows were delivered at will, one crushing blow to the heart and a hook that knocked him backward to the mat again. When he dropped to his knees, he could see the blurry outline of his opponent waiting to charge the second he got to his feet. The bell sounded. *Saved by the bell?*

Early in the third round, another right-hand punch split his eyebrow open and closed his left eye, which left him blind to the right hand of the big Swede. But it was an uppercut that took Aaron down. Quitting was still not in his heart, but it was his legs. Unable to climb the ropes to his feet, he rolled over onto his back. The bright white lights overhead had to be searchlights from hell.

That night, as he lay in the barracks in a pool of sweat, Aaron's hammer-and-anvil head pounding mixed with the jungle sounds of the sleeping men. Earlier, he had received a letter from Mary. He had held it close by all day, waiting for a private moment when he could read and savor it. In the dim light of the bathroom hallway, with only one open eye, he angled her letter to capture the light. He traced his hand along the sharp edges of the stitches in his forehead as he began to read.

Dear Aaron,

I miss you so much. Hearing from you is so precious.

I celebrated my birthday at the Casaloma with new friends from the plant. No cake. No candles. The next day, I moved in with Millie. Millie has two other friends from the plant living here until her husband comes home. It's so weird working there, making 50-caliber bullets. My boss said so far the plant has made over two billion. It's hard to imagine. Good for the war effort, more bullets.

Dad made a big fuss when I moved out. He keeps saying how things will change while you're gone. It's like he is wishing for that. It makes me mad. He said you might not come back. I hate him for saying that. And I feel terrible for hating him that way. I know you'll come back. There is no doubt.

I go back and forth. Do we wait until you get back from wherever you are off to, or marry now? My heart says I'm eighteen and I can do what I want, so let's get married. This war makes things so clear, so black and white. I want you to take my love with you wherever you go, wherever you are. Mom and Dad want me to be happy. But they're so old-fashioned. Father would never approve anyway.

I agree, forever is too long. So let's get married now.

I love you and miss you.

Mary, the Lucky One

Aaron dropped the letter to his chest and gazed up at the ceiling. He was surrounded by snoring, yet so alone. *What do I tell her? When? How?*

* * *

The end of boot camp was coming, and the habits of the soldiers shifted from barracks chatter about killing Germans and Japs to counting down the days until heading home. At the same time, it was being decided where the new boot camp graduates would be sent. What was becoming clear was only a few would end up together. Tony was assigned an artillery designation and after furlough was to report to Fort Sill. Fritz was invited to apply for Officers Candidate School and was to report immediately to Fort Hood, Texas. So much for the three blood-brothers staying together.

Aaron longed for his furlough and anxiously awaited news on where he was headed. He hoped his destiny wasn't foot soldiering. Every day more pieces fell into place for everyone but Aaron. The drill sergeant had shown an interest in him on the firing range, but when Aaron didn't show much promise for fighting in the boxing match, he thought maybe he'd lost his edge.

The last few nights, just before lights out, the barracks were especially subdued. Like a silent rite of passage, boys now were men and feeling like soldiers. Out of nowhere, the sergeant appeared in the doorway and shouted out for Aaron to join him in his office. Aaron stood at attention until the sergeant motioned for Aaron to sit. Being at ease around the drill sergeant was worse than standing at attention.

"How would you like to take a little trip to Georgia for some additional training? Fort Benning."

Most of the soldiers in his unit already had their orders, so pride once again brought a smile to Aaron's face. He was being singled out like Fritz and Tony had been. One day the sergeant was the devil and the next, he wasn't such a bad guy. Still, the sergeant's crooked smile was alarming.

"Sir, I never thought of the Army as providing soldiers with choices," Aaron said with a friendly smile.

The sergeant returned his smile. "Your marksmanship qualifies you for sniper training. This is a great honor. How do you feel about that?"

"I don't know. Sounds kind of—"

The sergeant interrupted, "This is not one of those opportunities where I can volunteer you. You get to choose."

What does a sniper do? Aaron thought. *It sounded like sitting in a tree shooting people.* "I don't know what it'd be like . . . shooting people."

"Shooting people?" The sergeant's expression turned sour. "This is war, dammit. Where have you been?"

Flustered, Aaron answered, "Sorry, I wasn't sure—"

"Well, I sure as hell am. You're not qualified. You'll get your orders tomorrow. We can't have reluctant snipers. You're not tough enough anyway. God damn it. What do you think we do in the Army anyway? Now get out of here."

As he left, the sergeant said, "You're in the Army now. Good luck on the front lines."

The next day, Aaron received his orders to depart for Europe, after a two-week furlough. Aaron quickly jotted a letter to Mary, telling her he would be home soon. When he arrived, he would catch a ride from the bus station with Tony's dad and call her. Maybe Betsy could give her a ride to Miller's Bend and they could meet there.

Aaron was surprised to receive another letter from Mary the day before he was to leave. Alarmed, he could tell it was brief as he tore open the envelope.

Aaron,

I've made all the arrangements. Millie has been a big help, driving me around and supporting me and teaching me to drive. She loaned me her car to meet you.

I stopped by the bakery. Tony's mom said Martin Claywell was killed. He was on a ship called Fiske that was torpedoed. Thought you'd want to know.

Call me at Millie's. Millie Armstrong. You have to call the operator. Counting the minutes till we're together.

Love ya,

Mary

7

LEAVING MISSISSIPPI DREW cheers from the soldiers, and before too long, they were through Memphis and heading into Arkansas, making frequent stops to pick up or drop off military personnel and civilians.

For Aaron, the bus ride home was unbearably hot. The windows could only be opened halfway, and the smell of testosterone, sweat, and cigarettes ate up all the fresh air in the first half hour, which lengthened the journey. It was through drooping eyes Aaron read the sign, *Entering the State of Iowa. Where the Tall Corn Grows.* Now only hours remained.

When he arrived at Tony's, he called the operator and asked to be connected to Millie Armstrong. After several polite attempts to break through the party line phone, he asked the operator to break in and explain he was a soldier who had just arrived home and it was important he reach his girl. Hearing Mary's voice twisted his tongue as he stammered in a hoarse, deep voice, "I'm home. Can you meet me at Miller's Bend?"

Mary squealed with delight. "Yes!"

Tony said his dad would take him, but Aaron insisted on walking the straight route across three farmer's fields and through Johnson's pasture. Home; he was home. Mary had farther to go, but she was coming by car, and her route was circuitous and potholed, so he'd beat her there and have time to cool off by the water.

As he was crossing the pasture, three grazing horses watched as he passed. "Hello, Mister High Socks!" Aaron called out. Mister High Socks was the first horse he had ridden. As a boy, he had used to stop by Ricky Johnson's after school, but when Ricky's father died, Ricky had moved away. The horse had stayed with the farm. Aaron didn't know if Ricky was in the war.

When he had left in early summer, the tall cottonwood trees that stood at attention along the roadside had dropped their fluffy, white seeds, covering the countryside like summer snow. Late summer had dried the field into brown stubble. At the end of the pasture, he hopped the barbed wire fence and caught his first glimpse of a car parked at the far end of the lane. Road dust, like fine, brown mist, made it difficult to see and turned the edge of the roadway brown. She must have just arrived.

When he broke free of the cloud of dust, he saw her standing with her hand shielding her eyes, searching for her first glimpse of him. At first, she was a splash of blue, the color of her regal dress. Seeing her looking for him made him smile, and he started to jog. Army training made this full-pack lope feel like a casual stroll.

Mary could see he was wearing his uniform with his duffle bag slung over his shoulder. He was taller than she remembered, but there was something else. The closer he got, the more there was something about his appearance that was off. When he was close enough to lock gazes, Aaron was smiling broadly, but Mary looked worried.

Aaron tossed his duffle bag aside and reached for her, lifting her off the ground and twirling her in a circle. When he released her, she stepped away. They held hands at arm's length, gazing into each other's eyes, stopping time, melding together. Her smile slipped quickly away, and when she grew serious again; he felt alarmed. She looked down at his swollen hands, then up to his two black eyes, with raw, still healing cuts around his temples. It had taken twelve stitches to close the gash over his right eye.

"Aaron, what happened?" She guided his hands to her waist and then, tugging at his arms, pulled them around her. "Are you okay?"

"I'm fine," he answered firmly. Inside, though, his confidence was waning and he was trembling.

"You're not fine, Aaron. What happened?"

"Base boxing tournament," he said. "I should've warned you." Aaron shrugged.

"I didn't know you were a boxer."

"Me neither. I wish I could say you should see the other guy." He forced a smile.

Mary was still searching for understanding in the awkward silence. She tugged at his hand. "Let's walk."

As they wandered hand and hand toward the river, Mary couldn't resist peeking over to Aaron. It wasn't the blackened eyes or the swollen face or even the cuts that bothered her most, but the dull look in his eyes. He had the concerned look of a man with responsibilities, not the look of someone happy to be home, but a look that said home might never be the same.

When they stopped at the water's edge, as they had so many times before, she was sniffling. She turned toward him, climbing back into his arms, in tears.

"Oh, Aaron, I'm so happy you are home. I couldn't wait for this moment, but you're so . . . different, and there's no time to . . . you'll be gone again, just like that."

Stepping back, holding both her hands, Aaron studied her face. The smile he'd dreamed of meeting with a kiss was replaced now by wide-eyed dread, running makeup, and bright red pursed lips. Her auburn curls danced about in the wispy wind, just like he remembered, but her brandy-colored eyes were sad, begging for good news when there was none.

His heart ached with racing thoughts of what he had to tell her. Bat'ko was adamant. He could not marry her and even threatened to stand in their way. The pastor would feel even more strongly that they should never be together. Because he was a Jew.

Aaron knew his own heart, but what about hers when she learned the secret? He thought he knew hers. But just a few words might start a change in her mind. Her religious upbringing could light a small fire of doubt, and the fear in her heart could become a raging prairie fire. He saw that fervor in Bat'ko and Maty. He knew that same zeal existed in the pastor and Mary's mother. He felt his whole existence was on the line, more now than the life he faced going off to war, which seemed trivial in the face of what he was about to tell her.

Shaking his head and dropping his hands from hers, he bit his swollen lip. "Mary. Oh, Mary, I have something to tell you."

Mary shivered, brought her hands together, and raised them up to her chest as if she was offering a prayer. The taste of her lipstick was still on his lips. She searched his eyes.

The words came out in a rush. "The night before I left for boot camp, I made Maty tell me what my religion is. For you. I had to know. For us. Maty told me I was Jewish. I never knew. I don't even know right now what being a Jew means. To me. Or what it means to you either."

"You didn't know?"

"I never thought . . . It never came up. We prayed like other families at dinner. Just like at Tony's or Fritz's. Maty said it was the same God as everyone's since I was a kid. I made her tell me, though. And Bat'ko was so angry." He took a deep breath. "I still want to marry you."

"Oh, Aaron. That is what you had to tell me?" Mary's smile returned to her face just like he remembered, just like he longed for. "You nut. I love you for you. Nothing can change that. Nothing." Aaron reached out for her and drew her into his arms, and sighed deeply. "Mary. You are such a blessing." He held her as tightly as he could and whispered in her ear, "So, did you?"

She pushed back, smiling dreamily up at him. "Yes. It's all arranged. We have to go downtown. You need to sign some papers. I begged a justice of the peace to meet us on Labor Day. Told him I was marrying my soldier before he had to leave. And Millie made a bedroom for us in the upstairs attic. Our first home. Kinda. I think you'll like it."

* * *

It was after dark by the time he arrived home. Cubby announced his presence with loud barking when he entered the barnyard, wagging his tail and smiling over gray whiskers in the moonlight.

He entered through the back door into a storage room that was crowded with coats, boots, dirty clothes, and shelves stacked with Maty's canning. There was an old, tattered rug in the corner where Cubby slept. He peered into the living area, with its familiar rocking chair, sagging wool-stuffed chair, and three rickety, rusted folding chairs stacked against the wall. He thought his parents might have gone to bed already, in their little room off the kitchen and living area, next to his room, and the storage room full of musty boxes and things waiting to be fixed. He hesitated. He should have thought to bring in some water for Maty from the pump outside, and to stop on the way at the outhouse, thirty tiny, hasty boy steps away from the house, so he wouldn't wake them with another creak of the back door.

Cubby crowded in with him, sniffing at his hand. "*Shhh*, boy!" he laughed. Everything was the same. Everything. "Don't wake them."

As he stepped in, he saw Maty in the low-ceilinged room, a pendant pull-string light casting an amber glow over her as she lifted herself, flinching in pain, from her chair to greet him. Motioning toward the closed bedroom door, she said, "He's down in the back." She studied him, as a mother would, and said, "You're so tall." In the dim kitchen light, she reached up and felt his face and ran her hand gently over his healing black and blue forehead. "What did they do to you?"

"It's nothing. Really. I fell." Pulling her into his arms, he said with a sigh, "Maty, I have to leave soon. A week from Monday."

Maty moaned. "So soon?"

"There's something else. Mary and I are getting married. Monday," Aaron blurted, wanting to make the declaration immediately, as he had planned.

She moved away and stood, leaning on the back of a kitchen chair.

He expected anger. In a pool of sweat in his boot camp bunk, he had gone over this moment in his mind, ready to fight for Mary. Instead of giving him the scolding he anticipated, she raised her eyebrows and said, "A maty knows her syn. I knew she was the one.

And you have a strong head."

"She is," Aaron said, smiling down at her. "Bat'ko won't accept, will he?"

"Not ever."

"That's a long time," Aaron said. "Maty, why does he do this to me? What is he afraid of? Why isn't my happiness as important as his religion?"

"You are too young to see." "But not too young."

"These are complicated times. He is a good man. When he can't make sense of it all, he is down-hearted, and—"

"We'll be moving in together," Aaron declared.

Maty's shoulders slumped, but she kept her thin smile. "Why can't we all be happy? We won't live forever. He will never; he is stuck. Caught between old and the new. But there is always the old and always the new. If you live long enough, old or new, who is to say which is better? But when it comes to the killing, I hope there is a new after, for you, syn."

"I didn't know you were so wise," Aaron said.

"Old age either makes you wise or kills you." She smiled.

"I hate that he wants me to choose between him and Mary. As if I must choose his God, even when he says we all pray to the same God. Let me tell him," Aaron said firmly. "Maybe he will accept it."

Squinting up to the ceiling, like answers were written there, she pulled a pouch of tobacco out of her apron pocket and packed a cigarette. She struck a match on the stove and lit it, sending a plume of smoke curling off the ceiling and down the walls. "You can try. We all have different ways. Your bat'ko has his reasons."

Aaron shrugged his shoulders. "So does my heart have to pick his way? Does God make me choose a religion?"

"Oh, Aaron, you'll always be Jewish. Keep God close and remember the best synagogue is in your heart." Maty abruptly changed the subject.

"You really leave so soon? This terrible war."

"It's a good war. You know they are killing Jews just for being Jewish. That's me. Who would do that?"

"Evil does that. Evil waits for weak people and then tells them religious stories." Bracing herself on the back of the table chair, she moved around the table to stand close to Aaron. "Evil is always out there. You may not recognize it. If God were living here, people would burn his fields."

* * *

The next morning, Aaron made his way through the property. After being gone for two months, seeing the farm in daylight was disturbing. Time and hard winters always tore away at the house, but now it seemed to sag. Everything was noticeably worse. How could Bat'ko shovel the roof with his bad back this winter? The rattling of windows in the constant Iowa wind had been opening small, unseen gaps that allowed the snow to work its way inside and accumulate on the window ledge, opening wider seams for the summer dust. The battle to keep outside dirt from taking over the interior of the house seemed to have been lost.

He crossed to the barn, where he knew he would find Bat'ko. He could see the defeated bean field, brown, scorched by sun and drought. Unfairly, the only green life that remained was the return of the grotesque giant ragweed, like statues with long strangling arms. Never so neglected, so pitiful, had Bat'ko's fields been. With great pride, he had tended them, like his barn, like his house. Anything that came under his domain endured the focus of his eyes and the care of his hands.

Last winter had been colder than normal, and Aaron could see the firewood supply was low for this time of the year. The woodpile should be shoulder-height by this time. Wood was necessary for cooking as well as heating. There was a stand of drought-limp dogwood, hickory and oak trees that grew alongside a seasonal stream that ran along the property's edge. But Bat'ko hadn't been there.

When Aaron entered the barn, Bat'ko smiled broadly as he painfully unhinged his back to stand and opened his arms to embrace him. Then, holding him by his shoulders at arm's length he shook his head. "You look like *dyyavo*."

"It's nothing."

"Nothing? I can see it's nothing." "Maty says your back is not so good?" "It's nothing. It'll pass. It always does."

"I can see it's nothing." Aaron smiled. "Looks like I have some work to do."

Bat'ko shrugged his shoulders in answer.

"I'll clean your field this week before I leave. What else can I do?" Aaron could see the stall was unkempt and the top rail was sagging. "How bad is your back?"

"It'll be okay. Everything passes. Everything. Even my back." "Not everything. Bat'ko, I know time passes, but I think you may still be upset about Mary."

Bat'ko shuffled away and leaned against one of the barn columns. Raising his eyebrows and shrugging his shoulders, he said, "Your maty says life is too short. That I am old, and I have my ways."

"I won't let you turn me out. Someday, maybe, you will accept Mary like your own. Life will go on. I will make you proud. I will be here to help you. I will clean your fields. I will fix the gate. And scrub this stall. What else can I do?

"You think I can't do this?" Bat'ko questioned. "Of course, you can. But while I'm here."

Bat'ko turned back to working the leather harness he had been holding when Aaron had entered the barn.

Aaron examined the stall, glancing at his father. "Bat'ko, there is another thing. I leave in a week. I have to go to New York. They haven't told me, but I am sure I will be fighting the Germans."

Bat'ko waved his hand toward Aaron. "We should be fighting the Russians. Not just Germans. Let's not talk about this."

"Yes, I don't want to talk about it either." Aaron took a deep breath. "Mary and I are getting married."

Startled, Bat'ko jerked his head up. Red-faced, he growled, "And I don't want to talk about that! You know how I feel. You are not just going against your father. You go against the Torah. You would do that and then put your life on the line in war? What is wrong with you?"

Aaron pursed his lips and went out to tackle the weedy field. There was no point in arguing. Neither of them was going to change their minds, not this week. Not today.

Sunday, Aaron paid his respects to Lloyd Claywell over his son's death. Lloyd asked if he wanted to buy Martin's car, and with a handshake and fifty dollars down, he bought it, with the rest to come when he could afford it.

From there he drove to Millie's, where they would live for the first week of their married life. Mildred and Butch Armstrong's farm was a mile north of the ordnance plant, just outside the Ankeny city limits. Before Butch had joined the Army, they had contracted to purchase it for eighty-five dollars per acre from Butch's folks, who lived across the road, a football field away. Butch had accepted a commission in the Marines, and like Aaron, he was waiving the farm deferral. Millie was serving her country on the home front, working in the munitions plant.

The story-and-a-half, cracked, white-painted farmhouse had a long front porch facing the road. A grove of trees protected it from the hot afternoon sun and wind, and a cinder drive circled a six-foot-wide oak tree. Butch's grandparents had built the house in 1888. In 1938, both had passed away. The land was still farmed by Butch's two brothers and his father, who lived on adjacent properties. Before leaving for the Army, Butch had replaced the roof and added an indoor bathroom and running water to the kitchen. Dreams for complete restoration had been interrupted by Butch's call to duty.

The plan was for Aaron and Mary to occupy the unfinished upstairs for the week he was home. A single pull-string low-wattage bulb light fixture hung from the center of the ceiling. It added spooky shadows to the open roof rafters, which pitched so severely Aaron could only stand in the middle of the room. They positioned springs and a musty mattress in front of the single open window on top of the wood-planked floor. A rag-quilt and two mildewed feather pillows completed their bed. One of the window-weight ropes had decayed and split in two, so the window was propped open with a stick. Dusty sheer curtains were pulled back from the window.

* * *

Labor Day Monday, Aaron and Mary tied the knot in a quick courthouse ceremony. Not another soul was around except the justice of the peace and two clerks who had volunteered to come in and serve as witnesses. Mary hadn't told her folks. She'd assured Aaron she'd deal with it when he left, knowing how upset they would be and wanting to avoid it until he was gone.

She was wearing a navy blue and white polka dot dress she had made just for this occasion. It was buttoned in front by four heart- shaped buttons down to a fitted waist tied loosely with a matching cotton belt in a perfect bow. A white cardigan sweater was tied around her waist. He wore his uniform, pressed and clean.

Afterward, they walked hand and hand on the streets of Des Moines and went to the matinee at the RKO Orpheum Theater. An Abbott and Costello movie, *In Society,* was showing. They sat in the back row and cuddled like the young lovers they were, and squirmed with side-splitting laughter throughout the movie, especially at the "everybody hates hats" Susquehanna Hat Company routine. They poked each other playfully the rest of the day, asking, "Where's Bagel Street?"

That night, they had dinner at the Casaloma, a nightclub restaurant on the north side of Des Moines, with Millie and her girlfriends, who were also living on the farm. A small local chamber orchestra played swing tunes, and Aaron alternated dancing with the three of them. "This is harder than boot camp!" he joked.

When Aaron and Mary danced, she nestled her head on his shoulder, and he pulled her close with his hand on her lower back. In between dances, they sat close, holding hands, which prompted glances and giggles from her friends. Nervously, they watched the time. When the band announced it was nearing midnight and they would play for two hours more, Aaron and Mary popped out of their seats to leave.

At home, clinging together, unwilling to be separated even for a second, they felt their way up the stairs to their second-floor bedroom. The cloud-covered moon on a dark country night offered not even a flitter of light through the open window. They couldn't see their hands in front of their faces. When they reached their bedroom, she moved away.

Reaching out for her, he whispered, "Mary."

There was no response, and he continued to feel for her in the pitch black. "Mary," he whispered louder.

A stifled giggle broke the silence. He rushed to her and found her open arms. Seeking her lips, he found a nose and a cheek, then another giggle, then her moist lips. Taking a step back, Aaron caught the edge of the floor mattress and fell, backstroking the air down onto it.

Mary burst out laughing.

Aaron collected himself and rose up to his knees and pulled her down onto the bed. Suddenly, she broke away and stood. In the black nothingness, he could hear her heavy breathing and the rustling of her dress being removed. Aaron held his breath and listened.

In the darkness, he could hear her tugging at the buttons on her dress, then a swish and the rustle of her slip as it fell to the floor. She paused and stood motionless. Aaron held his breath. When they met this time, there was no searching. Nature took over. He found her, and she found him, their hands exploring places no longer forbidden, their hearts beating out love and precious time. The mattress springs squeaked loudly, so they quickly slid the mattress to the floor, and found a rhythm in the still darkness, wanting more and more, climbing upward into the clouds, into heaven, still climbing higher and higher, never satisfied, reaching for the unreachable, until their breathing was overtaken by the silence.

* * *

Tuesday, Mary had to go back to work, and Aaron went to help his folks. For two days, he labored to rid the field of the giant ragweed scourge. How could Bat'ko keep up when he was away? He gathered as much wood as was available, felled two trees for curing, and split and stacked what he could. Unpainted siding boards were pulling away from the house, and Aaron spent one afternoon nailing the siding and stuffing what cracks he could to keep the mice and the elements out.

When they worked together, conversations between Bat'ko and Aaron were mostly grunts and groans and a few instructions. Bat'ko's silence ruled and what few utterances there were were short declarations.

Aaron wanted to talk about Mary. He couldn't get her out of his mind and wanted his Bat'ko to share in his happiness, but he dared not bring up that he was already married. Did Bat'ko know? Aaron figured he was working the matter over in his mind like he always did. Maybe he had softened to the idea, but Aaron knew not to mention it.

Throughout their days together, Aaron could feel Bat'ko's gaze on him. The silence was like screeching chalk on a blackboard. He also wanted to say something about boot camp and finally broke the silence and blurted out, "I got a marksman medal."

Bat'ko was sweating profusely, huffing and puffing as they weeded, groaning every time he bent over and straightened up. "You were always a good shot."

"The sergeant wanted me to be a sniper." "What, to sit and wait for people to kill?" "That's what I thought."

"Maybe that's how wars are won, who kills the most?" Bat'ko shook his head. "You could say no?"

"I did."

"War. It never ends. One war ends, and the devil starts his work over again on weak people." His voice dropped off into a whisper. "But always boys do the fighting."

Aaron pretended not to hear.

Saturday marked the beginning of another end. Mary had two days off work before Aaron had to leave Monday. For two days, from the porch, they watched massive thunderheads roll in from the west until fierce winds and sideways sheets of rain drove them indoors. It hadn't rained all week, and this weather reminded them of the May floods before he left for boot camp, and then on maneuvers in the heat of training.

"The last time I saw rain like this was in early August. We were bivouacked in the De Soto National Forest. It rained a solid week," Aaron said. "Nothing but wet. When we woke up in the morning, we were lying in pools of water. Even when it wasn't raining, the humidity dripped from the forest canopy like mist. During the day the temperature was over 100 degrees. The mosquitoes were like small birds. We were all covered with festering sores that itched. Everyone prayed we wouldn't be sent to some jungle island. That's where Tony is heading. Don't know about Fritz. Those of us who got orders for Europe felt lucky." Aaron laughed. "Imagine feeling lucky to go to war anywhere."

That rainy Sunday night, Mary cooked dinner: steak and potatoes with lots of onions. Aaron sat at the kitchen table and watched. It seemed they had run out of things to talk about. Several times in the last few days, they had shared plans for when the war was over, but always in the silence between, there were unspoken, dead-end *ifs* and *buts*. Over dinner, they sneaked sad peeks at one another, gazes filled with the hope that all would end well and the fear it would not. After dinner, they drove to Miller's Bend and sat in the car and listened to CBS reporter Douglas Edwards: "Two American forces are on the attack today. First Army forces are threatening the German city of Aachen and Patton's Third Army has moved six miles forward . . . "

Aaron interrupted. "Wow, we're about to invade Germany.

Maybe the war'll be over before I get there."

Edwards continued. "Today, they are singing in England."

We're going to hang out the washing on the Siegfried Line. Have you any dirty washing, Mother dear? We're gonna hang out the washing on the Siegfried Line. 'Cause the washing day is here.

There were also positive reports on Navy and Marine successes in the Pacific. Butch, Millie's husband, was a part of the Amphibious Corps

3rd Marine Division and had received a field promotion to major. Millie had already received word he was safe after the Americans recaptured Guam.

Cuddled together, they listened to *The Pepsodent Hour*, starring Bob Hope and Amos 'n' Andy. Following that, the crooner Bing Crosby sang "Don't Fence Me In" and The Andrew Sisters trilled "Shoo Shoo Baby." Later, there were songs by Judy Garland, the Milles Brothers, Ella Fitzgerald, and the Ink Spots. The rain beat on the roof of the truck until it finally stopped.

In the middle of the night, their last for what seemed like forever, moonlight found a path through a cloud break and illuminated the cobwebbed, moldy, rain-stained, open ceiling and the naked, single-pull bulb hanging over the bed. The world seemed to pause; night creatures watched and listened.

"Mary, you awake?" Aaron whispered.

"How could I be asleep? I don't want this night to ever end."

"Me neither."

Mary rolled over and laid her head on Aaron's chest as he put his arm around her. "I'm afraid to go to sleep. If I do, then tomorrow will be here, and you'll be gone."

"I just can't imagine what it's going to be like. When I start thinking about it, I'm scared," Aaron whispered.

"It's hard to make sense of it." "It won't be long." Aaron sighed.

"Three hours." Mary looked up in the dark, squinting to see his face illuminated by the moonlight. "Two hours, fifty minutes," she said, holding her wrist up in front of her face as if she was wearing a wristwatch, "and thirty-nine seconds."

"You counting the seconds till I'm gone?"

"And then when you leave, I'll start counting the days and hours until you're back."

Rolling over on top of Aaron, she pulled the quilt up over them, covering their heads. "There is no out there,'" she said. "There is only in here. Maybe morning will never come. No tomorrow, or the next day, just us right here."

Part 2

WAR

In Flanders Fields the poppies blow
Between the crosses, row on row,
That mark our place; and in the sky
The larks, still bravely singing, fly Scarce heard amid the guns below.
We are the Dead. Short days ago
We lived, felt dawn, saw sunset glow,
Loved, and were loved, and now we lie
In Flanders fields.
Take up our quarrel with the foe:
To you from failing hands we throw
The torch, be yours to hold it high.
If ye break faith with us who die
We shall not sleep, though poppies grow In Flanders fields.
—Lieutenant Colonel John McCrae
Canadian war poet

8

A FEW WEEKS after Aaron returned to Hattiesburg, he was transported by train to New York, where he boarded the the Queen Mary, repainted and named the Gray Ghost, bound for Scotland. The ship was crowded with faces he might never see again and men he might die with. The luxury liner had been refitted for soldier transport and quickly earned the reputation for outrunning subs, able to turn 30 knots compared to the 17 knots of a German submarine. Twice, he was ordered topside to don a life vest as they ran full speed to avoid enemy subs. The ship also earned a reputation for indestructibility when she accidentally rammed a British cruiser and cut her in half.

Soon after he arrived in Glasgow, Aaron was transported to Cheltenham, England, where he joined thousands of other soldiers in a tent city larger than many Iowa towns. By moonlight, along with fifty or so other men, Aaron marched up and down rows of loudly snoring and sleep-talking soldiers to their assigned bunks in their wood-floored tents. The marching arrivals grew smaller in number until he was the only one left. The private that guided him with a flashlight opened the tent door and scanned the interior. All the cots were empty.

Aaron threw his bedroll on a cot near the back. "Looks like I'm first."

Laughing, the private answered, "Before you wake up, it'll be full. Then it will be empty again. The guys here yesterday left this morning. This place is like a bucket with a large hole. Don't get comfortable." As the soldier walked away he turned and added, "On second thought, get comfortable. Later, this place is gonna seem like the Waldorf Astoria."

At night, the soldiers were free to roam the streets of Cheltenham, where they mostly sat in local pubs and drank English stout. Three days later, Aaron was loaded onto a train bound for Southampton and immediate transport to France. There, he boarded the Duke of Wellington. After a long day on rough seas, the soldiers roared cheers when land was sighted, but as they neared the city, twilight revealed the ragged outline of a bombed-out Le Havre, France.

How different the view from the Duke's deck was from the newsreels Aaron had seen. The harbor was littered with sunken ships, so he was loaded onto an LCI to get ashore. He debarked in a fog so thick he had to feel his way on rubbery legs onto the temporary dock. *What time is it in Iowa? What is Mary doing right now? Is she thinking about me?*

When Aaron arrived at the reception depot, he was marched to a transitional area, where he waited for deuce-and-a-half truck transportation to Red Horse. Red Horse comprised several camps named for American cigarettes: Camp Chesterfield, Lucky Strike, Old Gold, Philip Morris, Pall Mall, Tareyton, Wings, Home Run, and Twenty Grand. Aaron's destination was Camp Lucky Strike, which could house up to 58,000 men. Located between Canny and Saint-Valery, France, soldiers called it *repple-depple*, replacement depot, or sometimes *the pneumonia hole*.

After two hours of waiting, Aaron wandered on wobbly sea legs in the Army-mandated darkness, cold to the bone in the soupy fog, along with soldiers as bewildered and lost as he was. When he arrived at his tent, in the dim glow of a hell-hot heating stove, he groped his way to a cot, where he found folded blankets and a musty pillow neatly stacked at the foot of the bed. He removed his boots and rolled onto the canvas cot while in his uniform. Exhausted, he thought he would immediately fall to sleep. But his head was still riding the seas, listening to the muffled voices of fellow soldiers echoing in the black tranquility.

In the dim morning, Aaron woke in a crowded, roasting tent of strangers, many of whom had continued to arrive throughout the night. The dirt floor was now mud. When he stepped outside, he was amazed to find himself in the middle of row after row of drab, Taj-Mahal-shaped canvas tents.

The tension was palpable. Every replacement soldier was inching toward the time when they would replace the killed and wounded on the battlefield. Every day, sections of camp cleared out. Now Aaron was ticking off precious moments before he would move to the war zone. The war was going to be won by the biggest army in history, expendable boys who waited like mounds of dirt waiting to fill potholes. Some men would be there only a few days, and others a few weeks, depending on the evolving war strategy and the number of casualties.

In a tent city for replacements, a soldier's time was measured in minutes, hardly enough time to remember the names of soldiers he met. The instinct of camp soldiers, even if the wait was longer than a day or so, was to resist making friends anyway. Veteran soldiers, what few there were, stayed aloof, too. Aaron had never felt more alone. For the most part, the soldiers he met were lost in a blur of various shapes and sizes and unintelligible accents. He was accused of sounding like a hick.

One of the soldiers who arrived that first night was an exception. It was early morning. The loud snoring had kept Aaron awake throughout the night, and the tent was suffocating hot. When he stepped outside, Jack Post was smoking a cigarette, leaning against a large barrel of water, which each tent had in case of fire. The clanking of mess tent pans echoed in the fog-shrouded, otherwise empty pathways.

"You must be new here," Jack said.

At first, Aaron didn't understand the humor, but then he chuckled. "Yep."

Jack was Hollywood good-looking, a scrappy, scruffy, sandy- haired 5-foot-10-inches-tall Californian with a linebacker build from the waist up and spindly legs like a racehorse. Aaron and Jack couldn't have been less alike, as far apart as Iowa and San Bernardino, California, but they bonded.

Their kind of friendship could only be understood by others who forged foxhole friendships. Jack was from the rolling hills of California, where he bragged they made the best burgers in a diner called McDonald's Bar-B-Que; Aaron was from a small Iowa town that didn't appear on the map.

On the first day in Camp Lucky Strike, M1 training was the priority. The M1 rifle was a magnificent killing weapon, ten pounds of what legend had it could shoot through a small tree and kill the German standing behind it. The second day, soldiers completed a mandatory course in front-line hygiene, taught by one of the medics, who issued ominous warnings about foot care in cold weather. Every day, there was marching and additional training that could keep you alive: digging foxholes every time you stopped, donning gas masks, reviewing first aid, and learning German weaponry.

On most nights, dame talk, bragging, movies, or radio were the most popular pastimes. They gathered around the radio, listening to Charlie McCarthy and Edgar Bergen, the music of Glen Miller, and BBC news about the war. The BBC reported the Allies were bombing Berlin—a hopeful sign.

Standing around the radio, they had an air of nervous optimism. "Hell, the war'll be over before we get a chance to fight," Jack said. "If we don't get there soon, there won't be any Krauts left to kill!"

When they returned to their cots, they lay in restless silence for a while, and brave talk shifted to secret hopes and prayers.

Aaron passed on going to see *The White Cliffs of Dover*, which he had watched with Mary. Instead, he and Jack picked *This is the Army*, starring Ronald Reagan, and a John Wayne western, *Tall in the Shadow*, which they watched twice. Jack said Reagan was a California guy and Wayne had played football at Southern Cal, where Jack had gone to school before enlisting.

Sunday was a day of rest and mail. Early in mail call, Aaron heard his name, and two letters were tossed high over the heads of fellow soldiers. One he snatched out of the air, and the other landed at his feet. He held Mary's letters to his nose, hoping to capture her scent. Then, pressing them to his lips, he kissed them and stuffed them into his shirt. All through breakfast he felt them rubbing his chest. After chow, he rushed back to his tent, pulled his shoes off and flopped onto his cot. The first letter from Mary was postmarked September 29, a few days after he sailed for England. She had received his postcard. There was nothing new to report on the home front. She said she was missing him terribly and was praying he would come home soon. *Remember what I said right before you left. I know you said I didn't have to. But I am going to, as soon as I get the courage.*

Aaron set the letter on his chest and stared at the canvass ceiling. He pictured the commitment on her face. The promise she was talking about had been one of the last things she said. He smiled at the thought of her introducing herself to his maty and bat'ko. She also said she broke the news to her parents. He assumed they were angry. *She must be sparing me the details*, he thought, hoping he was wrong.

The next letter from Mary was postmarked October 3rd.

Dear Aaron:

I'm not sure where this letter will reach you, or when, or if you're on the move somewhere. And I hear a lot of mail is lost. But I hope it will find you safe and, I pray, some distance from harm. I look at maps and try to guess at where you are, but it's confusing. You're heading for France or maybe you're there? I went to church this morning and prayed and really feel good about your safe return. Everybody here thinks the war will end soon, at least the one where you are.

I know you want me to keep you informed about Tony and Fritz. All I know is Tony is in the Pacific. Fritz is in your area. Maybe you can find him.

Well, I did it. Told you I would. I went to your house and introduced myself. I was scared, but got my courage up and went anyway. I figured you're at war, so how could I be scared of anything. Your dad didn't say much, but I think he's a pussy cat. He wanted to talk to me. I could tell by the sad look on his face he had something to say.

I'll start another letter today. I will send you a box of stuff, so write soon what you need. Please write. It is all of you that I have right now. I miss you and love you and pray hard every night for your safety. Be careful.

Love and kisses, Mary—the Lucky One

Staring into the canvas sky, he daydreamed about Fritz and Tony, fishing on the banks of Miller's Bend. He remembered roller skating with Mary, swooping in and lifting her off the floor in an embrace that was magnetic, pulling her close, longer then he should have, all memories he was clinging to. Above the din of morning horseplay outside his tent, he could hear soldiers singing hymns in the mess tent church.

The next morning, Aaron saw and heard the first movement of troops out of camp. The excitement was palpable. Everyone was out of their tents to witness the exodus with brave hoorays, subdued good lucks, and silent stares. Half his tentmates were gone by the end of the day. That evening banter was more subdued. Not knowing was a new enemy, and any soldier who passed through Camp Lucky Strike was imprinted with a strange, unrecognizable smell thought by some to be fear.

Tuesday there was no drilling, an ominous warning that Aaron's number was up. His anxiety was building, and just before noon chow, the chilling announcement came he would be departing the next day. The rest of the day moved in slow motion—packing, eating, small talk, and mind talk. Jack said, "Eat now, because you'll be eating rations from now on."

His pack included sixty pounds of clothing, three days of rations, shelter canvas, an entrenching tool, canteen, utensils, and a first aid kit. In addition to the pack, he would carry his M1 rifle and ammunition belt. Nothing proved more that this was really war than when he clipped hand grenades to his chest.

The next day, there was a massive movement of men, material, and supplies. Half the men were loaded into French train boxcars known as *40-and-8s*, an old expression referring to forty men and eight horses. Aaron and Jack were assigned to a caravan of deuce- and-a-half trucks that headed off northeast across France toward Belgium. It was uncomfortable, aggravatingly slow going with several unexplained stops. Along the way, they passed caravans of trucks heading away from the front lines, some loaded with German prisoners, others with the wounded and the dead.

Aaron and Jack sat across from each other nearest the open back of the truck. A fight nearly broke out when they first claimed their seats, ones that gave them a clear view of the countryside, like looking in a rearview mirror. They passed through scared villages, abandoned and bombed-out homes, and wheat fields gone to weed. Occasionally, a few locals were seen clinging to their spot on the map: women, boys and small children with their heads poking up in the wheat. In one field, a farmer worked a horse pulling a two-seater mower, and a woman followed along, tying the wheat in bundles, using ropes made of twisted wheat stalks. The scene reminded Aaron of home and boyhood, and long days shadowing Bat'ko.

Curious survivors clinging to their homes watched from doorways as the truck passed, inoculated to the fear and numb to the back-and-forth of the nearby sounds of artillery and small arms fire as they watched the comings and goings of moving armies. German soldiers had moved in and out, and now Allied soldiers did the same. On the southeast edge of Waregem, Belgium, the convoy ground to a halt when Aaron's transport broke down. When it was determined the rear axle had snapped, and it would be several hours before they could continue, the restof the caravan moved on without them.

It had been drizzling all morning. Most of the soldiers opted not to wait it out on the uncomfortable metal backless seats. Instead, they took shelter under the truck or in a nearby grove of trees, where they napped. Aaron and Jack stayed put, clinging to their preferred seats.

Jack could tell jokes better than most and loved to tell stories, always the entertainer. As he pulled a cigarette from the pack and held it between his lips, out of the corner of his mouth, he said, "I could use a drink."

Aaron handed him his canteen.

Jack held his hand out, refusing it. "I mean a real drink. Why don't they provide us with something to drink? A little Wild Turkey would make us better soldiers."

"Braver, maybe," Aaron chuckled.

"And women. What's up with that? We're not supposed to fraternize with the locals, but the recruiter said the girls over here loved soldiers." Jack fished his lighter from his pocket and lit his cigarette. He took a long, satisfying drag, smiled, and blew a perfect smoke ring that floated up and out of the truck and quickly disappeared.

"You're gonna run out of smokes. Might not be so easy to come by. "Got a whole backpack full of 'em," pointing to his pack. "Guess you're right, though; we might be here a few days."

On and on, Jack told stories about California. He said the girls were loose and wore two-piece bathing suits. "They wear two-piece swim-suits where you live? Iowa. Where is that?" Aaron had never seen a girl in a two-piece swimsuit. He thought about how they used to go swimming in the river, but the girls watched from the bank.

Late in the afternoon, the drizzle stopped. Aaron stretched out his arms and slid out the back of the truck. "Gotta take a leak."

"Better take this." Jack held out Aaron's M1 rifle to him.

Aaron cringed. He had been warned so often in boot camp never to leave his weapon, to always keep it within easy reach. How could he have forgotten already? Across the road was a grove of trees and, beyond that, row after row of bone white crosses. He could see there was a memorial not too far away. Slowly, reverently, he made his way between the white crosses of American soldiers who were buried there. He stopped at a marble monument and read the inscription.

In Memory of those American Soldiers who fought
in this region and who sleep in unknown graves.

Flanders Field Cemetery was the final resting place for many World War I soldiers fighting on the Western Front. It was not that long ago that men had died fighting for this same piece of land soldiers were again dying for, Aaron reflected. *Who sleeps in these unknown graves?* All around the cemetery, beyond the perfect rows of white crosses, as far as he could see, were wilted and forlorn poppies of the dead and the near-dead. One war after another. Why so soon? Why at all? What could be learned from this war, from the last one, except how to fight? How to improve the killing?

Across the road, a replacement truck had arrived, and men were stirring, unloading, and reloading their packs. The sun poked through just in time to disappear over the horizon as they continued their journey to the front.

As darkness set in, the clouds cleared and opened up a heaven of stars, but a shifting wind also brought a chill to the air. They passed through the city of Eupen, Belgium. The road narrowed as they entered the Hürtgen Forest, at the northern edge of the Eifel Mountains. The forest canopy obliterated the stars and threw a black curtain over everything.

Aaron, Jack, and their truckload of comrades were assigned to a recon unit in an Army division that had been battling German fortifications in a 50-square-mile area east of the Belgian–German border. The Army division he was joining had been fighting for months and was badly depleted.

When the truck squealed to a stop, Sergeant Richard Collier ordered the men out. The sergeant was a tall block of wood with a bristly chin and steel-gray eyes. Pushing and shoving, confused soldiers scurried out the back of the truck, shielding their eyes against spitting snow.

The sergeant's growl startled them. "Out. Now. Move." As the men were offloading, he pointed and pushed them, scattering them in different directions. "Move," he commanded in a hoarse loud whisper. "Dig in. Keep your head down." This unit had earlier attacked a German fortification and, two hours before now, had blunted a surprise counterattack.

Aaron leaped from the back of the truck and found an abandoned foxhole less than fifty yards away. Jack rolled in behind him. He could hear the groan of the truck engine as it drove off. The sound of small arms fire and the distant rolling thunder of artillery kept Aaron in wide-eyed confusion and wonderment. In the darkness, for all he knew, the forest was all around him; he could be staring at the base of a tree. A German could be yards away.

The slightest breeze was unnerving; every movement of the brush and rustle of the trees could be the beginning of a German attack. In the pitched darkness, the muffled voices of men around him was eerie. Adrenalin coursed through his veins as he gripped his weapon tightly. Listening to the sounds of the forest, he tried to discern the good from bad, fearing any minute they would be overrun. Occasionally, Jack peeked over the top of the bunker. A thin layer of snow covered his helmet.

Off to the side and ahead, Aaron heard soldier's voices. "Do you see them yet?"

"They're not coming."

"You think?"

"Sarge says they're dug in. They want us to attack them."

All along the front, Germans had well-fortified positions in the event the day would come when the Fatherland might be invaded. The final defense.

Jack was leaning out over the foxhole, looking out. "What's going on?" Aaron asked. "Shouldn't you keep your head down?"

Jack responded. "Should we contact Sarge? Are we in the right place? Are we supposed to shoot if we see something? He just dumped us here and didn't tell us shit."

"He'll tell us. Just keep your head down."

The small arms fire seemed to be moving closer, but it was too dark to make out anything, and no one wanted to look over the bunker's edge for very long. Without warning, a German artillery shell exploded and shook the ground. Aaron slid to the bottom of the foxhole, clinging to the earth, his hands over his head. He could feel the concussion in his chest and his temples. His ears rang, and he felt like his eyes would pop out of his head.

Aaron strained to hear his platoon sergeant's shouts. He knew Sarge was shouting commands, but he couldn't understand. Soon, the soldiers nearby began to fire into the darkness at any suspected target—usually at nothing.

More ear-shattering explosions rocked their position. In the brief, nearly imperceptible time between them, one after another, the experience was seared into Aaron's memory: raining earth, the pinging sound of M1s, zinging artillery shell fragments, the smell of gunpowder, the blue cloud that hung over them, the sights and sounds of death.

Some explosions came with warnings, a distant whistling, growing louder, heightening the terror, taking his breath away, tightening his chest. An eternity squeezed through the eye of a needle: uncertainty over what was going to happen next, relief the shell wasn't for him when it landed nearby.

And always, terrified men crying out for help.

"Medic. I've been hit."
"Mother of God, help me."
"Jesus, save me."
"Mother, I love you."
"Please someone help me."

Should I stay and keep firing or try to help the wounded soldiers? Aaron worried, but he stayed put.

Silence came as abruptly as the bombing. Even the stranded wounded stopped to listen. Aaron noticed that Jack had wrapped his arms around him.

When the morning gray first outlined the nearby forest and the scars of last night's hell, he heard the platoon sergeant's voice announce that the Germans had retreated. Aaron peeked over the top of the foxhole and brushed a thin layer of snow from his shoulders. The snow-covered tree branches, like a landscape artist's canvas, were a peaceful contrast to the fiery pandemonium of the night before. But the dense conifer forest wall still could easily hide a German.

Aaron stood and could see soldiers and medics carrying the bodies of the wounded and dead. On one of the stretchers was the blanketed lump of a soldier's corpse. On another was the surreal sight of two arms next to one another. Aaron had never seen a dead man. He slumped back onto the ground.

Suddenly a face appeared above him and yelled out, "Hey, Sarge, gotta see this. We got another one." Looking back to Aaron and Jack, smiling, the face said, "Looks like you had company last night."

Aaron's gaze was drawn to an unexploded shell lodged in the side of their foxhole. The French resistance was sabotaging German munitions production and had defused some of the shells. They hoped this was one of them. Standing over them was a diminutive private with small, sunken, dark eyes and a long, thin, twice-broken nose. Alvin Purdy, smiling through yellow, crooked teeth, hailed from Rabun County in northeastern Georgia. He spat and gave Jack and Aaron an unpleasant sneer, as if there was some joke they were too stupid to understand.

"Hey Sarge, the new guys cuddled up with the enemy last night!" He laughed, an eerie sound in the cold morning air. Aaron and Jack were sitting in the foxhole, leaning against their packs.

Sergeant Collier appeared beside Purdy. "Get it out of there," he said. Then, motioning toward Aaron and Jack, in a kind and commanding voice, he said, "You guys come with me."

As they followed, the sergeant turned and studied the two soldiers. "Where you from?"

Jack answered first. "Southern California."

Looking over to Aaron, he continued, "I'm from Maryland. What's your name?"

"Aaron Vanko, sir. Iowa. Saylor. South of Ankeny. We live on a farm outside of town."

With a second glance, Sergeant Collier exclaimed, "Ankeny, huh? Drop the sir crap. You call me Sarge or you call me Richard. I don't care. Just do what I tell you. Find someone and help clear this mess." Looking back to Jack, he added, "You come with me."

As Aaron was making his way across the field of battle, he came upon a man lying face down, dead, in the bottom of a foxhole. He could have easily been asleep. Aaron didn't know his name, but he recognized him as one of the men who were on the truck with him, from Minnesota, he thought. He reached down to roll him over. His chest was an empty pool of blood. His face looked like freshly butchered meat, a mass of blood from his hairline to his lower jaw, but a few teeth showed through it. Aaron turned away, gagging. He hadn't eaten since yesterday, so all he could do was dry heave. *He probably never even fired his weapon. All this way for what—just to die? What good is his death to the war? To the country?*

9

AARON'S RECONNAISSANCE UNIT had always been on the move until now—stuck in a deep, thick, treacherous, well-protected forest. His division had suffered nearly 5,000 casualties before he had arrived, and he didn't know how many had died since he had got there. They waded ashore at Utah Beach on D-Day and fought their way northwest toward the port city of Cherbourg, to protect Allies transport lines bringing supplies into France. From there, they battled through the hedgerows, south toward St. Lo, then helped to liberate Paris in August and celebrated there. Still, the war didn't end, and they pushed to the Hürtgen Forest, at the northern edge of the Eifel Mountains at the German border.

When they first arrived in the Hürtgen, the goal was to take the town of Schmidt and secure the dam, which was still under German control. If the Jerrys blew up the dam, it would flood the American position. German fortifications at the border were designed to be impenetrable, with thick concrete structures surrounded by minefields, booby traps, and barbed wire. All along the Westwall, the battle raged to a standoff, and recon missions were limited until there was a breakthrough. Aaron's recon platoon had been trying to solve the puzzle of German Hill 500, camped in the middle of a base of 100-foot, close-quartered towering trees that manufactured gloom, filtered the daylight, and obscured the night sky. The fighting ground on as the weather yo-yoed for several days, snow and bitter cold alternating with drizzle and mud.

Desperate for a solution, Sergeant Collier assigned a small squad to gain enemy intelligence and explore an area south of the German fortification. The four-man squad included Aaron, and to his dismay, Purdy, who was considered the best scout and nicknamed "the Indian" by his fellows. Despite his skills, Purdy was universally feared. Any soldier in the unit could easily handle him in a fight, but every man knew he would slit his throat in the dark of night or shoot him in the back.

They left camp at the first gray light of day. The melting snow and drizzle made the going slow. They moved carefully, at times silent and standing still for what seemed like hours, assessing for mines and booby traps. By mid-morning, they were shivering and nearly defeated by the thick growth along the stream, but they pressed on in ankle-deep mud and climbed up the steep bank, pulling themselves up by the roots until they came to a small clearing. Aaron was the second man to make it through the thick undergrowth and up the bank. With his rifle in the ready position, Aaron waited for the others to clear. Purdy was next, and then came squad leader Bob Stump.

Once assembled, they froze at the sounds of snapping twigs and the rustle of forest undergrowth. Two German soldiers appeared in the clearing not twenty yards from their position, looked around, leaned their rifles against a tree, and lit cigarettes. Stump was lying next to Aaron, nudged him, and pointed to the German soldier on the left and then to himself, then to the other man, then to Aaron. They shouldered their rifles.

As Aaron steadied his aim, he couldn't help but remember what his father said after he missed shooting the buck. "What happened? You're a good shot. Are you blind?"

Aaron knew it wasn't his eyes. There was a time when he couldn't shoot a skunk. A skunk, no less. It had bothered Aaron. Still bothered him. There was nothing special about the skunk, not like the six-point buck. Aaron had weakly defended himself, "Why are we shooting skunks? We can't eat 'em."

Tony had guffawed. "Because they waddle. Because they stink. Because nobody likes 'em. Hell, nobody cares if you kill a skunk."

Aaron brought himself back to the present. He mustn't get distracted. *Nobody cares*. The Germans exhaled smoke and whispered to each other.

Stump pulled the trigger, and one dropped to his knees and looked in his direction, grabbed at his chest, twisted and fell face first. The second German looked back in shock. His gaze locked onto Aaron's, as if a sixth sense told him he had arrived at the end of his life. It seemed like an eternity but was mere microseconds. Aaron saw that the man's mouth was open, his eyes wide with horror. Aaron pulled the trigger. The German fell to the ground, then scurried to his knees and into the bush and disappeared.

Purdy sniffed, and gave Aaron a long, sneering look, gearing up for one of his best insults. Stump poked him before he could say anything and gestured toward the camp. Silently, they headed back. Aaron made sure he stayed behind Purdy all the way.

When they returned to camp, Sergeant Collier gathered the scout squad. While they broke out K rations, Bob Stump reported. Collier listened intently, his steel-gray gaze locked on Stump. "Seems like the south edge through the slough might be a good approach, but I wish you hadn't killed the two Germans."

"One," Purdy jumped in. "Our new boy here chickened out." Aaron jerked his head around to face Purdy, who went on. "You know I watched you. You froze and missed the shot.

Hell, he was right in front of us. You could have spit on him. You chickened out."

Aaron searched for a response. "I missed," he said weakly. "Yeah, you missed all right, chicken. Stay away from me. You'll get me killed."

Sergeant Collier looked over to Aaron and back to Purdy, then to Stump. Soldiers on the front line could be hard on one another. They could love each other like brothers, but to a man, they didn't like re-placement soldiers. Replacements were undertrained, not real soldiers in the eyes of battle-hardened veterans, who had seen too many of them do stupid things, seen too many friends try to rescue them, seen too many of them die trying. Experienced soldiers knew immediately who had a chance to survive, who would get it, and who would get everyone else killed.

Stump looked away, then back to Sergeant Collier. "It was an easy kill."

"Just don't ever put me with the chicken again." Purdy made his point again. "I ain't gonna get killed for him."

"We shouldn't have shot either one, Stump," Sergeant Collier exclaimed. "Easier to send them a letter. Well, they know we were there, so let's cool off a couple of days. And Purdy, you do what I want and when I want it." Looking back to Aaron, he added, "And you take better aim next time."

* * *

Jack was scraping for the last bits of canned meat. "Hey, Aaron, I'll give you my sugar packets for your cigarettes." Without answering, Aaron flipped his four-pack of Chesterfield cigarettes in his direction, rose, and returned to his foxhole. It wasn't until two hours later that Jack joined him. Not a word was spoken between them.

The darkness accentuated every crackle or rustle in the forest, interrupting the muffled conversations of soldiers in their foxholes for a moment. Was it the Germans? At midnight, Aaron moved to a different foxhole to serve a sentry shift with a veteran soldier, Bart Humphries, a cowboy from Montana. When he arrived, Humphries was leaning out, looking toward the forest. Without saying anything, he watched Aaron settle in and nod. Not too much later they both stiffened at the sound of footsteps moving in their direction and then the sergeant's voice in the dark, "Humphries. Take a break. I got this."

Settling into a comfortable position, with his arms leaning on the top of the foxhole, he popped some chewing gum in his mouth and offered a piece to Aaron. "Iowa boy, huh? Be great to be back in Iowa right now. We lived a stone's throw from the Mississippi. Grew up fishing catfish from the river bank."

Aaron grunted. "Our rivers are smaller, but we got catfish too." After a few moments of silence, he asked, "Sarge, what were you doing before the war?"

"Schoolteacher. Third graders."

"We farmed."

"My mom is from Ankeny, but I've never been there," Sergeant Collier added. "Her father was a coal miner there. She was a nurse in World War I, met my dad and eventually moved to Maryland after the war. Brooklyn Park. It's a small town, about the size of Ankeny, I guess. Everybody knows everybody."

They turned their attention to night sounds, then Collier said, "My brother is a conscientious objector. It's not like he's any more religious then I am. Hell, I went to synagogue as much as he did. Prayed just as hard. Can't explain it."

Aaron interrupted. "You're Jewish?" Aaron shifted uncomfortably in the silence that followed.

"Yep. You act like you never met a Jew."

Aaron snickered. "Well, yeah, I've met a Jewish person. I guess. Mom told me I was Jewish the night before I left. I'm not real clear what a Jew even is. "

Sergeant Collier looked in Aaron's direction with a raised eyebrow, trying to find his face in the dark. "Imagine that. Well, anyway, maybe my brother just didn't want to die. Who does? Oh, well, he's my little brother. Glad he's not here."

Aaron listened to the sound of the sergeant chewing his gum wildly. Then the chewing stopped, and Aaron held his breath. A crack from the trees, then silence again. Alarmed, both men looked out and watched for several minutes, but it was nothing.

Collier's quiet voice was the only sound in the black night. "My father was a sergeant in World War I. He told me the battlefield was full of conscientious objectors. He said it was tough to get his men to even shoot at the Germans, that a lot of men never even fired their weapons. Never. Men on the front lines. He said men would die helping others but wouldn't kill the enemy." The conversation halted again as both men held their breaths and listened. Aaron's heart was beating fast. He knows. Sarge *knows*.

"Aaron, I suspect you have some decisions to make. Only way home alive is killing Germans. The alternative is earning a white cross in some cemetery. Not the kind of award I'd want. Now, a guy like Purdy belongs here. Heaven help us when the war is over; they'll need to lock him up."

Aaron pondered his words as the sergeant went about chewing his gum. "I'll do fine. Don't worry about me."

Aaron wanted to talk, to ask questions, but he kept quiet. Jewish. He wasn't sure he had ever met a Jew other than his parents. *This guy is just like me.*

The sergeant stopped chewing his gum. Aaron wondered what he was thinking. Had he fallen asleep?

After a long pause, the sergeant continued "You know, there are people back home who feel this war is unnecessary. Thou shall not kill. Well, tell that to the Germans as they take one country after another, seize property, and enslave and murder people. You know they're killing all the Jews."

"I know," Aaron whispered.

As Sergeant Collins got up to leave, he said, "You'll figure things out. Keep the faith, whatever that is. I'm planning to survive this damn war, and I'll do whatever it takes. You should, too."

* * *

Over the next two days, several patrols went out to check the perimeter. Sergeant Collier went to battalion headquarters for a briefing and to discuss strategy. The Germans were entrenched and had the advantage of higher ground and fortifications. Fighting was still occurring up and down the line, but since the last surprise attack, their sector had been quiet.

In the lull, the men sat alone or in small clusters around their foxholes. Aaron sat in his, writing a letter to Mary while he listened to the quiet chitchat. Tonight, Jack was in a perimeter hole with Humphries and Purdy.

Dear Mary:

You probably already know this, but sometimes my letters may have blacked out portions.

I have to be careful what I write. I received your last package with the sugar cookies. How'd you get the sugar? I loved the hard candy and will savor each piece, maybe ration two a day.

He eavesdropped as Humphries boasted, "If there's a bullet with my name on it, I sure as hell will be taking a few Germans with me!" "There's no bullet with my name in it. But there's a gal back in California that's got my name on her," Jack said. "More than one.

Blonde and brunette."

Aaron smiled and continued to write.

Good news. I forgot to tell you. When we first landed in France we were told we would be paid $5 more a month. You'll see an increase in what I send home. Don't need any money here.

Hard to make friends here. Any news about Fritz or Tony? Nothing here reminds me of home. Except Sarge. His mom's from Iowa. Right there in Ankeny. He's a schoolteacher in Maryland. I think any man in the unit would jump in the fire for him. There's something about him.

"So what's up with your chicken friend?" Purdy asked Jack. "Lay off him, Purdy. He can take a bullet as easy as you. He's a good guy. He'll hold his own."

"Well, I'm here to kill Germans. Why be here if not that?"

"And the way I see it, after we kill all the Krauts, the local women will want an American soldier as a love trophy," Jack announced. "Think of all the easy pickin's!"

The conversation went back and forth, from sex to killing, babes to Krauts, back and forth. *Taking life and creating life*, Aaron thought. He put his pen down, thinking about his last night with Mary. Killing and making love, both a man's most private moments, both first times always locked away in breathless memory. Gentlemen didn't brag about either, and the ones that did were the ones who hadn't done it. Aaron grinned, reading through the letter again. His Mary. He wished he could tell her better.

"I figure shooting Jerrys is like shooting melons." Purdy's voice rose above the others. "When I was young, me and Billie went to Farmer Hanks' melon patch and started popping melons with our shotguns. Hated that Farmer Hanks. Shot every goddamned one, one after another, pop, pop, pop." Purdy pointed his rifle out toward the forest to demonstrate. "My father beat the crap out of me. I mean he really beat the crap out of me." Purdy hesitated and then added reflectively, "He'll never do that again." He pulled his helmet back to show off a scar that extended from the top of his eyebrow down to his cheek. "I thought he was gonna kill me. Had to eat soup for two weeks." He aimed his gun at the woods and made a popping sound. "When you shoot a Kraut in the head, it makes the same sound."

Humphries asked, "How would you know? You ain't done that." "I done that," Purdy argued.

"Why'd you hate the melon farmer?" Jack asked quietly.

Purdy jerked his head up. "All those melons in the sun. His whole field full. Why do you think? Now I'm popping German melons, and they're gonna give me a medal."

In the distance, Aaron could hear the hushed conversations of the other soldiers in their foxholes. There were twenty-five men in his platoon. He could make out the voices of Bob Stump, the son of a Baptist minister, and Tommy Woods, who had just graduated from high school in St Louis. He was quarterback on his state champion high school football team. Sometimes he shared a foxhole with Dan Carney, also from Missouri—Springfield. Nearby, Cory Wheeler, a West Virginia coal miner, was saying he wanted to go to college. He was going to make something of himself, not like his father. Fran Cathcart was a life insurance salesman from Chicago. Jim Gartner from Kentucky started college and dropped out to join the fight. His father was a banker. Jim Schwinn, Jimbo, was from Omaha, the largest man in the unit, so clumsy he was sure to step on a mine.

Everyone had a story, all from different places, all finding the going different then they imagined, caught up in the war, the life and death. Most of them with dreams, girls back home, moms they weren't embar-rassed bragging about. *"Mom cooks the best fried chicken in the county."* *"Mom can out-spit my dad and ride a horse better than any man."*

When Collier returned from headquarters, he brought a bag of letters and dumped them out on the ground. Bob Stump called out the names. There were four letters from Mary. Her first two reported on a fire in the building next to Jamison's Bakery. Turned out, there was little damage to the bakery, and they were open for business. She had talked to Tony's mom, and he was in Saipan, somewhere in the Pacific. Fritz was nearby, but even though Aaron kept asking soldiers from other units, it was impossible to find him.

The third letter was more news about home, ordinary things. He felt his shoulders relax, almost as if hearing her voice again. He traced the return address on the fourth, knowing it was her last word for today and he wasn't sure when he'd get another one. Taking a deep breath, he peeled it open. Pastor Woodruff's nephew, his godson, was missing in action in the Hürtgen Forest. She wasn't sure where that was. Aaron put the letter down. *That's where I am. She doesn't know.*

Missing in action wasn't good news. So much of the fighting was in a thick forest and retrieving bodies was difficult to impossible. The letter continued to explain that Pastor Woodruff was close to his brother and nephew, and they were praying he'd be found soon and alive. She reminded him her uncle was one of the coaches for the Iowa Seahawks football team. Missing in action. The news hit the pastor hard, she said.

She reported a bad storm had destroyed one of his folks' chicken coop. Half the chickens were dead or scattered. Aaron gasped as he read on.

Dad went over and helped him build a new one. That's like Father. He has a wonderful heart. He still hasn't said anything to me about our marriage. But in my heart, I'll always be his little girl. Just like I'm your big girl. Everything will be okay. I know it. The last thing Fritz said to me was he promised me you'd come home safely.

Always remember I'm the Lucky One and you're Lucky Two.

I love you forever, Mary—Lucky One

* * *

For Aaron, surviving each day was a relief, and each restless night was a hollow search for hope. Some of the soldiers used quiet time to make deals with God. Aaron wondered if his Jewish God was different from the one his fellow soldiers prayed to when they thought no one could hear them, or even from that of the Germans he was here to kill. During boot camp and then again on lonely rainy nights in Le Havre, waiting for his assignment to this graveyard, Aaron had allowed himself to wonder if he was going to die. Now his thoughts more often drifted off to wondering what it would be like when he did. When images of home drifted so easily off in a cloud of his cold breath, he began to feel it was his destiny to die here. And then, when he lived another day, the searching began again. Around and around, he went.

On Thanksgiving, they ate cold turkey sandwiches, a treat compared to their usual rations. General Eisenhower had committed hot turkey dinners to the soldiers on the front, and on November 22, 1,604 tons of turkey arrived in France. Transporting supplies and ammunition soldiers to the Hürtgen Forest was a challenge, because the few roads available were weather-beaten, slushy, and narrow. Sandwiches were the best they could get, but the change was something to celebrate.

The next day, Sergeant Collier pulled the platoon together. "We just got orders to take Hill 500. That damned piece of earth has been in our way too long." Along the Westwall, for eighty-five miles, Allied forces were poised to enter Germany, awaiting a breakthrough. "This target is considered a soft spot. We have to get through. The good news is, the Germans can't rely on tank support because the forest is so thick here. The bad news is, neither can we. Air support and artillery support is limited. Fortifications on Hill 500 aren't as formidable as other German fortresses along the Westwall, but they're well protected. It's going to be mano y mano sometimes, men. Stay alert."

Collier paused to let his words sink in as he surveyed the faces of his men. "I know we're a recon platoon and this is a combat mission, but this is key to a breakout. We've defeated the Germans in Aachen and now is the time to push through. Captain Jardine got these orders from high up, the very top of the chain. We're going to take that damned hill and drive the Huns all the way to Berlin." Sarge laid a map in the ground as the men crowded around. Pointing to the map, he said, "Here's the plan. We'll be going through the slough and Echo Company will go through the front door. They'll be here tonight. We know where the Germans have set up their machine guns and artillery units. They have positions here, here, and here," he said, pointing to the map. "Don't get caught in a crossfire. We also know they planted booby traps and mines and strategically positioned snipers, but we don't know where." The men stared down at the map, glassy-eyed. Every man knew the secret sauce to winning the war was having the largest army and a willingness to spill large amounts of blood. Many attempts had failed. Would this be different?

Soldiers jostled closer to see the map, some on bent knees and others standing. "Echo Company will set up mortar positions here and here and raise a lot of hell. The Germans are going to see this as a frontal assault. Our job is to blow up the main battery." Looking back to the solemn faces studying the map, he continued, "As soon as we blow the battery, the direct assault will push through here." He pounded his finger on the map. "Right in their face.

"While Echo hits them up front, we're going to move up through the slough. Stump, I want you to carry the TNT satchel." Grasping Aaron by his shoulder, Collier pulled him close. "Vanko, you stick with him." Then he traced his finger along the map south of the German position. "When we get through the slough, we'll split off." Sergeant Collier laid out the assignments to set up covering fire while Stump and Aaron made their way behind the pillbox.

"We want to get as close as we can and lay down fire to allow Stump and Vanko here," he said, pointing to the map, "to do their job. Half of you will stay in reserve." He divided the men into teams and told them when they would be called in. "After the assault force takes out the German position, you reserves will come up to this zone, set up a defensive position in case of a counterattack."

At daybreak, they moved out. By 9 o'clock, the sounds of the rifle company's Browning automatics and mortars could be heard showering the German position. It was raining hard, and the temperature was in the thirties. It was hard to grip anything with cold hands. Collier and his men were still struggling to wade through the muddy stream and climb the embankment through the thick underbrush littered with branches and slippery moss-covered fallen trees. They moved slowly, fearful of mines and booby traps, as unfair and seemingly random as a 500-pound bomb dropped from an airplane. One wrong step and, without a fight, a soldier could lose his leg or his life.

In the distance, Aaron could hear the angry *rat-tat-tat* of machine-gun fire and the *thunk-thunk-thunk* of mortars launching and exploding shells bursting high up on the hillside. The German machine guns were relentless, firing at a rate of 1,200 rounds per minute. It was difficult to tell what was happening, but so far, the brunt of the German reaction seemed to be directed at Echo rifle platoon.

Stump and Vanko made it fifty yards further and hunkered down in a ditch, behind the pillbox. So far, they hadn't fired a shot or tripped a mine. The trees thinned out in front of them, and in the murky light, they could see mounds of dirt covered with leaves and bushes where the Germans kept up steady fire, in front of the main bunker, their target.

As they approached the concertina wire on the pillbox perimeter, they could see Purdy and Humphries break out from their position, firing their weapons wildly. Suddenly, there was an explosion, and

Humphries flew into the air and landed face first. The blast knocked Purdy off his feet. He scrambled to cover behind a tree. Sergeant Collier, directly northwest of their position, was firing from the cover of fallen trees.

The open ground to the pillboxes had some small depressions where Vanko and Stump could find cover. They inched their way closer, pulling themselves along on the bellies. Stump dragged the twelve pounds of TNT, six pounds on each side of a saddle-shaped canvas bag.

There was a burst of German machine-gun fire in their direction. They had been seen. They rolled for cover, landing in a rocky swale behind a moss-covered pine. Bullets ripped through the trees and underbrush, raining splinters of wood and dirt down on them. When the firing paused, Aaron lifted his head and looked skyward. It had stopped raining, and through a small cloud break, a sliver of sunlight glistened through the trees. Aaron felt something wet on his face and rubbed it. Rain? It wasn't raining. But when he took his hand away, he saw it was blood.

Stump was at his side, their bodies entangled where they had tumbled to take cover. "Bob." Aaron nudged him. He shoved him harder, and Stump rolled back. Stump was staring up with a fixed gaze. "Bob!" Blood was streaming out of Stump's chest and formed a pool of blood beneath him. A trickle of blood began to flow out of his nostrils. Aaron's chest was covered in blood. He felt his own chest and arms to see if he had been hit.

Mesmerized, Aaron's eyes kept trying to connect with Bob's glassy ones. He heard his own men firing to his left. Still, he couldn't take his look away. He was no longer there. The satchel was still tight in his grasp. Finally, Aaron pulled on it and rolled back until it came loose and landed on his chest.

On his left, down the hillside, he could hear mortars and more explosions. Aaron peeked out to see where the other men were. Jim Gartner, under heavy fire, began to crawl to the side to change position. Aaron thought Jim was about to make it to safety behind a tree when his body lurched. Bullets found their mark. Jim fell face down in the dirt.

Sergeant Collier yelled out. "Jim. Where are you?"

Aaron shouted back, "He's been hit."

Aaron stared at the TNT satchel and then up through the forest canopy at the thin line of sunlight reflecting off the glistening tree branches. Taking a deep breath, he pulled the detonator cord on the satchel and, with all his might, flung it over his shoulder toward the bunker, then covered his head. The explosion was deafening, like standing next to thunder. The earth quaked with the impact. Even though he had expected it, the blast shook him to his soul. He lurched forward, as if a nightmare had awakened him out of a dead sleep.

Then it was quiet. The devil took a deep breath. When the machine-gun firing began again, it was not in Aaron's direction. He slumped back and looked up into the trees and closed his eyes. Should he run or hunker down? Suddenly, a rush of footsteps startled him, and as if dropped from the sky, the body of a German soldier fell on top of him.

Aaron cried out as he tried to push the body away, waving frantically like he was caught in a giant spiderweb. Trembling, his heart pounding, he reached for his rifle and pointed at the unarmed German soldier. He was a young man about Aaron's age, his eyes wide with fear. Tears began to stream down the soldier's cheeks. Aaron searched for what to do, what to say. *Should I shoot him?*

Aaron knew a few German words but nothing for this situation. His mouth began to move, but unformed words hung on his trembling lips until unintelligible unconscious mumbles broke free. "I'm sorry."

The German soldier flinched. He was bleeding from his abdomen, a thin red line trickled from his nostrils, and his mangled left arm hung to his side, muscles and ligaments showing through his torn uniform. Aaron slid closer. "I'm sorry," he repeated. Aaron fumbled around in his pack for a morphine syringe and injected it into the soldier's hip. "I'm sorry," Aaron repeated softly, barely above a whisper.

"Mutter. Helfen Sie mir, Mutter," the German soldier murmured, tears rolling down his cheeks.

The morphine took effect quickly, and the German's eyes grew heavy. Aaron watched him, unable to break away. The German appeared to find some peace and slumped back. The sounds of battle drifted away, mortar blasts and gunfire faded into a silent forest.

Aaron's hands were folded under his chin, his gaze locked on the German's, silently pleading for understanding, for a miracle to turn back time. Maybe the war had never happened, maybe Aaron had stayed on the farm. Maybe the German was a farmer too. Aaron showed him his picture of Mary. He expected he might smile, or nod, anything but those judging, suffering eyes.

He lost track of how long he'd been sitting there, staring. The wet pine straw, one minute glittering like fine diamonds in the sunlight, suddenly turned lifeless and gray, as if a curtain had been pulled. When he looked up into the forest canopy, he could see Mary's face in the treetops and hear her voice. *"Remember you're Lucky Two. We'll always be together."*

A voice jolted him back to the rocky swale. Sergeant Collier was standing over him. "Vanko, you okay?" How long had he been there? "Vanko, did you hear me?"

Collier looked at the German soldier. His eyes were open wide, unblinking, staring. "Aaron, he's dead."

Aaron looked up at Sarge, back to the German soldier, then to his bloody hands. *How long has he been dead?* He lifted his hands and held them up in front of his face, flinching back, trying to stand. Falling forward on his knees, he began to throw up.

10

BACK AT CAMP, survivors returned to their foxholes, nibbled at K rations, smoked, and watched medics tend to the wounded. The more severely wounded and the dead were evacuated as quickly as possible. Captain Jardine was at Sergeant Collier's side. This was the first time Aaron had seen the captain in camp. He eavesdropped as Sergeant Collier reported that eight soldiers from his platoon died, ten had been wounded, and seven were being evacuated. Aaron strained to hear as the conversation continued in a hushed tone. Collier's head was bent between his knees. The captain laid his hand on his shoulders.

The Battle of Hürtgen Forest was fought from September 1944 to December 1945, the longest battle fought on German ground and the longest and deadliest US Army battle ever. The human toll in the fight for fifty square miles of timber was 33,000 Americans killed and wounded. German casualties were 28,000. Aaron's platoon hadn't seen the worst, and if he didn't know it that day, he somehow felt it. The image of Bob Stump, the Baptist preacher's son's, his eyes wide, lifeless, and unblinking, kept interrupting Aaron as he watched Sergeant Collier and the lieutenant. Jack had survived, along with the other soldiers in the reserve unit, stationed down the hill, but the cowboy was dead, as was Jim Gartner, the Kentucky banker's son.

Up and down the Westwall, American boys were loaded onto the backs of trucks like sides of beef, robbed of all their tomorrows— Christians and Jews and former atheists, foxhole-convert atheists. The dead were Italians, Mexicans, Germans, all ethnicities except for blacks and Japanese, who weren't allowed. Lost were the quick friendships founded on nothing in common but respect, common cause, and tragedy. There were rich kids and poor ones from high school classes of '39, '40, and '41, replaced by boys from the classes of '42, '43, and '44 who didn't want to be there once they got there but had enlisted for patriotism, pride, families, wives, or girlfriends. No soldier was immune to the battle fatigue, and no amount of glory could overcome the exhaustion. It was like a wet blanket on a cold rainy day, damping all emotions. Shoulders slumped, eyelids drooped, and conversations diminished to grunts and groans. At the same time, the soldiers' springs were wound so tightly they could break at the touch, triggering tears and rage. Members of the attack force were awarded ten Silver Stars, six Bronze Stars, and eighteen Purple Hearts. Aaron won the Distinguished Service Cross, but he didn't much care, not now. The platoon's will to fight, what was left of it, was going cold.

Holding their coffee cups in their cold, trembling hands, they watched the bodies of their comrades carried off to the waiting trucks. Any youthful notions of heroism, of returning with a chest dripping with medals, were replaced by a single desire—to return home in one piece.

Aaron had not let his comrades down, but duty and honor now conflicted with the remorse he felt every time he saw the image of the young German soldier's face and echoes of his voice ringing in his ears, *"Helfen Sie mir, Mutter."* There were also the nightmares of Bob's bloody face that kept him from sleep.

* * *

Aaron's unit was relieved in early December and moved back to Spa, Belgium for rest. Spa, called the Pearl of the Ardennes, located in a valley surrounded by a wooded hillside, was famous for its healing mineral springs. Officers were put up in heated hotels and houses with running water and baths, electric lights and radios, and meals in dining rooms with white linen. Soldiers were put up in a field outside of town. Aaron and Jack shared a pup tent. Jack, who hadn't seen the worst action, bragged how they had destroyed the German defenses. Aaron just nodded, letting him crow.

The mixed snow and rain of the Hürtgen Forest followed them to Spa, but relative safety and conditions improved with three hot meals a day, predictably hash and beans. Aaron and Jack listened with passive interest to German radio broadcasts, Lord Haw Haw, an American-Brit, who broadcast in an aristocratic accent, and Axis Sally, an Ohio woman named Mildred Gillars, as they spewed their German propaganda. More entertaining were the movies, *Gaslight*, *Mr. Skeffington*, and *Cover Girl*.

The mail didn't find them until three days after they settled in. There were four letters from Mary and two packages. The first letter he opened had been written Thanksgiving night. Earlier, she had gone to see her folks, but for the first time in her life hadn't had Thanksgiving dinner with them.

We girls prepared our own Thanksgiving dinner at Millie's. All our husbands are overseas, and we thought it would be nice to be together. This was our first-time cooking Thanksgiving dinner. We cooked a turkey with oyster dressing, green beans, mashed potatoes and gravy, biscuits and cranberry sauce. Millie has been saving up sugar and made a pumpkin pie. We had so much fun. After dinner we listened to Abbott and Costello and laughed till we cried. In one routine Abbott wouldn't invite Costello to Thanksgiving dinner because of his table manners. He explained the last time he was at his house he kept reaching across the table to grab food. Costello said, "What's wrong with that?" Abbott said, "You got a tongue, don't you?" Costello says, "Yeah, but my arms are longer."

It's not so funny now I guess, but we laughed and laughed. And when we finished laughing we all cried. We miss our hubbies. We're so blessed that you're okay, but we think how lonely it must be where you are. We'll make it up when you come home.

She finished the letter saying she had stopped by to see his folks. They were okay. She hoped he liked the shortbread cookies and explained again how her father had a way of getting more sugar, given he was a pastor . . . *And did you like Millie's beef jerky? Did the socks I made work out?* She closed the letter with some good news. *Ever since Pastor Woodruff received the news about his godson's death and our wonderful announcement, he has been so nice to me. Even asked about you.*

Aaron's heart raced. Our wonderful announcement? He looked at the smudged date on the envelope. He rifled through the unopened letters and found the oldest one and tore it open.

Dearest Love:
I'm pregnant. We are going to have a baby. I just got confirmation from Doctor West.

Aaron dropped all the letters to the ground. Tears in his eyes, he looked around to be sure no one noticed and stiffened his jaw. They were going to have a baby. At the end of the letter, she said she had gone to his parents and told them the good news. His mom had cried. Mary said she thought Bat'ko was happy too.

As I was leaving, your mom said, "I'm glad Aaron has you. I know he must love you a lot". See, I told you!

That night, Aaron shared the news with Sarge and Jack. At last, something to celebrate.

Aaron's division began to fill up with new men, as easily as a coffee refill. Aaron was no longer a replacement soldier. He was a veteran, albeit a reluctant one. Now he understood what the more experienced soldiers felt. Sure, replacement soldiers could die the same as any other, but they weren't immediately accepted by the already tested.

He watched as they awkwardly went about their business, trying to understand the zombie-like sidelong glances and cold shoulders of the other soldiers. When Aaron was a mere replacement soldier, just a body thrown into battle, he too had found friendships hard to come by. Now he held back, too, sticking with Jack and the few men who had made it back from the forest. They'd figure it out. He had.

Cold and rainy days held the upper hand and kept the men in their tents, writing letters home, playing cards, reading books, watching movies, listening to the radio. Soldiers booed when American crooner Bing Crosby was interrupted by the down-home voice of Midge-at-the-Mike, Axis Sally, an American Catholic girl, a cog in the German propaganda machine.

On the few days when sun breaks reflected off the flocked pines, soldiers wandered between halls, cafes, bakeries, chocolate shops, and taverns, to drink famous Belgian beers and liquors. Some of the men, like Jack, trolled for women. Aaron sent a box of chocolates to Mary. He explained it was an early Christmas present, since he didn't know where he would be from day to day.

One Sunday morning, Aaron went to the mess tent after breakfast to read Mary's old letters and write her back. The cook's crew was cleaning up and making preparations for lunch. When he arrived, there were only a few men in the tent. He took a place in the far back corner. Before long, men began to file in, and Chaplain Liam O'Shaunessy began to set up in the front of the tent.

He recognized the chaplain from Hürtgen Forest. He was a happy, diminutive, portly New Yorker in his early thirties, wearing field khakis. His chaplain's flag was attached to the front of his Jeep, covering its radiator. Soldiers sitting at his feet, he had conducted sporadic church services on the battlefield dirt. He had even baptized several of the soldiers on the front lines, something Aaron shrugged off, its meaning lost to him. There were only twenty chaplains for the front to cover thousands of soldiers. Just a handful of those were Jewish, but at the beginning of the war, there were none.

Aaron listened with one ear as he watched the other men, some with reverently bowed heads, others crossing themselves like he had seen Tony and Fritz do when he went to Catholic church with them. He was surprised to see Jack sitting up front. *Is church a magnet for sinners, or is he in the army of the church?* Are German soldiers in the same army? It all seemed pretty random to Aaron.

Still, every seat was taken. Men were standing in the aisles and out the door. Aaron stayed tucked away in the back corner, anxious to write his letter, hoping the service wouldn't take too long.

Chaplain O'Shaunessy opened the service with a prayer, and then led the men in the singing of several hymns. The tent was quiet, except for the sound of the Chaplain's Irish brogue and the rain on the tent canvas overhead. Starting out softly and rising to a furor, he held the men captive.

This war is personal. It is a personal decision for each one of us. Sure, we are fighting for our country, for Mom and Dad, for our wives and children, and Uncle Sam has given us the tools to fight. But what is in your heart? Every day you choose. And it comes from your heart. It's what makes you a good soldier. A better one." Holding his Bible high over his head, he paused and watched the men. "Evil has been allowed to spread unchecked. Before the war, the world was tired. The last war hadn't been that long ago. Everywhere heads were turned, and evil men seized control over good men's hearts. We must pray we never let that happen again."

The men watched in thoughtful silence. "The Bible gives us some instruction in Ephesians 6:10–17. 'Finally, my brethren, be strong in the Lord, and in the power of his might. Put on the whole armor of God, that ye may be able to stand against the wiles of the devil. For we wrestle not against flesh and blood, but against principalities, against powers, against the rulers of the darkness of this world, against spiritual wickedness in high places. Wherefore take unto you the whole armor of God, that ye may be able to withstand in the evil day, and having done all, to stand. Stand therefore, having your loins girt about with truth, and having on the breastplate of righteousness; And your feet shod with the preparation of the gospel of peace. Above all, taking the shield of faith, wherewith ye shall be able to quench all the fiery darts of the wicked. And take the helmet of salvation, and the sword of the Spirit, which is the word of God.'" Chaplain O'Shaunessy ended with a prayer, and for several minutes, the men sat in silence. Then they slowly trickled out.

Lunch was more than an hour away, but the refuge of a warm, dry place held a few back and brought others in early. The mood changed as quickly as Iowa weather as platoon members joined Jack on the far side of the tent. Soon, he was holding court. Aaron admired him, always the center of attention, confident, funny. So much for Aaron's hopes of a quiet place to read old letters and write Mary back in solitude. Still, he continued as best he could.

There was so much he wanted to say. Every day, the war added new experiences and yesterdays were stacking up. Mary was the one person he could rely on, but words were hard to find, and he was restricted by censors. He was left to brood in silence in the crowded mess tent, shaking his head to loosen the images of the Hürtgen Forest battles and the dead German boy who seemed to follow him. His blood was on

his hands and still in his heart. Enough. He had to write Mary. She's
pregnant! He had to think about the future, too.

Dear Mary,

*I nearly conked out when I got the news. Of course I didn't cry, but I
sure couldn't sleep. I keep seeing the face of a little baby in your arms.
It's a weird feeling. You'll be such a great mom. I hope I'm a good dad.
Thanks for telling my folks. I knew Maty would melt. Don't worry about
Bat'ko. He's a hard one to read.*

*Your letters and packages were delayed so I got a number of them at
once. We were in an area where mail was hard to come by and now we
have moved. Hope you got my letters. Thanks for all the goodies.*

*Cold and wet here. Thought hell was supposed to be hot. We're in Spa,
Belgium. I guess I can tell you. A beautiful city, but it has started to
snow and living in a pup tent takes the shine off of being here. There
are mineral baths here that are supposed to be good for you. I haven't
been there, but some of the men have. Jack, my tentmate, went to town
and brought back a loaf of bread and shared it with me. He's a hard one
to figure. He's as windy as March, but with the heart of summer.*

While he was writing the letter, he listened to members of his platoon.
He watched Jack standing before a tableful of soldiers. "I'm telling you
she had the biggest Babylons you've ever seen." Jack held his cupped
hands out, a cigarette hanging from his lips.

"So what happened next?" Tommy leaned forward.

"I crawled out the window with my pants in my hand and ran like hell.
Hell, I didn't know she was married! Her husband was a mean son of a
bitch, too."

The soldiers were howling with laughter. "Aow-ooh!" Fran Cathcart
howled appreciatively. "You're such a wolf."

Jack smiled. "I'll tell you what a wolf is. It's when I take out a sweater
girl and try to pull the wool over her eyes." The mess hall erupted
with laughter and back slapping. Aaron shook his head and smiled. Jack
wasn't the kind of guy you wanted to be, but somehow, he still made
you feel jealous.

Sergeant Collier entered the tent and took a seat across from Aaron. "I see Jack's entertaining the troops. Hell, he should get a medal for raising morale."

Aaron smiled and nodded. "Happy Hanukkah!"

Aaron pinched his eyebrows and nodded.

"Happy Hanukkah, yourself." Aaron looked back to the letter he was writing, then back to Sergeant Collier, adding under his breath, "Whatever that is?"

Sergeant Collier smiled. "Well, it's a celebration of the end of war. People think it's Jewish Christmas. We Jews have been at war a very long time."

"I don't want to be Jewish."

A sympathetic grin broke across Sergeant's face. "Yeah, I don't want to be here in this goddamned war either. But I am. When I was back at battalion, I ran into Hemingway. He was our eyes and ears in Paris. He thinks the Germans are done." Sarge slid a picture across the table. The picture was of his two-year-old son wearing a sailor outfit. "Is that the cutest kid you've seen? Ignore the outfit. Her dad was in the Navy."

"That's something to live for," Aaron said reflectively.

Aaron admired Sergeant Collier. He had fought his way onto Utah beach and watched 75 percent of his men die there. To a man, everyone respected him. Purdy had been one of the D-Day survivors. Aaron wondered if that was why Sarge tolerated him, the crazy man and the warm glass of milk.

With a glint of sadness in his steel-gray eyes, Sergeant Collier shrugged his shoulders and narrowed them. "And to die for."

* * *

The Germans hadn't given up, in spite of Allied momentum, and on December 16, they launched a major counteroffensive along the eighty-mile front. Hitler called it *Unternehmen: Wacht am Rhein* (Operation: Watch on the Rhine). The Allies referred to it as the Ardennes Counteroffensive. The public called it the Battle of the Bulge.

Aaron's unit quickly packed up and moved out of Spa, ahead of the German line of attack, to rejoin the fight along the southern shoulder of the battlefront. They arrived midday in Luxembourg, a beautiful, tranquil city liberated by the Allies in September. German railway guns had shelled it for months, and it was still war-torn, but its sunny streets were full of citizens to greet them. Women, men, and children were quick to approach the soldiers, using the English they had learned in school. Collier allowed the soldiers some latitude, knowing how soon they would rejoin the fight, and let them have a few days to play.

On the streets, they were serenaded by accordions playing Yankee songs. Shop windows were decorated, and nativity scenes were displayed in front of the Catholic churches. Christmas gifts had already been exchanged on St. Nicholas Day, and the deeply religious community was preparing for the real Christmas ahead. Most everyone could only think about the holiday and, of course, rejoining the battle. Except Jack.

Ice cream shops attracted the soldiers, and a striking, long-black-haired teenage ice cream scooper named Bridget lured Jack. After two cups of ice cream, in between customers, Jack complimented her English, told her how much he liked her city, and launched into stories about Hollywood. Aaron listened in the background, smiling at his stories about how he had gone to school with John Wayne. Even Belgians knew of John Wayne. Anybody listening would swear Jack was a movie star himself. He had the looks. Aaron gave up and left him there, but ran into him not too much later.

He was being escorted by Sarge, who was rounding up soldiers and sending them back to camp. They were moving out in the morning. On their way back to camp, Jack obtained a two-liter bottle of cheap red wine.

* * *

Sarge secured a barn east of town for the night. It had a pungent, aged aroma that said it was a century old and out of use, but it was warm and out of the wind. They lit a small fire, less useful for its warmth than for flickering shadows and companionship. Aaron and Jack moved to the back, where Jack slyly poured the fruity pinot into their steel canteen cups. On the far side of the barn, they could hear the voice of Tommy Woods, the quarterback.

"We'll be in Germany soon. Wonder what that's gonna be like.

We gonna be fighting the locals?"

Aaron recognized Cory Wheeler from his slow West Virginia drawl. "Well, I doubt ther gunna kiss us like thay did in Paris!"

"The only good German is a dead one," Purdy's voice came out of a dark back corner of the barn, from one of the horse stalls.

"Nah, I'll bet there are good Germans, a lot of them." That sounded like the new guy, Levi Johnson, the Mormon son of a Utah Rancher, who had joined the platoon in Spa with three others. The recon platoon, the eyes and ears of the regiment, was again at full strength and had returned to its original reconnaissance mission.

"Then I say we kill 'em all and let God sort out the good ones." Purdy had a way of speaking for no one.

Levi was quick to respond. "The Apostle Paul said, 'If possible, so far as it depends on you, be at peace with all men.'"

Purdy's voice shot out of the dark. "Somebody shut him up."

Jack took a full gulp of wine and poured another. Aaron held out his empty cup. The Schlitz beer he had drunk at Miller's Bend with friends was bitter but drinkable. The wine was sweet and warming, and it added a comforting daze to his hard-ground misery.

"I wish they'd go to sleep," Jack lamented.

"You're not thinking of sneaking out to see that girl?" "She said she'd meet me."

"You know you're nuts? You'd get in all kind of trouble! If you don't make it back in time, they'll shoot you for desertion."

Jack just laughed. "What are you talking about? They need me. They're not going to do anything. Besides, whatever they do couldn't be any worse than this crap."

Close by they could hear a voice muttering. "What the hell does Jesus Christ have to do with us? Quit your preaching. He ain't here. Why in the hell would he be anywhere near this hell-hole? God, or Jesus, whoever you're praying to nowadays, doesn't give a tinker's damn. I say he gave up on us a long time ago."

Levi's voice grew angry and loud. "You'd better get down on your knees and beg for forgiveness!"

Jack shook his head. "You're Jewish, aren't you?" "Yep, I guess so."

"You guess so?"

"Long story. No churches—I mean —synagogues in my upbringing. My parents hid their religion."

After a long pause, with only the creaking of the old barn rattling in the wind, Jack said, "It's something, what they're doing to the Jews, huh?"

In July of 1944, the Russians had liberated several concentration camps in Poland— Majdanek, Sobibor, and Treblinka, confirming rumors of the of the death camps. Until their liberation, there had been many who hadn't believed the stories, horrors beyond even the understanding of the most hardened soldier. Boneyards were piled with babies and children, and skeleton survivors would die of disease and malnutrition right before their liberators' eyes.

"Do you believe all the stories?" Jack continued.

"I guess. Sarge said that's why we have to keep fighting. And the Chaplain too." Aaron answered. "I saw you at church service. You religious?"

"No religious upbringing for me either. My father was too busy selling cars. I was just checking it out. So your dog-tags say you're Jewish right?"

"Yep, the big 'H.'"

"I'd lose 'em if you're ever captured."

Across the way, Levi barked out angrily. "All you guys are going to Hell anyway unless you accept Jesus Christ as your Savior!"

Before another word could be spoken, Sergeant Collier's commanding voice cut through the fusty, smoky barn. "Shut up and go to sleep. If I hear another word, we're gonna take off tonight. Wouldn't bother me a bit to get going right now, so don't test me."

The barn went silent. Aaron whispered, "Jack, you still there?" After a pause, Jack groaned.

"I don't get it. Why are there so many different religions? What do you call a person who just believes in God?"

After a long pause, Jack's snoring was the first sound to break the Sarge's spell.

Aaron leaned over for the bottle and filled his cup.

11

The next day they moved to the northeast toward Osweiler, Luxembourg, in a thick and gloomy fog, which limited scouting missions as well as enemy encounters. En route, word reached them that the German surprise offensive to the north had overwhelmed the American defenses. In some places, Allied lines had collapsed, and thousands of soldiers were surrendering. Territory they had fought and died for, including Hill 500, was retaken by the Germans. On the second day of the German counteroffensive, eighty-four American soldiers were taken prisoner and executed near Malmedy, Belgium. A few escaped to report the horror. It wasn't until January that most of the snow-covered bodies were found, with the last recovered in February and April. One American unit gave orders to take no prisoners. Germans were to be shot on sight.

Aaron's platoon, sent ahead of the battalion to locate German positions, was the first to approach Osweiler. The day was the coldest it had been, and Aaron's feet were numb. On the outskirts of town, just when they thought the way was clear, they saw the enemy scurrying to take up positions. Mortar shells burst overhead in the treetops and on the ground.

Every man raced for cover and waited for the regiment to catch up. Sarge sent a runner to alert Captain Jardine. Casualties mounted. Fran Cathcart took a round in the thigh. Jimbo, the amiable, clumsy Omahan, was shot in the back while rescuing Fran.

Machine guns sent bullets zipping through the forest and cut away at their cover. The attack was so fierce it was difficult to return fire. Pinned down, the Americans fought the Germans to a draw, expecting they would either be overwhelmed or rescued at daybreak. They waited in the winter darkness. Jimbo painfully bled out during the night as fellow soldiers listened to his pleadings.

Lying in the ready position, they listened to German officers barking orders, wondering what was being planned for the next attack. As the dark gray dawn was breaking, they heard the friendly groan of tanks behind them. They cheered the rescue and watched the German retreat.

Sarge ordered an accounting of the men, and when there was no answer from the ditch to his right, Aaron crawled out to check. A soldier was face down. When Aaron turned him over, he could see he had been hit in the chest, probably in the initial attack. Pulling loose his dog tags, Aaron examined them. This man had been one of the replacement soldiers who joined them in Spa. The dog tag read *Wilder Rutherford B O 37467991 T44 44 Y*

Rutherford. Aaron had never heard his first name. Never talked to him. His religious preference was Y, which stood for none. Aaron recalled Rutherford had been close to Levi and had heard him praying with the preacher the night before. He had said he had never fired his gun. *He traveled all this way to die*, Aaron thought.

As the regiment engaged the enemy, Aaron's platoon was ordered to maneuver around the fighting toward Dickweiler, about three- quarters of a mile south of the Sauer River. They were to reconnoiter the area. The wind-whipped, side-spitting snow was piercing to the core. The dark sky was a sign of worse weather to come. For two weeks, they slept on the hard ground, trying to find places out of the wind, shoveling snow as best they could to make a camp.

Tortured by the lack of sleep, battle-ready but worn, they were reduced to grunts and swear words, nonverbal I-don't-give-a-damns, and piercing glances checking to see who was about to crack.

Water was brought in from several miles back in five-gallon cans. In the short time it had taken to get there, a layer of ice had formed on the surface. Canteens had to be stored under their parkas to keep the water from freezing. As the snow accumulated, some men ate it. Twice they were able to secure one of the sturdy stone houses common to the area, which had safe cellars with stores of food and beer and wine. But most days they ate K-ration canned eggs for breakfast, cheese for lunch, and Spam for supper.

After three weeks of daytime scouting and sleeping in ten inches of fresh snow, Aaron heard the voice of Levi, the Mormon rancher's son. "Aaron, you there?"

"Yep," Aaron answered halfheartedly.

"Do you remember, I said everyone was going to Hell unless they accepted Jesus?"

Aaron considered saying no. The last thing he wanted was a lecture on Jesus. "Yep."

"You know I wasn't talking about you. You know that, right?" "Okay."

"You're Jewish, aren't you? You're one of God's chosen children." Aaron was tired of being Jewish, of not knowing the first thing about it, and heading toward a land that was wiping out the entire race—his race.

"I doubt there are many Jews who feel chosen right now," Aaron lamented.

* * *

In Bitburg, the mail caught up with them. He first opened one of the boxes from Mary that was chock full of shortbread cookies stacked in tomato soup cans, and a large can of khrustykies that, no doubt, Maty had cooked for him. She also sent socks, hard peppermint candy, and Millie's beef jerky.

Biting into a cookie, he sorted her letters with one hand, first looking at one, then the other, trying to decide which to open. Before opening her first letter, he held it to his nose, hoping for a hint of her. By the Army transfer stamps, it had followed him from Le Havre.

Aaron smiled when she said the Iowa winter was hard and that she was already looking forward to spring. There was nothing new with her folks or his. Pastor Woodruff's godson's death still weighed on him. He asked about Aaron. Mary reported she was now stopping by to see his folks on a regular basis, and they seemed happy to see her—even his father. His back was still hurting. His mother was better, but still coughed a lot.

I pray you'll be back by the time the baby arrives. Doctor says it should be the first week in June.

Aaron put the letter down and gazed into the eerie, late- afternoon light, alert for any movements or sound. Unless he looked right at a picture of Mary, it was getting difficult to conjure up her image. When he had crossed the Atlantic, and again on the caravan across France, it had been easy to imagine her. Standing before the memorial in Flanders for the first time, he had labored to see her face but had sweet memories to call on—her auburn curls, how she closed her eyes, scrunched her nose, and shook her head whenever he told her how pretty she was. It had worked then. Now it wasn't so easy to remember. *What does the fading memory mean?*

He tore open the last letter. It was recently dated January 11, just a little over a week ago.

Dearest Aaron:
Perhaps you know already. I pray you don't know, but oh how I hope you do and that I'm wrong, or somehow there is an error. Fritz is missing in action. Somewhere outside of Malmedy, Belgium. I pray he'll show up.

Aaron dropped the letter. The stories about the massacre at Malmedy were well known. So many times, the missing turned up dead. Was Fritz really there? What had happened to him? Was he murdered as he surrendered? Did he cry out for help in the darkness? Fritz said he could kill, but didn't think he would survive.

He turned back to her letter.

We're so sad here. I know how sad this is for you. I wish you were here. We want so badly for the war to end and you to be home. I pray for your safety, but every day I wake up wondering where you are and what you're doing.
Your mother is depressed about things and I worry she has the whooping cough. It's going around. She agreed to let me take her to the doctor. I just don't know how she gets by. When I go over to see her all she can

talk about is you. Your dad always goes outside. Remember your job is to end this war and get home fast and help me with this baby. I'm still having morning sickness, but halfway through my shift I'm okay. Big deal, huh?

Please write and tell us you are safe. Tell me you're coming home. Tell me life is going to be great. I haven't heard from you but hear reports of fighting where we think you are.

I want to say cheery things to you, but I don't know what to say. I love you. I pray and pray and pray until my knees are sore.

Oh, Aaron. End this war and come home.

Mary

Aaron's nearly frozen fingers made it hard to hold the pen, and there wasn't much light. And censors laid down so many rules about what he could say that he worried his letters would sound evasive. Anyway, he didn't want to tell her how it really was or how he felt. *What should I say?*

In just a few short months, Aaron felt he'd become a man. Memories of his past were being covered over by heavy snow and cold and a thick layer of fear. Yesterdays were now mere dates on a calendar and tomorrows were hard to find and difficult to hold. As he began to write her, he tried to conjure up glimmers of Mary and his folks, all those days at Miller's Bend with his friends Fritz and Tony. But there were only lightning bolts of random images: a lifeless fishing line floating on top of the water, a bobber swaying in a gentle breeze, the innocence of three boys drinking beer sitting on the hood of his car, gazing at stars and wondering if those same stars would look the same thousands of miles away, the girl talk, and all the hopes and promises of blood brothers. Memories came in a flash, sparked, and in the blink of his eye, were gone.

Send me news about Fritz and Tony. It's so frustrating not knowing anything. Can't be true about Fritz, he was always on top of things. They'll find him. He'll be okay. So will Tony.

Got the socks you made. Dry socks are worth their weight in gold. Guess I can't tell you where we are or where we've been—doesn't really matter. I want to forget it anyway. Passed through a big beautiful city at

Christmas time. They were pretty serious about the holiday. It made me homesick. Nothing special about Christmas here in camp. Levi, we call him Preacher, tried to get everybody to sing Christmas carols. Nobody was in the mood. It was two days after Christmas anyway.

Not feeling so lucky. I love you.

Aaron

P.S. I put a letter in here for Maty and Bat'ko. Also, and I hope you won't think this morbid, but I've written a letter to Baby Vanko. I've been thinking June is a long way off before Lucky Three is born. Just stick it away and forget it. Save it for a special day, maybe a birthday or special occasion, in case.

* * *

It wasn't until the end of January that the counteroffensive was defeated. Germans surrendered en masse or retreated across the border. The Allies had finally won the Battle of the Bulge. The land was overpriced, paid for with the blood of 8,706 dead Americans and 68,283 wounded or missing. But the march toward Berlin was on.

Aaron's platoon lost more men. After the clumsy Omaha boy and the replacement, they picked up in Spa, two wounded soldiers were evacuated and two others sent back to have their frostbitten feet treated. Both of them lost toes and were sent home.

Aaron's division faced more of winter's roughest weather. Always, in camp and on the move, Aaron kept one eye on Purdy and the other on his surroundings for hints of the enemy and hidden bouncing betties. Bouncing betties were landmines that, when triggered, launched into the air and sprayed shrapnel in all directions.

In February, the regiment fought their way toward Olzheim, Germany and crossed the Kyll River as March unfolded. Every day, Aaron went off to work across, around, and in front of new battles, often for a small stretch of land, a hill, a town. At night they slept in trenches on frozen ground, or in abandoned farmhouses or barns.

When they crossed battlefields on recon missions, the sights dazed them: human remains ground into the icy tracks of military equipment, grotesque limbless and headless torsos, disregarded women and children stiff in the snow, mutilated corpses of Germans and Americans frozen to the earth, a few with beseeching hands outstretched skyward. The sights were horrifying at first but then became numbing.

The goal was staying alive and warm. Each day, they hoped to find a farmhouse or decent shelter for a warm night. But most nights were spent in trenches on the cold ground, fresh snow their blanket. And when the day's work was done, they were expected to take pride in bloody victories. But Aaron only felt cold and empty. Oh, how he wished he could shake the feelings deep in his gut, but the only purging was that of undigested K or C rations left on the field of battle. The platoon's last engagement cost the lives of two more— Tommy Woods and Dan Carney, friends, foxhole mates, both Missouri boys. The platoon was ambushed by German soldiers who had seen them coming and set up an MG42 machine gun, Hitler's buzzsaw, which fired 1,200 rounds a minute. They were ordered to withdraw and were lucky to get away with only two losses. They had to leave the two soldiers behind. Two well-equipped rifle platoons were sent in to take the Germans out and recover the bodies.

They moved off to the east and then north along a narrow farm road, thick with trees on both sides. Their recon goal was to determine where the retreating Germans were setting up defensive positions. It began to snow again, large flakes seesawing back and forth. The line of soldiers was strung out, with Sarge in the lead. Aaron found himself near the back, Purdy ahead of him. Suddenly Purdy moved sideways, and like a dog picking up a scent, he left the road, trudging through the snow toward the tree cover. Aaron and nearby soldiers stopped and watched.

Purdy had spotted a dead German soldier leaning against a tree, covered to his head in a foot of snow. The German soldier had crawled there with his last strength. Whistling, Purdy began picking through the German soldier's coat and pack.

"Hey Aaron, want to shoot a German?" Aaron turned away.

"Aaron, come here," Purdy said in a commanding voice. "I got one for you. Come on, shoot him." Purdy pointed his M1 toward the dead German soldier. "He ain't gonna move. You can't miss."

Aaron tried to ignore him. He could feel the gaze of others. He looked around for Sarge who was well ahead of them.

Purdy was smiling, his yellow teeth a stark contrast to the white winter scene. "Shoot him. Come on. It'll be good practice," Purdy mocked.

Aaron turned away.

"You chicken? You too chicken to shoot a dead man?"

Aaron jumped back at the crack of Purdy's M1 rifle. The German soldier's head was split open like a melon, fresh blood splattered on the white snow. What was left of his face was red pieces of splintered bones.

"You can't even kill a dead man. What kind of soldier are you?" Purdy chortled.

Aaron looked around for sympathetic faces, but the numb soldiers were moving on, staring blankly, bracing themselves against the snow.

Aaron didn't move. At times like this, he felt like a small boy in a man's uniform, holding a gun, clinging to the only part of himself that made sense—his youth. Purdy was the reincarnation of a Dark Ages soldier—take no prisoners, rape and pillage. Aaron felt like a stranger in a faraway land. Standing there, his feet frozen to the earth, his mouth agape, he wondered if the others feared Purdy. He had to stand up to the man, but he was trembling. "I can shoot *your* ass."

"Not if I shoot your chicken ass first," Purdy retorted. Purdy raised his M1 to his hip.

Sarge's footsteps swished past Aaron toward Purdy and stopped, their noses nearly touching. "You do that again, and I'll send you back so fast . . . " Sarge's face was red with anger as he spit out the words, "You want out of this goddamned war? Just do that again. I'll get you a nice warm cot in the stockade, waiting for a court-martial." Sarge recognized that Purdy was not like any other soldier and wouldn't want to go back. As an afterthought, he added, "Better yet, I'll take that goddamned rifle away from you, and you can fight with your hands."

Aaron looked over at the German soldier. What a way to die, alone, no one there to cradle him, no one there when he died. No one to take him home. He would rot there in the spring.

* * *

The snowfall finally stopped, but the buildup of fresh snow had complicated supply capabilities, so hunger was added to the misery of the cold and snow. Any tracks in the snow ahead of them were covered up, so for now, tracking was difficult. When they came to the end of the road, they took a break in the cover of a nearby stand of trees and broke open smokes and rations. Jack began to barter food for cigarettes. Aaron was always quick to offer him his four-pack of Old Golds. As Jack lit up a smoke and began to tell Hollywood stories, not far away, Preacher Levi was citing Scriptures to a growing audience.

Sarge noticed Aaron move to the edge of an embankment under the cover of a tight cluster of trees. He cleared a spot and sat across from him.

"If this war doesn't end soon," Sarge said, "I'm either going to shoot Purdy or myself. Look, we've all had our fill of him, but he's a damn good scout. Good to have him on our side, that's for sure. Wolves are 99 percent dogs, but make no mistake, God help us all after the war."

As the allied forces pursued the retreating enemy, they crossed the Rhine, the Germans fanned out, and the war entered a new phase, in some ways more dangerous. German soldiers were on the defensive and close to home, which at first made some more willing to die. Their backs against the wall, they fought like trapped animals. In addition to the regular Army, the soldiers the Allies faced were old men and children, the *Volksstrum* and the Hitler youth called *Hitlerjugend*, units made up of boys as young as twelve. Others fought on under the threat of being shot or hanged by SS soldiers who had secretly infiltrated infantry ranks. So long as the Nazi party was in command, and Hitler was alive, there would be fighting. At the same time, German surrenders were common because many towns saw the Allies as liberators.

* * *

February's war conditions were different from January's cold and deep snow, but not better. Mixed snow and rain produced mud, just as accursed. Allied forces were gobbling up the land and killing and capturing the enemy. Annihilation of the enemy was the soldier's path home, and fighting on German soil added the element of revenge to the faint smell of victory.

Germans, now defending their homeland, sometimes seemed to Aaron no different than his friends back home, except for the color of their uniforms. *Why do regular people fight?*

When the day's work was done and others celebrated victory, all he felt was cold and empty. He still couldn't shake the image of the of the young German soldier who had died in his arms or Bob Stump's face staring back at him, as if he was sitting right next to him. Aaron wondered, until he was long past wondering, if each day was his day. As they advanced, they found many German cities reduced to rubble by Allied bombing, creating a cruel real-world game of pick- up sticks and bricks. The more populated areas were good only for plentiful beer and wine. Jack was the ideal drinking companion, always one to lighten the mood, impervious to the slashes and gashes of the carnage. Whenever they found bombed-out or abandoned houses, they rummaged through the cellars, sometimes even finding vodka and whiskey.

Many German citizens were tired of the war, wanting to be conquered. Soldiers started surrendering by the thousands. Surprised at how friendly Americans were, some greeted them as heroes, anxious for the war to end, but their desperate civility was complicated, too. Among the citizenry of each town was an indistinguishable faction—Nazis—who could be swift and often cruel, punishing their own people by destroying entire towns poised for surrender.

American soldiers were warned not to fraternize with the locals, but that didn't dissuade many, especially not Jack, who was always on the prowl for women and bottles. In the town of Kriegsfeld, Jack met a sixteen-year-old girl named Bertha, who took him home to meet her parents. Her English mother chatted away about England and how they hoped to go to America one day. Eating sauerkraut and beets didn't appeal to Jack's California sensibilities, nor did the warm wheat beer. When the family offered him a bottle of wine, he shared it with Aaron, along with the story of his latest conquest.

* * *

After crossing the Kyll River, the Americans fought their way toward the City of Worms. Dug in outside Kitchleimbolanden, they waited for orders and watched waves of Allied bombers light up the night sky. On the horizon, explosions flashed like lightning strikes and rumbled like thunder. Over 300 planes dropped 1,100 tons of bombs, destroying half of the buildings below. When the Allies were able to enter Worms,

Aaron saw homes, stores, factories, churches, and synagogues lying in rubble. A statue of Martin Luther was toppled in the public square along with ancient temples to the gods Jupiter, Juno, Minerva, and Mars. Always the schoolteacher, Sarge said Worms was one of the oldest cities in Germany, once home to one of the largest Jewish populations.

As they slept in trenches outside Kitchleimbolanden, hay from a nearby field added an unaccustomed comfort to the still-cold ground. The spring snow covered them. When it warmed in the morning, the campsite was a mess of mud and green slime.

Three replacement soldiers had joined Aaron's platoon. Seven fellow soldiers from his platoon had died, and four had been sent back because of wounds and frostbite. Aaron recalled his first night, learning names, the camp mores, who to avoid, who might be helpful. It had been like being a new kid in a strange town. Aaron could see the fresh fear in the recruits' eyes and wondered what they made of the dull resignation in his and the other veterans' faces. He tried to be friendly.

Gayle Erickson was a wiry, prematurely balding farm boy from Ogallala, Nebraska. Mike Talbot, a meek, fair-skinned, slightly built soldier from Alexandria, Virginia, talked about working in Potomac Yard, a large Eastern seaboard railway hub. Bob Wells was a Chippewa Indian from Walker, Minnesota. His animated personality reminded Aaron of Tony. The men called him Chief. Jack said, "All the comings and goings are making this place look like a parking lot."

Sarge called his men together the next morning, gathering them around the map on the ground. Pointing to a nondescript spot, he outlined their new assignment. "In three days, we're going to connect up with the Fourth right here. There's supposed to be a cluster of abandoned farmhouses here, where we can stop on the way. I'd like to find one where we can hole up for two days before we meet up. Get out of this mud."

Soldiers loved breaks and abandoned farmhouses. Sometimes the houses were already stripped, but sometimes they found potatoes, beets, spirits, and beds, and even if they didn't, a hard floor was better than the trenches they slept in most nights.

Looking up to the attentive smiles of his men, Sarge continued. "We've heard sporadic small arms fire, 88s, ahead of us for some time, but today, it's been silent. Headquarters says they are nowhere near where we are heading."

"Sounds gud to me," Cory Wheeler said in his West Virginia drawl as he scraped the green slime off his boots with a stick. "Reckon we kin holt out, long as we git there b'night. Cain't sleep in this shit agin'."

"It's just a couple of miles up the road." Sarge studied the faces of his men. "I need a couple of guys to check it out. Don't engage the enemy, just find out if the area is safe."

Heads turned, and soldiers began to lean back out of Sergeant Collier's direct view, knowing he was about to make assignments. Purdy spoke up. "I'll check it out."

Sarge wasn't surprised. Purdy was always restless in camp, more comfortable on the move. He was like one of his squirmy third- grade students, when he wasn't just being mean. Of course, now, even more men looked away. No one wanted to go with Purdy. Sarge made a mental inventory, listing who he had recently sent out, who was new, and who was in line for an assignment.

Selecting anyone to go with Purdy needed some thought, but since this was just a half-day scouting trip, anyone should be fine. So Sarge said, "Aaron, you're up. I expect you to be back before we lose daylight, but if you don't, the password is Betty Boop. Everybody got that?"

Sending Aaron out with Purdy made sense. It was his turn, and doing otherwise wouldn't be fair to the other men who had recently been on patrols. Sarge respected Aaron's quiet strength and thought he'd be able to endure Purdy's goading. Compared to the reckless Purdy, he preferred men like Aaron. The kid could handle himself. He had proven that. He may not be the killer Purdy was, but he was reliable and took orders.

As the meeting was breaking up, Levi Johnson lingered and addressed the sergeant. "Is it a good idea to send Purdy out with Aaron?"

Sergeant's answer was loud enough to be heard by all the men. "If Aaron doesn't come back, I'll shoot Purdy. Simple as that."

When they left camp, the evergreen trees along the road were still heavy with snow, and soon, the snow of poets turned to devil's sleet. As the ice covered the snow, the boughs of the trees began to droop to the ground. So thick was the forest there was no escape, and the bowed trees offered perfect cover for the enemy. At least the sleet washed away their footsteps as if they had never passed this way.

Still, it battered at them and, with rising wind, forced them to take shelter for a half hour. Not a word was spoken between Aaron and Purdy. When they were able to return to the road, Purdy said, "I like the snow better." It was the nicest thing he had ever said to Aaron.

Walking like drunks, meandering from side to side, they turned in circles, looking for landmines and watching their backs Purdy insisted on taking the lead, which was a relief to Aaron, who preferred having him where he could see him.

Moving up the road in single file, like an angry father leading a small boy, Purdy broke the silence and called back, "You still back there, or have you run off?"

"I'm still here." A few minutes later Aaron asked, "So Purdy, what have you got against me?"

Without hesitating, Purdy replied, "I think you're gutless and you're going to get me killed."

"You're gonna get yourself killed."

"I think you're a chicken." Turning in the road, Purdy leered, flashing his yellow teeth, ice fangs extended from his nostrils. "I'm watching you, Aaron. If I ever feel you're jeopardizing the platoon, I'll put a bullet in you. I might just do that out here. Nobody'd knows." He turned and began to walk on.

Aaron decided to leave it alone. There was no reason to talk anymore. It's not like it was really news.

A few minutes later Purdy broke the silence. "I know you're Jewish, too. That'd be another good reason to shoot you. I saw the H on your dog tag."

Aaron shook his head. He was tired and cold. "I can't figure you, Purdy. What are you so mad about? Save your bullets for the Germans. Lay off me."

For fifteen minutes both men were silent. Without turning back, Purdy declared into the wind, "This is all I got. This war. Nothing to go home to. This is it." After several beats, he added. "I ain't gonna shoot you."

In the distance, a farmhouse appeared in the fine, frozen mist, gradu-ally replacing the sleet. With studious eyes, they watched for activity. If there were Jerrys around, there would be some sign of them, or sentries posted. They moved to the edge of the road, still and silent, waiting.

The farmhouse was built of fieldstone and had a thatched roof. There was a large barn not fifty yards away. When they finally decided there was no one there and approached, the sun was breaking through fast-moving clouds. Beside the barn was an old, abandoned wagon. The peek-a-boo sun brought out the sounds of chirping birds. The song of a red crossbill, a series of short, warbled clicks and whistles, reminded him of cardinals back in Iowa. In the field beyond the barn was a lonely, weathered scarecrow.

There was no sign of life. They paused at the front door and listened before entering. Purdy reconnoitered the upstairs and Aaron the lower level. The house reminded him a little of Fritz's home. When was the last time he had felt that safe and comfortable, with walls, a roof, windows, doors, a ceiling overhead, feet on a hard-planked floor? Empty jars and cans, cups and saucers were abandoned on the counter. Behind the kitchen was a small back bedroom. From the large, stone fireplace that smelled of years of ash, soot crawled out into the room and climbed up the wall.

The sun had broken free and was shining full force through the window, directly onto a large overstuffed chair set to look out into the yard. Pulling his knit hat off, then his wool finger gloves and parka, he threw them in a pile on the floor next to the chair, pulled his heavy, wool sweater over his head and sat. He removed his four- buckle galoshes, leaned back, and sighed. He could hear Purdy's footsteps on the second floor. Someone's father and mother looked out of two curling, faded unframed pictures on one wall. On the fireplace mantle was a porcelain statue of the crucified Jesus and on the wall behind, a picture of Jesus talking to a crowd on the top of a hill. The sun was warm through the window.

When was the last time he felt this comfortable? Mary's image popped into his mind. She was wearing the skirt with the white dog's face embroidered onto the bottom, the same one she was wearing that night at Riverview Park. She was smiling up at him, her hair pulled back in a bun. Suddenly she was here, so vivid he felt he could reach out and touch her. He laid his head back and closed his eyes.

His eyes blinked open wide. He had dozed off. How long? Like an invisible tap on the shoulder, there was something he had missed. Jerking his head toward the far corner of the room, he saw a German coat laying in the corner, an open, half-eaten German ration kit, a pack tucked behind a table. It made him shiver. A noise behind him startled him. He stood. "Purdy!" He called out, about to turn.

Suddenly, large arms were reaching around him, the ends of a rope in each hand. Large, strong hands, not Purdy's, looping the rope around his neck, but not before Aaron grabbed on to it. The rope was pulled tight against his throat. Kicking wildly, he pushed up with his feet and flew back and forth like a rag doll.

Gasping for air, he reached back to find flesh, and strong arms continued to jerk him from side to side. When the man attempted to ram Aaron's head against the wall, Aaron was able to pull the rope free from his neck. When he pushed away, he saw the German soldier for the first time, in his field gray uniform with a death's- head patch on his arm. He was Aaron's height and muscular, with the shoulders of a footballer. His sad Aryan blue eyes and well- kept white teeth were smiling confidently, as if he felt like a lion in the final takedown of a wildebeest. Before Aaron could move, the German rushed him and struck him in the face, knocking him against the wall and striking him again and again.

Aaron braced his feet on the wall and pushed with all his energy, knocking the German to the floor. The tussle continued until Aaron was pinned. The honed black carbon commando knife was held above him, out of reach, looking for the killing spot in the center of his chest. Aaron grabbed the German's forearm. They wrestled as the blade inched slowly toward his chest.

The German leaned in. Aaron gasped for air as he attempted to push the knife away. Aaron was losing strength as the knife point inched closer. He felt it pierced his skin in a slot between his ribs, drawing blood. He was microseconds from death.

Their gazes locked in a battle of kill or live. Aaron's strength and will was dwindling. *I am about to die.* He could feel the sharp knife point moving deeper. He saw his Maty hanging clothes on the clothesline and Bat'ko lifting him on the horse when he was a little boy . . . *Mary. Where was Mary?*

The German's eyes softened as he relaxed his grip on the knife and pulled it back. A smile crept into the corner of his mouth. Aaron was still gasping for air. "*Jüdische*. You are Jewish, no?"

His respectable English surprised Aaron. He had heard all the stories about how Germans were slaughtering Jews. There were warnings about a captured Jew being a prize to be paraded. His parents hid their Jewishness. Aaron rolled his head to the side in resignation, trembling.

Holding Aaron's dog tags in his hand, the German soldier continued, "*Liebe die Bruderschaft,*" The German rolled off his chest, dropped the knife to the floor, and sat beside him.

Aaron rolled his head to the side and studied him, still fearful, not understanding what he said.

"Honor the Brotherhood. The Torah teaches." The soldier said, smiling down, placing his hand on his chest.

Aaron looked puzzled. He couldn't move. Blood was trickling from his mouth, like an old man's drool. The German reached out for his pack and pulled out a handkerchief and dabbed at the trickle of blood. Aaron stared back, his mouth open.

The German soldier picked up Aaron's dog tags and pointed to the letter H. "I am *Jüdisch*." Reaching back, he pulled a picture of his wife and two children out of his pack. Pointing to his wife, he said, "Lulu." The German soldier followed Aaron's gaze as it shifted to the staircase. "I'm sorry for your friend. Such is war. Was he a friend?"

Aaron was surprised when the corner of his mouth turned slightly upward. Shaking his head, half laughing, he said, "No. He was a horrible person. Still, I feel sorry for him."

"Of course. Sorry." The German shook his head. "War, *Ich kann nicht für Deutschland zu kämpfen.*"

Aaron steadied his gaze, searching for understanding.

"I don't fight for Germany." Pointing to the death's-head patch on his uniform, he shook his head angrily. "*Nicht.* Just stay alive." He pulled a cigarette from his pack and pulled out a lighter. After lighting his cigarette, he dropped the lighter to the floor beside him, and took a long draw and blew a cloud of smoke to the ceiling. Offering one to Aaron, who just shook his head, he continued, "Like you, huh?"

"But you are Jewish?"

"There are Jews in the Army. More than you think. Not by choice. Hiding."

Looking at his watch, in a panic, the German soldier rose to his feet. Aaron was sitting on the floor. Reaching out his hand, he pulled Aaron to his feet. "I must go. I am Bernhard Klaus. You?"

"Aaron Vanko."

Bernhard opened a closet door, pulled his parka, hat, and gloves on and threw his pack over his shoulders, picked up his rifle, turned, and said, "Good luck."

Aaron stared in disbelief as the soldier opened the front door and looked to see if it was safe. Looking back to Aaron, he asked, "Where is your unit?"

Aaron shook his head.

Bernhard stepped in the doorway then looked back up the stairway. "Again, sorry about your soldier. It was unavoidable."

After he was gone, Aaron gathered his stuff and prepared to head back to his platoon. He confirmed Purdy was dead and grabbed one of his dog tags. Before he exited, he looked back and noticed that Bernhard's lighter was on the floor where he dropped it. The lighter was a black-matte finished Zippo. Several of the men in his platoon, including Jack, had Zippos. When he turned it over, he saw an engraving:

Bernhard
Ich liebe dich
Lulu
1940

* * *

Aaron straggled into camp as darkness closed in. All heads turned to see that Purdy wasn't with him. He immediately found the Sarge and climbed into his trench beside him. "Where's Purdy?"

Aaron explained that a German soldier surprised Purdy when he was checking out the house. He handed one of Purdy's dog tags to the Sarge. "I left him there."

"We'll get him picked up." With a tilt of his head, Sarge said, "A lot of people didn't like him. Some said they wanted to shoot him. What happened to the German?"

"He rushed out the door. I couldn't stop him." "You look like you've been in a serious fight."

"I tried to stop him. We fought before he took off," Aaron lied.

Sarge looked at him askance. "You okay?" Not waiting for a response, he continued, "I wouldn't blame you. No one in this outfit would blame you. But that doesn't make it right. There may be questions."

"The German slit his throat. I was downstairs."

"I'll look things over when we get there." Sergeant Collier said sympathetically. "On the other hand, I'm not sure anybody will care. Glad you're all right, Aaron. Go see the medic."

12

AARON'S PLATOON WAS tasked to scout out a location for a bridge-head across the Main at Ochsenfurt. After crossing the river, they headed south toward Munich. April brought a warm, drying wind, and news that President Roosevelt had died. America seemed far away. Here, the hillsides were greening and trees budding. Yellow dandelion fields did little to lift the spirits of Aaron and his mates, now more ragged, with many more replacements than experienced men. Soldiers with fresh recollections of home mingled with battle- weary veterans trying to shake memories of fallen comrades. Even in the face of a renewed optimism that the war might soon end, many moved like zombies. Half of the platoon was hollow, fatigued from the unremitting pressing forward deeper into Germany, dragging one foot after the other, with K rations for the body but without hope for the soul. The other half were naïve soldiers filled with fear, dragging their feet hoping to prevent the inevitable.

For Aaron, only the numbing effects of alcohol seemed to provide an escape from haunting images and the racing thoughts that had taken over. *What can a soldier do?* To be shocked or horrified wasn't even an option anymore. Crying like a baby in a fetal position on the ground was no option. *I'm a man. Be a man.*

Drinking was the preferred medicine for treating what ailed wartime soldiers. Aaron drank to dull the stress, the loneliness, and the terror, never to celebrate victories—he drank to bad news just as easily.

Drinking himself into oblivion, he celebrated another day alive and suppressed another day of feeling dead.

Since leaving Luxembourg, they passed through more and more small towns and clusters of farming communities. They regularly found accommodations in houses, barns, and schools. Supply conditions improved, which meant better food and cigarettes for Jack. As they moved toward the beer capital of Germany, the beer flowed more freely. Soldiers carried it back in kegs, bottles, canvas bags, carts, on anything with wheels, sometimes filling their canteens or even their helmets. They scavenged from abandoned houses and bombed-out taverns. *Löwenbräu, Hofbräuhaus*, and *Augustinerbräu*, the beer of monks. Sometimes they received it as welcome gifts from hospitable local Germans or bought it from the few operating taverns. Occasionally they confiscated bottles of Schnapps and Jägermeister.

Tonight, Jack and Aaron had secured a nearly full, already-tapped keg from an abandoned bar. Using a commandeered wheelbarrow, they rolled it a mile down the road to their camp at an abandoned farmhouse on the outside of Augsburg. Everybody drank except Preacher. When Jack was setting up the keg on the kitchen table, Sarge watched, wondering if all the drinking the past few weeks was actually good for morale. Drunkenness and hangovers could be deadly if the men were in battle, but the fighting had largely stopped. The fight now was with boredom.

"Aaron, do you ever worry about getting used to this stuff?" Sarge asked. "Someday you'll be going home. To your family. You can't keep this up."

"That's the least of our problems," Jack broke in.

The sergeant recoiled, shrugged, and tipped his helmet. "I'll drink to that."

Jack filled a stone stein with beer and handed it to him.

* * *

Nights and days of drunkenness and hangovers would have made any fighting difficult, had there been battles to fight. The thought of facing more fighting, though, was good for the drinking. Mail caught up with the platoon again in Kissing, Germany, including a shoebox of goodies and a stack of letters from Mary. Seeing the letters brought flashes of images of home, Mary's face, her auburn curls, her smile, her soft, warm skin.

Mail call was a solemn event. Anticipation filled the air as the soldiers waited for their names to be called. Some tore open mail where they stood while others, like Aaron, savored the time alone. In the quiet that followed, soldiers anxiously watched for signs of good and bad news on the faces of fellow soldiers. Sometimes care packages were shared, along with stories and pictures. Sarge's dark, whiskered face beamed with pride as he passed around a new photo of his son with a baseball bat slung heavily over his shoulder in a DiMaggio pose. Mike Talbot held up a picture of his girlfriend to Jack Post's catcalls.

Jack later told Aaron, in a hushed conversation, he'd received a letter from Bertha, the girl he met in Kriegsfeld. With the help of her English-speaking mom, she had written that she hoped to see him again. Aaron expected a comment about putting another notch on the stock of his M1, but Jack's face was serious, so Aaron left the moment dangling.

Mary was thorough in reporting on the news from home. Spring had sprung in Iowa. Aaron's father was plowing up the fields and his mother's garden. Mary continued to support the war effort making bullets, and life on the farm with the girls was "wacky." She said they still cried and laughed and then cried again. He was glad she had company.

She said she'd offered to help his mom write a letter, but Maty refused. Aaron remembered she avoided reading and writing. While Bat'ko sat at the kitchen table eagerly learning along with Aaron from his schoolbooks, Maty ignored them and went about her business.

Pastor Woodruff's praying hard for all the boys and especially you. He's got the whole congregation including you in theirs. Remember, he's got a special audience with the Man Upstairs.

Aaron had asked for another picture of her, which she had enclosed. It was taken on the front porch of Millie's farmhouse, a week before he left. He wore his Army uniform and she his favorite blue print dress. His heart melted seeing them together, his arm tight around her. She was so beautiful. Also, Millie sent him a cartoon from the newspaper about Roosevelt's death.

Before going to sleep, he penned a letter to Mary.

Dearest Wife.

I receive a letter from you every mail call without fail. There isn't much to look forward to except your letters. They always bring me back to life. And now I have another picture of you. I'll keep it close to my heart. I keep thinking we've seen the worst. Then it gets worse. Sarge said he felt like he was someone else, not himself. Funny hearing him say that. I feel that way. Will I ever be me again? I need you to remind me I'm human.

We are pushing the Germans back. We all talk about this war ending, but every day the same stuff. I saw thousands of Germans captured last week. Funny, a number of them were wearing belts with the words 'Gott Mit Uns' imprinted on them. Sarge said it meant 'God with us.' Chaplain O'Shaunessy, the regiment chaplain, says God is with us. That we are on his side. Must be a different God.

I remember that night at Riverview. Remember, I brought you a bouquet of lilacs. I'm sitting next to a budding lilac bush, thinking of that night. Let's go to Riverview when I come home. We'll ride the coaster and of course the Tunnel of Love.

When I joined this unit I was a green soldier.

Now I'm an old hand.

I can see the first star of the night. Can you see it? Tonight, I am feeling alive and Lucky Two looking at a picture of my Lucky One.

I love you, Aaron—Lucky Two

They moved farther south to Egenhofen and, two days later, got more mail. There was only one letter from Mary. Aaron got away from camp to find a private place. His helmet was on the ground beside him, next to his M1 leaning against the tree. In the distance, he could see Chaplain O'Shaunessy walking toward him. He placed his helmet on his head, pulled it down low over his eyes, and leaned back against the tree. Aaron only looked up after the chaplain passed. The day had been mild. In the damp earth under the tree, there were daffodils, just opened. He picked one and held it for a minute before opening her letter. As he opened the envelope, he could tell the letter was ominously short. His heart raced.

War manufactures the worst moments and touches so many lives. And it produces some of the best moments too, the good and bad woven together in a single strand. Mary confirmed that Fritz had, in fact, died in the Massacre at Malmedy, where over 100 American soldiers surrendered to the Germans in an open, frozen field, where they were shot—machine-gunned, given small-caliber shots to the temple or behind the ear, or even killed by rifle butt. A few escaped to tell the story. Not Fritz. Then came a double shock.

Sorry, we just got the news that Tony was also killed in action in the Luzon, Philippines.

Writing the letter had been the hardest thing Mary had done. Reading it was worse. *Fritz and Tony. My blood brothers.* The recruiting sergeant had promised them they could stay together. *I'm not going to cry.* He ripped the letter in so many pieces it fell to the ground like confetti and was picked up by the wind and blown away. Now, only Mary and Aaron and the wind would know.

Aaron moved farther from the camp, out of earshot of the small talk, to a bluff a hundred yards away. *Is it safe?* He didn't care. Night clouds covered the faintest outline of a brooding quarter moon. As he stared into the nothingness, despair and hope twisted together in the black night. He was fighting his own war, the one between his heart and mind. Part of him wanted to forget what the rest of him never would. Looking up to the heavens, he cried out, "Why don't I have a God?"

Making the rounds at midnight, Sarge found Aaron curled up on the ground and escorted him back to camp. He never asked what was wrong. He knew it was the same thing wrong with everyone. Sergeant Collier had seen it, had been trained for it. Men crack. Every man had a bottom. Some find it, others die first.

"Do you want me to send you back?" he asked Aaron. Aaron tried to focus on his words.

Sarge pressed him. "Aaron, I can send you back. Away from here."

"No." Aaron mumbled. "No. I just want to sleep."

* * *

Thoughts of dying and staying alive occupied Aaron's thoughts. Having walked from frozen, snow-covered northern France through Belgium and then into German mud, Aaron had crawled to the very edge of hell and thought he might escape, until the devil himself had jerked him back to face another horror, then another. Was there an end to the madness? Was the devil lurking in every shadow? Was this the devil's domain, where every day he set out to outdo his last torture? Was death the only way out?

New orders and they were on the move again, farther into Germany the next morning. Riding in a deuce-and-a-half for two hours over a bumpy road kept conversation to a minimum. Then they were on foot. Soon they would either find shelter or dig in for the night. They were to scout the area and continue south. When they arrived in Bergkirchen, the wind shifted around to the east. There was a peculiar, rancid smell. Jack was first to comment. "So this is what Germany smells like?"

Cory Wheeler ground out his words. "Like rott'n gut-shot deer."

Gayle Erickson, the boy from Ogallala, quickly followed up. "Worse than the feedlots back home. Worse than skunks." The stench stayed with them for several miles, so overpowering that soldiers covered their noses and mouths until the wind shifted.

Aaron was mesmerized by the rocky road, watching the footfalls of the soldiers in front of him, tuning in and out of the conversations. He hadn't said a thing all day, still brooding over Mary's letter.

Gayle was so much like Tony, Aaron recalled. When they were young, Tony said one of the older boys, Tall Carl, had told him you could plunk a skunk out of his hole and hold it up by his tail he couldn't release his stink bomb. If you were fast! Because skunks never go off in their own burrow.

Snickering, Fritz and Aaron watched from a distance as Tony crept up on the skunk's den, reached in, pulled a skunk out by his tail, fumbled it, and caught the full blast. Unafraid, the skunk dropped to the ground and looked up to Tony, then back to Fritz and Aaron, as if it knew they were too far to be a threat, and simply started to waddle away. Halfway out of the clearing, it stopped and looked around to see Tony jumping up and down and tearing off his shirt and pants.

When Fritz's laughter subsided, he turned serious. "Skunks don't fear anything. When God created skunks, knowing they didn't want to be a vicious killing predator or have to compete for carrion, He so loved the skunk that He gave him the ultimate defense: the Stink!"

They're dead. Fritz and Tony. Both of them. They're dead.

The next day his platoon learned that Hitler had committed suicide. Every man said the war had to end, that the evil leader had ended the war with his poison pill. Eight days later, Germany surrendered unconditionally. German soldiers turned themselves in to the Allies in droves. In towns they passed through, citizens greeted them with chants of *Gott sei dank!*

News of Hitler's death improved Allied morale, but still the fighting continued, now against the SS and the Gestapo and the most hardened Nazi soldiers, and sometimes a few loyal Nazis blending in with grateful citizens.

In a small area in the Dachau district, well north of the city center, Aaron's platoon found a schoolhouse. They shared it with members of a recon unit of the 45th Infantry. Members of the 45th had liberated the death camp Dachau just days earlier, coincidentally the day before Hitler's suicide. They'd found thousands of ghostly humans, barely alive, and the remains and ashes of thousands of men, women, and children. Aaron's platoon sat in silence, awed by the horror shared by the men who had days earlier witnessed one of the greatest atrocities in history.

"There were dead men standing, staring back at us as if they were ghosts."

"Alive skeletons, naked from the waist up."

"Bones wrapped in a thin wrapper of see-through skin."

"Large dark holes for eyes."

"Gaping holes smiling up to us with no teeth."

"Women and children."

"Clergy too."

The broken soldiers poured out their hearts. Aaron listened with reverence and amazement. They had witnessed the devil's work first hand. Approaching the compound, they had seen stacks of garbage that, on closer inspection, were human bodies. The vision was burned into their memory. The smell forever. The surviving Jews, gypsies, and Christian clergy, nearly three thousand, would bear witness to the torture and death of neighbors and loved ones. General Eisenhower said, "The American soldier might not have known what he was fighting for, but at least, after seeing the concentration camps, he knew what he was fighting against."

Aaron continued to receive letters from Mary and finally mustered the strength to write back. He knew she would worry if he didn't write, but he didn't know what to say. That he was happy the war was over? That he didn't know if he'd be sent to the Japanese front? That war was so much a part of the new Aaron that he didn't know if he could ever come home? Could he wash away the smells, the sights and sounds, the faces in the night, the stories?

Where could he find positive words? It used to be the censor's black marker that directed his pen. Now, when he held the pen above the paper, he struggled to find any words. He wrote, *I guess the war here might be ending and maybe I can come home. Might be sent to the Pacific to fight against Japs?* For several more minutes, nothing came. Did she know that the war wasn't over as long as he was wearing the uniform and carrying a rifle?

There were always rumors of where the platoon was heading next—Okinawa, Manila, Melbourne, Florence, somewhere else in Germany, Amsterdam, Paris—or, perhaps, home. Captain Jardine said they all should expect orders to join the battle against Japan. He said they would now fight the Japs just as they had the Jerrys.

Aaron's platoon, now as an occupying force, stayed in the Dachau district north of Munich. Air raids, seventy-one of them, had left Munich in rubble; 41 percent of the citizens had left the city. Aaron's platoon patrolled daily, watching locals pick through the debris and begin to put their lives together, always on alert for zealots who would die for their county.

Beer halls were open for business for the GIs, and local women were feeling especially liberated while getting so much GI Joe attention. Jack was surprisingly restrained; Bertha was his new religion.

Aaron and Jack slipped into a beer hall and had already guzzled a steinful when they heard commotion on the streets. The Aryan devil was clinging to the few remaining souls he controlled. Aaron and Jack rushed from the hall. A crowd of soldiers was standing over a soldier on the ground. A medic was tending to him. A boy in the street was dead a few yards away, a pool of blood spread outward.

As Aaron was weaving his way through the crowd, he overheard one of the soldiers. "Some kid stabbed the sergeant. I shot him. Sarge could have shot him."

Sergeant Collier was writhing in pain. A knife was protruding from his rib cage. Aaron knelt beside the medic. "We've got to get this thing out of you and patch you up. We'll get you to the field hospital," the medic said.

Blood was spreading across the front of his shirt. Aaron stared in disbelief. *Not Sarge.* "What happened?"

Struggling to breathe, his eyes were wide. "He was just a kid.

How the hell do you shoot a damn kid?"

Aaron looked back to the dead German boy in a pool of blood, so close he could touch him. He hadn't even shaved yet. Looking back to Sarge, "You're gonna be okay."

Taking a deep breath, he turned his head to the side. "I hope so." A Jeep pulled up and a litter was set on the ground beside him.

Aaron gripped his hand and squeezed it. "You'll be home before me." As he heard his own words, it occurred to him that he wouldn't see Sarge again. War had taught him the unexpected was the expected, that each morning unfolded on its own terms. There were no goodbyes on the battlefield, only false hope and lies.

Sarge's breath was shallow, and a trickle of blood appeared in the corner of his mouth. "I'll make it." Squeezing his hand tightly, he smiled, "Look me up after the war."

* * *

Aaron's unit relocated to a school south of Munich, with the luxuries of running water, bathrooms that worked, sinks to shave and clean up, and hot showers nearby. At one point, over a million men had been amassed on the German front, but now, most of them weren't needed. For days on end, Army boredom was treated by movies, card games, and drinking the nights away. And more beer during the day.

The Army did their best to entertain the troops with movies like *Blonde Fever*, a comedy-drama, which was accompanied by a variety of GI shorts on the war's aftermath and news from home, footage of the new President Harry Truman going about his business.

Starved for dames and anything about America life back home, soldiers crammed into the USO shows. Everyone made sure to go to the big show in Munich, with headliners Bob Hope and Marlene Dietrich, a German-born Hollywood star. Giddy soldiers ogled and catcalled when she showed off her gams and sang, in her smoky, trademarked voice, every soldier's favorite song, *Lily Marlene*, the story of a soldier's love affair.

Underneath the lantern By the barrack gate,
Darling, I remember
The way you used to wait,
'Twas there that you whispered tenderly,
That you loved me, you'd always be,
My Lili of the lamplight, my own Lili Marlene.

Aaron declined promotion to sergeant, although Captain Jardine told him Sergeant Collier had pegged him for it. Al Blick, an unfriendly, gung-ho Philadelphia city boy who couldn't ever fill Sarge's big shoes, was promoted and reassigned from another platoon. Learning that Al was short for Adolf did little to endear him to the men. He was a stickler for Army regulation. His speeches on fraternization were as effective as prohibition laws were for quitting drinking.

Jack said, "He ain't my sergeant. The Army can have him. I'm going home, and I'll take Bertha with me."

The next day, a few of the soldiers decided to go check up on Sarge. Jack, Aaron, Cory, and Mike Talbot, the new guy who loved working on the railroad, crowded into a Jeep. When they arrived, they were sent to the wrong room and wandered up and down rows of infirmed and wounded soldiers. With new instructions, they went to a tent with ten beds and scanned the faces of soldiers. There were several empty beds, but no Sarge.

A nurse approached them. She was a short, broad-shouldered, over-weight woman in her forties. A lifer. "You guys aren't supposed to be in here. You see the sign?" Unsmiling, filled with duty and the everyday, she added, "Who you looking for?"

"Our sergeant. Sergeant Collier. We know he's here," Jack added. "Well, if you don't see him, he's not here. They come and go."

"He was here yesterday," Cory said.

"Told you they come and go. He probably didn't make it. Some guys don't. Now get out, or I'll call the MPs." The nurse widened her stance, prepared to take whatever steps to get them out.

"He was okay! He was supposed to be okay," Aaron mumbled.

Shrugging her shoulders, she said, "Happens." She pointed her stubby finger toward the exit.

Aaron thought back to the last time he saw him, how his eyes flashed when he looked down to see the knife sticking out of his chest. How he rolled his head to the side in defeat. He said he was going to make it. His little boy in the sailor uniform. *I'm not going to cry.*

* * *

Aaron often returned to his unit drunk. Tonight, when he arrived back at the schoolhouse, there were two letters from Mary.

He felt guilty seeing them. He had only written her twice since the war in Europe ended. He offered no explanation. He hid his feelings in short letters about Germany and the people and how surprised he was at their friendliness. Why weren't they the enemy too? He mentioned Mike Talbot the Potomac railroader. And Jack and Bertha. *He's serious about marrying her.*

Mary's recent letters were mostly about how soon Baby Vanko would be arriving. She was well and full of anticipation. Beyond ready. Finally, her last letter announced the birth of their son. Millie called the doctor to the house in the middle of the night, but it wasn't until the sun was just peeking over the horizon that the baby was born. One minute her bedroom was dark, just the amber glow of the bed lamp, and then morning light filled the room, and he arrived.

We have a boy. He's laying right beside me as I write this letter. Baby Vanko cried out at 5:40, just as the sun was announcing a new day. He cried out for his daddy. Oh, Aaron, it is a new day. You'll be coming home now. I feel it.

What shall we name him? Something strong like Robert, David, or Ronald or a biblical name like Joseph or Samuel, like your father? Do you want to name him Aaron?

I know it's hard to pick a name by mail, but please tell me what you like.

He won't have to be a soldier. You have ended wars. What kind of world will it be?

In closing, she announced that she had moved back in with her folks so they could help with the baby. He should send letters to their house.

Aaron quickly penned a response. He was a father now like Sarge had been. He asked, *What does he look like? Can I get a picture?* He wondered, *What kind of father will I be?* As he wrote about his joy, he worried she could feel the sadness behind his words. *How about the name Richard? It would mean a lot to me.* He had told her in a previous letter that Sarge had died.

While he was waiting to hear back, in late June, Aaron received new orders. He was going home. Not everyone in his unit was leaving. The new replacement soldiers' platoon was staying, eyeing the veterans with a little jealousy. They might still end up in another theater of war, or maybe they'd stay in Europe for a while. Jack surprised everyone but Aaron when he wrangled an extension so that he could stay with Bertha, making plans to marry her and take her back to the States. The Army interviewed Aaron to sort out whether she was of legal age. Aaron tried to help. He remembered Jack had said she was sixteen, but now he said she was eighteen, and kept the details to himself. They'd still be investigating when he reached stateside.

As Aaron packed his gear for travel back to Camp Lucky Strike, his next stop, he felt strange. It was over for him. Or was it? He might be reassigned to the Pacific front. Or he might go home. *Home. Home.*

Part 3

FINDING THE WAY HOME

But after the fires and wrath
But after the searching and pain
His mercy opens us a path
To live with ourselves again

The Choice
—Rudyard Kipling

13

CAMP LUCKY STRIKE was better than Aaron remembered. Tents and outdoor chow lines had been replaced with wooden barracks and mess halls, where well-fed German POWs helped serve. Coffee and doughnuts were available 24-7, and cigarettes could be purchased for next to nothing in the new PX. Asphalt streets and walkways meant less mud. Every day, soldiers lined up before bulletin boards hoping for their transport announcements, and every night they celebrated with whatever alcohol they could get. Secretly, they were all nervous. What if their orders changed? Finally, a week after he arrived in camp, Aaron was assigned to the SS *Sea Bass* out of Le Havre.

The boat ride home started out as a continuation of the celebration that began VE Day. Three times a day, the hot Navy food met all expectations, and for the first three days, the men shared the bottles they'd tucked into their bags, mostly Schnapps and gin. In all-night poker and dice games, they bartered and bet their souvenirs, armband swastikas, and larger wall hangings. Their duffles bulged with worthless German currency, splinter bullets, the fancy Walthers with eagles engraved in the handle, china dishes, cuckoo clocks, and anything else that could be smuggled on board. The deck was used for dice games. Sleeping quarters were crammed with hammocks stacked six high, with aisles only wide enough for one man to pass. This drove some, even the manliest of men, to escape episodes of claustrophobia to sleep on the open decks. If you had a lower center hammock, it was used for all-night card games. And lower bunks, no matter what time of the day, were the first step for those in the upper berth, evoking groans, pranks, and sometimes fights.

All the celebrations ended when they encountered rough seas. Dizzying, fifteen-foot-high swells brought an end to the flow of liquor. The smell of vomit and perspiration turned Aaron's face Army green. He moved his bedding topside and stayed there until they reached land. The crossing was scheduled for seven days, but it wasn't until nine days later that they entered the Hudson River and passed the Statue of Liberty. After docking at the Staten Island pier, they were transported by train to Camp Shanks, northwest of New York City. Built at the beginning of the war, on farmland purchased under the War Powers Act, Camp Shanks had displaced about 150 farm families.

With over a half a million soldiers arriving back in the States, so many were being processed through Camp Shanks that the logistical bottleneck was mindboggling. Soldiers hunkered down, bored and restless, killing time in a mass of humanity.

Arrival, though, was a big deal. Soldiers were treated to an all-you-can-eat steak dinner and a chance to call home. But that meant standing in the telephone lines for hours. Army patience reached the breaking point as tempers led to fights over the length of calls and jammed telephone lines. The New York telephone company asked residents to clear the lines, as thousands of soldiers were trying to call out.

When Aaron was finally able to get a line, after three hours of waiting, Mary wasn't home, so he left a message with her mother. His mother-in-law seemed excited to hear his voice, but avoided uncomfortable small talk, knowing the cost of the long-distance call and the limited time he had.

He next hurriedly called Millie's, to the curses of those in line behind him. He held the earpiece away from his ear when she screamed loudly enough for everyone to hear. "Aaron! Crap. Mary's not here. When are you coming back?" She said Mary was moving back in anticipation of his homecoming. Butch, her husband, was a captain now and still in Guam, and she sounded sad. "He has no idea when he might be coming home. But he's safe. I know he's safe! Oh, Aaron, we can't wait to see you!"

Aaron's furlough was slower in coming than others. He had to wait for the official ceremony to receive his Distinguished Service Cross for the Hürtgen Forest campaign. He knew it was a big honor and would be for anyone, but for Aaron, the price had been steep, too steep. He lay awake at night reviewing bloody images that wouldn't let him rest, wishing he could just skip the whole thing. He didn't feel heroic. *So what, I threw a sack of TNT and ducked.* So many others deserved the award. Every man there. It must have been Sarge's doing. When they pinned the medal on Aaron, he saluted, and then he hid it away in the bottom of his pack. *No big deal. Even Purdy deserved this medal more than me.*

He assumed the other part of the delay was deciding where he would be ordered next. Camp White in Medford, Oregon was rumored as a jumping-off place for the Pacific campaign, and he crossed his fingers he wouldn't be assigned there. But he figured he would go to a whole new division, since his platoon was being scattered. He kept an eye out for Jack, who was probably still wrangling to marry Bertha and gain a visa for her passage to America. When they'd said goodbye, Jack was rushing off to town to be with her. Jack had changed. So had Aaron. War changed everything.

Most of the men stayed in camp, because the Army went all out to take care of returning soldiers: six theaters, a number of post offices, a hospital, chapels, bakeries, ball fields, bowling alleys, a swimming pool, gymnasiums, and several beer halls. USO clubs hosted dances with the live music of Harry James and Benny Goodman, and an amphitheater featured a constant flow of celebrities: Betty Grable, Frank Sinatra, Louis Armstrong, Jackie Gleason, Shirley Temple, Jack Benny, Mickey Rooney, and Judy Garland. Aaron went through the motions, but he just wanted to go home.

It wasn't until the third day at Camp Shanks that Aaron gained his land legs and any appetite, which coincided with the arrival of orders for a thirty-day furlough in three days, then to go to Camp White and the Pacific. Sick of the Army and sick of camp life, he found a local off-base beer joint, Smokey's, in Orangetown, New York. For the next two days, as soon as he could escape camp, he headed for Smokey's, and while the town celebrated on July 4th, Aaron pressed his elbow to the bar and small-talked with the bartender and owner, a friendly, balding guy with a gray, bushy mustache. At closing, he was so inebriated he had to be escorted back to camp by MPs. He sleepwalked into the train the next morning, and slept through most of the long trip home.

* * *

When Mary first saw Aaron step onto the Rock Island train platform, three train cars away, she was again startled, this time not by the bruises of a boxer, but the mysterious aura of an impenetrably sad man. A man with stories, secrets.

She knew there would be stories, plenty of them, from the newsreels, radio accounts and newspapers report that had flooded the country. She hoped he would tell her everything, half afraid of what she'd find out but longing to know what his time had been like. No one, though, could have predicted that most of the soldiers' stories would be locked away, either taken to graves or buried in memory.

She had never seen a person die, although she knew about death. She was the pastor's daughter and had seen the dead peacefully in their coffins. The news stories were crushing, cold, dirty, faceless stories about death of biblical proportions. What had he seen of it? But he was home, when Fritz and Tony weren't. They would have to deal with secrets.

When Aaron didn't see her, he stopped and steadied his gaze. Soldiers and civilians rushed by him. Thick smoke swirled around him. Soldiers rushed to waiting brides and pulled them up into their arms.

As the smoke cleared away, he found her and tossed his duffle bag over his shoulder to weave between the other soldiers and their families toward her. She was struck by how gaunt he appeared, how he moved differently than she remembered—his head was lower, his shoulders drooped, his jaw was tight, and the expression on his face was resolute under a smile that looked a little forced, a little hard. She shivered and waved.

His pace quickened as he approached her, but then, a few feet from her, he stopped.

She was holding baby Richard swaddled in her arms. He was nearly a month old. Frozen to the train platform, he stood stiffly and directly in front of them. His head moved ever so slightly side to side. His feet twitched, but he couldn't walk. He held out his outstretched palms, open, almost pleading. His shoulders began to shake, and suddenly there was a flow of tears. He tried to stop, tried to wipe away the streams with his sleeve. His nose started to run, and he wiped his face with the back of his hand. He couldn't stop shaking. He reached out, but his legs couldn't move.

Mary looked down at his outstretched hands, tears streaming down her face. "Oh. Oh, Aaron, you're back." Reaching out, she took one of his hands in hers and forced it around her waist, wrapping Richard between them, and looked up, studying him. It was like meeting someone you knew well but seeing something different, not knowing what it was, but feeling it was something big. She hoped it was the time apart, or all her worrying, the relief from the plague of thoughts she might never see him again, or the relief of seeing him here.

The other girls had moved out, so only Mary was living with Millie. Butch was still in Guam. Mary insisted they take the attic room. It was just as Aaron had remembered, musty, opened beams, hardwood floors, cobwebs and all. What a strange sensation, being home, surrounded by loving people, well-wishers everywhere, little Richard. He had a son. And being with Mary for the first time again, so soft and warm, like wrapping his arm around a velvet blanket, not the scratchy wool ones he was used to.

Outside, it was windy, and cooling off from a daytime high of seventy-four degrees. Inside, it was still warm from the second-floor heat trap. Lying there without any covers, locked in embrace, bare to the night, Mary clutched him tightly, like she would never let him go. Logically, he should have slept like a baby, but when, at last, sleep came, Aaron blinked wide awake an hour later. *I don't want to go back. There's nothing I can do about it. Nothing. Nothing I would do*. Exhaustion quashed his worries as Aaron dozed off, dreaming.

Outside his house, there was a wind and an unlatched gate swinging back and forth—squeaking, and the clatter of tank tracks. Death had arrived. The earth trembled. The clatter stopped, the turret turned toward the enemy, then spit out hell.

Fran Cathcart was shot in the thigh. He made it. Jimbo didn't. His pleas were so real. "Help me. Lord Jesus, help me." Purdy said someone should shoot him, Jimbo cried out for help, Purdy said, I'll shoot him," and back and forth. Aaron opened his eyes wide, searching the ceiling in the low light of a half-moon. He was in Iowa. He was home. His mind raced. His time home was short, and then he would be off again. A lot of guys said it was going to be worse in the Pacific. Germany had been bitter cold alternating with mud everywhere, on the roads, on his boots, where he slept, so thick it was hard to walk. He was about to trade it for sweltering hell-hot days, the white snowy gray sky replaced by a blinding hot sun.

And a different enemy. What were they like? What God did they worship? Everyone said they were godless. That their God was killing American soldiers. Dying was an honor. What kind of thinking was that? Was life so hopeless? Doesn't there have to be faith in there somewhere? Would there be a Purdy in his new unit? A Sarge? For sure, there wouldn't be any Jap soldiers like the German who spared his life. Why hadn't he just killed Aaron? Because he was Jewish? Because he felt sorry for him? *Maybe I will be a killer in the next war.*

Aaron dozed off again. He could see the knife above him, feel the German's power as he slowly inched the knife blade toward his chest. Aaron flipped back to the past, pushed the knife away with all his strength. He felt his strength leaving him. His will. Always the same dream. He was about to give in. Let the knife plunge into his heart. Give in to the inevitable. End it. He could feel the German's knife piercing his chest.

Aaron jerked upright.

Mary lurched. "Aaron, what's wrong?"

His chest was heaving. His skin glistened with beads of sweat. As he was trying to catch his breath, he looked around. Slowly the room came into focus. Where was he?

Mary put her arms around him and pulled his head onto her chest. "Everything is okay. You're home, safe. You know that?" Aaron could hear her breathing and feel her warm skin against his cheek. "What's wrong?"

"Nothing. There's nothing wrong. Just a bad dream." His breathing slowed. He sighed. "This is all a bit new to me. That's all." Looking down to the mattress on the hardwood floor, he continued, "I just haven't had such nice luxuries," he chortled.

* * *

Mary continued to work at the ordnance plant while Aaron helped out on the farm. She was able to take only two days off. Aaron had plenty to do during the day, anyway. Bat'ko was older than he remembered. His face was wrinkled and thinner. He was still down in his back, seldom smiled, and kept mostly quiet. The farm had been neglected in Aaron's absence, and now there was a lot of work to be done: field work and repairs to the house, the barn, and the fences.

Maty was an even more troubling picture. Her white hair, usually pulled back tight around her face, now was unkempt and unruly. Her bout with whooping cough had inflicted years on her. She looked frail, much more so than when he deployed. She was unable to get through a cigarette without a coughing spell, and some of those seemed without end.

Sometimes, when working beside his son, Bat'ko seemed to be on the verge of asking questions, but only a few ever reached his lips. Once he took a nail from his mouth, and before he hammered the new barn board in, he asked, "So we won the war?'

Aaron looked at him quizzically, wondering how much he knew. *Didn't he sit around the radio at night like other Americans?* "That one," he answered. Bat'ko never asked what was next. Several times, Aaron wanted to tell him where he was heading. It was always on his mind.

Sometimes, Bat'ko seemed to want to talk about Mary. "Mary came by while you were gone."

Aaron waited for more, hoping he might say something about her. After a long silence, Aaron gave in. "I heard." But there it ended.

All the while they worked together, Aaron kept an eye toward the house, looking for Maty. This time of the year there was work to do in the garden, but he hadn't seen her there since he arrived. More often, she rocked on the porch, wreathed in smoke, swatting flies, the sounds of her coughing fits cut across the barnyard out into the fields where they were working. Bat'ko either didn't hear her or was used to it.

There was peace with Pastor Woodruff and Mary's mother. Ricky was the great healer. They had a grandson. More than a grandson, baby Ricky was a Woodruff. He would grow up in the church. Sunday dinners seemed normal enough, but still Aaron wondered what was behind the silent moments when he caught Pastor Woodruff studying him. No doubt he wished Mary had married within the church. Well, it was done, and Aaron was glad.

Aaron never asked Mary if her folks mentioned him being Jewish. Mary never said a word about that, and Aaron didn't ask. He knew they had. He avoided the subject altogether.

Mary hinted they should go to church, but never insisted. Aaron went twice and sat stiffly in the pews, feeling staring eyes all around him. When he dared to look around, the faithful quickly looked away. The last day he went was a communion Sunday.

Wearing a white robe, Pastor Woodruff stepped out from behind the pulpit and stood behind the altar. "Today we celebrate Holy Communion." Holding his hands out to the congregation, he smiled and made his invitation. "Today, I invite you to accept Jesus into your life."

Aaron thought he was looking at him as he spoke.

Holding up a basket of small pieces of bread, the pastor continued. "In communion, we use bread as a symbol of Jesus' body and wine as a symbol of His blood. Jesus started the tradition of communion when He instructed His followers to use bread and wine to remember the sacrifice he was going to make when He died for our sins on the cross. This tradition will continue until the end of time."

Aaron watched as members of the congregation solemnly paraded to the altar, sneaking glances at him sitting alone. He was the only person who remained seated. What did it mean to not take communion? What did Pastor Woodruff think of him sitting there alone? He never wanted to experience that again. Mary squeezed his hand when she sat back down, but he wondered what she really thought of it all.

Two weeks home, he began to help out Lloyd Claywell again. It was good to be paid for his work. And at the end of chores, he was always invited up to the house for a drink. As Claywell wiped out water glasses with a dish rag and poured two full glasses of Old Fitzgerald Kentucky Bourbon, he said in his British clip, "Here's to killing Japs." Few words were exchanged about his son Tommy, except when Claywell said his body was never recovered. He always concluded with, "He went to the fishes."

Aaron had never tasted bourbon but found it had the warming qualities of the wine he drank in Germany, only with a greater and quicker effect. His return to Millie's at the end of the day was delayed, later and later. At first, his late arrivals weren't alarming to Mary. She knew they had a drink or two after chores. That was okay. She had seen her father share a nip of whiskey now and then.

When Aaron entered the house, he was red-faced and unsteady. He moved awkwardly around the kitchen. His wavy black hair was mussed, and the long scar over his eye, a remnant of the boot camp boxing tournament, stood out against his flushed face in the bright, overhead light. His eyes were red and glassy. Bristly chin whiskers were as coarse as 400 grit sandpaper when he kissed Mary.

"You guys work late?" Mary offered.

"Well, yeah, but I told you Claywell likes to have a drink after work. I think he likes the company."

"Or two."

Aaron was standing in front of the cupboard, looking for something to snack on, then stopped and turned. Mary was still wearing a kitchen apron. Millie could be heard in the other room laughing along with the radio.

"Yeah, a couple." Aaron looked forlorn.

"Ricky's asleep." Mary wanted to say more and wondered if he could read anything into her declaration. Aaron hadn't paid much attention to his young son, not a minute with him this past week. When he had first returned from Europe, he couldn't take his eyes off him. Mary decided not to say anything. Time was so short.

As sure as birthdays pass, Aaron's furlough expired, and he was scheduled to depart on a train heading for Camp White in Medford, Oregon for more training before entering the Pacific war. As the summer sun cast early morning shadows on the white painted plaster walls of the Armstrong living room, Aaron dozed on the sofa. Packed and ready to go, his duffle bag stood at attention by the front door. Millie was at work.

Mary sat in a rocking chair across from Aaron. Looking down at Ricky, who was asleep in her arms, smiling dreamily, she whispered, "It's a crazy world. What would you like to be when you grow up? Not a soldier, I hope."

Aaron hadn't taken to Ricky as she expected. Her mother said that was the way of fathers and babies. Maybe they needed to be big enough to hold a ball. Life keeps advancing into the unknown, even when nothing seems to be changing. Being apart doesn't affect love, but it can put a grip on people.

When she looked over to Aaron, his eyes were open, but glazed over, like a dog sleeping with his eyes open. He was somewhere off in a distant land, far from the warm quiet of Millie's farmhouse. In his mind, Aaron was approaching a farmhouse in the desolate, frozen mist. The wind whistled in his ear. Purdy was beside him. They watched for signs of any German soldiers.

Aaron snapped to and looked at his wife. He looked up, and their gazes met. She smiled. He blinked and squinted through dry, red eyes, still blurry from a night of little sleep and a late night at Claywell's.

Mary could see he was about to get up. "I can't believe you'll be leaving so soon, to go to another—"

Aaron saw that Ricky's eyes were open and seemed to be focused on his as if to ask the same question. *Another war?* Aaron smiled at his new son, then looked up at the wall clock and watched as the large hand clicked to attention, covering the twelve and perfectly aligning itself with the outstretched little hand.

"It's six, Mary; I've got to get going."

A half hour later, he was back, clean-shaven and in full uniform, his Army hat folded neatly hanging over his belt. "I've got to go," he said without conviction.

"I wish there was something—"

For months, Aaron had prayed he would see Mary again, picturing Baby Vanko, the fearsome little miracle, his own flesh and blood who had already crawled up inside of his heart. But he also had resisted the thought, a new regret to be avoided. He was stuck in the Army. They had talked about the cruelty of going from one war to another, and in private thoughts, he even explored his options, but only briefly. They were few, and even dangerous to think about. Like standing on a ledge when you have a fear of heights, and the image of falling appears before you like a warning that takes your breath before you quickly jump back from the ledge. Survival was his only option.

"I can't desert," he cut Mary off. "It's the Army. There are no options. But maybe—" Aaron, in his darkest moments, had pondered self-inflicted injury, or maybe seek a farmer exemption as Bat'ko had implored him. Both options seemed cowardly.

"I sure as hell ain't gonna hurt myself just to get out," he scolded.

"Or claim hardship, beg them to let me be a farmer. I've seen those types of guys. I'm not that."

Now, just as quick as the words "I've got to go," he shuffled over to Mary and leaned down to kiss her. Prying himself from her firm embrace, he hoisted his GI bag and slung it over his shoulders. He stood soldier tall, then paused stoically at the doorway, looked back, turned, and walked away.

* * *

Upon arrival at Camp White, he was assigned to a new company that would deploy on September 1 to Okinawa, a Pacific island, which had been won by the Americans and was now a major base of operations for both land and sea soldiers. Fortunately, Aaron's deployment would be short.

The Japanese surrendered on August 15, following the US attacks with atomic bombs on Hiroshima and Nagasaki, ending the war. The war with Japan was over. World War II was over. Aaron's war was over, and in the spring of 1946, he was granted an honorable discharge.

Iowa opened its arms to returning soldiers—proud mothers, fathers and wives, even strangers on the street. Aaron was a hero to family and friends, and for families who had paid the highest price for freedom, he was a survivor. Bat'ko momentarily broke character when he embraced him, in stoic relief, with a big bear hug and said, "You made it." Maty greeted him with flowing tears as she touched his face like a blind person might test reality, verifying his well-being. Pastor Woodruff and Sarah welcomed him home like a returning son. Chewing on his pipe, smiling broadly, Pastor Woodruff puffed heartily, sending jubilant smoke signals into the room. With a tear in his eye, he asked them both to attend church Sunday. The congregation had prayed so hard for him and the other soldiers. He encouraged Aaron to invite his folks, although he knew they would never set foot in a Christian church.

After a month of hero's welcomes, relief and joy, life found a new normal and summer passed quickly in Millie's attic and their small town. Aaron landed an apprentice job fixing cars at Barney's Garage in Des Moines. He learned of the job from a stranger he met at Dewey's North

Side Tavern, where he had stopped to have a beer on his way back from job hunting in Des Moines. "Gotta help our boys," said the man, and bought him a beer.

When Aaron showed up to apply, Barney, a WWI veteran, closed the shop for lunch and they went across the street to the Forest Tap. Over beers and hardboiled eggs, Aaron landed the job. Barney looked like he never bathed, his sleeves black and greasy up to his elbows, and Aaron soon learned he wore the same black-stained overalls every day. But he was a good boss and felt like a friend. For a while, the job, liquid lunches, and after-work camaraderie at the Forest Tap was a welcome relief from wild, sleepless nights.

Soon after he landed the job, he and Mary purchased their first house on the new GI Bill. The one-story, two-bedroom house with cracked white paint was in the Drake District, on a small lot overgrown with weeds and wild mulberry bushes. There was a dining room and living room. Without much money for furniture, they found a bed, chest of drawers, wooden folding table, rocker, and dusty well-worn overstuffed chair with matching threadbare sofa at the Salvation Army Thrift Store.

The pace of life throughout the country was easy and uncomplicated. It was as if the world had released a collective sigh. Making goods and babies seemed to be the business of the day. For Aaron and Mary, regret and long sighs were replaced by daylit smiles. When Aaron first returned from the war, climbing into bed with Mary at the end of the day on a civilian mattress in their own home was a satisfying confirmation that all was well and safe. But too soon, well and good by day became nightmares at night, leaving Aaron sleeping in the living room.

* * *

Thanksgiving Day recorded Iowa's first snowfall of the 1946– 1947 winter season, the first layer of white-on-white-on-top-of-white that remained until March rains finally washed away the last dirty, gravely remnants of plowed snow. Aaron and Mary had a strong baby boy to be thankful for, as well as the unspoken thankfulness to have survived a war when many hadn't. But it was also the beginning of a harsh interruption to their marriage, the harvest of seeds sown in war. The ride home from the Woodruff's Thanksgiving ham dinner turned out to be as cold inside the automobile as the snowy parkway itself.

After a long silence, Aaron said, "I wish your father would get off me about going to church. You know how I feel about that."

"He never said a word," Mary huffed.

"I know what he's thinking when he makes his little comments about church. Looking right at me. Everything I do, it's not enough for you and Ricky?" Aaron took a deep breath and sighed, gripping the steering wheel tightly, his jaw clenched.

For baby Ricky, swaddled in the back seat, the warmth and rocking motion, and the crunching sound of tires pulling through the heavy snow was lullaby music for baby dreams. But his peace was interrupted when the car plowed into the drifted snow in the driveway, and halted suddenly, spilling him onto the floorboard.

Ricky began to cry.

"Crap." Aaron pounded the steering wheel.

Mary looked at Aaron and scowled. In a flash, Ricky was in her arms. She rushed him to the house, carried him to his crib, pulled the blanket snuggly up around him, and kissed his forehead. She felt her way through the darkness until she found Aaron in the overstuffed chair, his feet stretched out on the ottoman.

"I'm going to bed, are you coming?" Mary asked calmly in the darkness.

"I'll sleep here tonight," he responded.

Which Aaron is home tonight? The happy one or the one with bees swarming inside his head.

"You've been sleeping here a lot." Mary dipped her toe in the water to test it. He didn't wave his hand as if to dismiss her, so it seemed okay to jump in, at least up to her waist.

She put her hand on his shoulder and squeezed it affectionately. "Oh, Aaron, you can't stay up all night. You can't sleep on the sofa every night. We're husband and wife. What are we going to do?" Tears welled.

"I don't like this either. Nobody can do anything about it. It'll go away."

"Can we talk about it?" Mary pleaded.

"What is there to talk about? I don't understand. I don't know what to do. And I'm not going to church and sit there and pretend."

"Mom says we need to baptize Ricky."

"Sure. Do it. It won't hurt him," Aaron blurted. "And he can go to church with you. Just don't drag me into it. I told you I'd never stand in your way."

"Will you ever consider it?"

"How can I? I'm Jewish. You know that. You knew that when we got married. My Sarge was Jewish. Did I tell you that? You know, the guy killed by the Nazi kid. A boy. You should have seen it." Aaron dropped his head into his hands. "It's hard to figure." Mary leaned in and put his arms around him and laid her head on his shoulder.

"All I want is for you to shake this thing."

"Men were praying at night and getting killed in the morning. Or they were killing Germans who the night before were doing their own praying. To the same God? Or did they have their own God? Can you explain that? Can your father? I don't think I'll find the answer in your church, or some synagogue. Besides, what is my religion anyway? Is that the way it works? You just pick a religion? Or does religion pick you?" Aaron reached back and clasped her hand resting on his shoulder, and held it. "Maybe, someday. But you go. I want you to. Your folks will like that."

The snow continued throughout the night, and by morning the sidewalk and driveway were piled high with the downy white, except for the indentations of car tracks that ended at the foot of the driveway, the barely discernible footprints to the house and clumps of long grass and weeds of the unkempt yard that poked through.

In the morning, as Mary made her way to the kitchen, she could see Aaron slouched far down into the chair, his head cocked to one side, using the armrest as a pillow, his large frame balanced over the tattered, green ottoman.

After a while, the smell of fresh coffee roused him, and he stiffly made his way to the bathroom to splash cold water on his face. He changed clothes and twenty minutes later appeared fully dressed in the kitchen doorway. Ricky was lying on his back, on a blanket, just outside the kitchen, both his hands and feet flailing joyously.

"Hey there, little fella, you wanna fight?" Aaron made a big fist and held it to his nose and rubbed his big knuckles across his cheek.

"You aren't so tough. Come on, put up your dukes."

Taking his tiny hands in his, he bent down close to him. "Oh, I didn't see that right cross," he said as he guided his tiny hands upward toward his face. "Oh, here comes a jab."

He guided his other hand to his own face. "He's down," Aaron rolled back onto the floor, feigning a knockout. "He's out." Aaron arched back into a sitting position on the floor in front of Ricky.

Looking up to Mary, he said, "Smells good. I forgot today was Sunday. I think I'll go outside and dig the car out and see what the streets are like. Might go to the shop. We're stacked up with work. Seems like the cold has been hard on starters and alternators."

"You eating breakfast first?" Mary stood at the stove with a spatula in her hand.

"Sure." Aaron rose to his feet and looked at the sizzling bacon. "I'll take my eggs over easy."

* * *

Aaron returned home well after dark, though, fumbling at the door, long after dinner went cold. Ricky was asleep, and Mary was sitting at the table.

When he entered the door, he ducked his head. "Sorry I'm late. The phone was out at Barney's. Snow too heavy for the phone lines." Leaning on one foot, he untied one boot, then the other, and as he was pulling his boots off, lost his balance and slammed back into the door. Laughing, gaining his balance, he said, "Wanna dance?"

"Aaron, have you been drinking?" Smiling, "Just a little antifreeze." "You're joking?"

"Of course. But it was cold in there. Took all morning for the heaters to kick in, so there was a bottle . . . to keep me warm."

"Does Barney care if you drink on the job?"

"Barney drinks too. But he wasn't there. It was just me. Me and a '40 Ford and a '42 Plymouth."

This wasn't the first time he'd come home after drinking with friends, but it was the first on Sunday. Occasionally, after work, he'd stopped off at the tavern with guys he worked with. She'd ignored it, and tonight, she pushed her worries again to the back of her mind.

Mary reminded herself that drinking seemed to be his silver bullet for warding off night terrors. He was a good person. Time would resolve this thing. *He'll lick this thing, won't he?*

For Mary, change was marking the passage of time as reliably as the hands of a clock. Now she was housebound, dreading days stamped out with mentally exhausting familiarity.

Her world was trips to the kitchen and basement to wash clothes and hang them on a makeshift clothesline from one end of the dark basement to the other, much like the electric lines across the streets. A long wooden pole supported the center of the line when it sagged from the weight of wet clothes. Each morning after she prepared breakfast, and after Aaron departed for work, she washed and dried dishes, cleaned the kitchen, picked up his discarded, dirty, greasy clothes, washed diapers, dusted, swept, scrubbed boot prints, and, in the afternoon, prepared dinner. It was the same thing, day after day. And now, after twenty straight days of subzero temperatures that kept her and the baby inside, the tedium of daily sameness lowered her spirits even more. Housebound, worrying about Aaron and making ends meet on Aaron's paltry salary, Mary's spirits became as bleak as Iowa's subzero landscape.

When she got up the nerve to suggest she find a job, Aaron offered no resistance. Most husbands wanted their wives at home, but he didn't seem to care about anything—not even his son. Sometimes he played with Ricky, rubbing his chin whiskers on his belly to make him laugh, other times he went days without even a glance at his son, or at her.

Mary was hired as a pool secretary with Meredith Corporation for the magazine *Better Homes and Gardens*. She'd learned Gregg shorthand and typing in high school, which qualified her for the job. Weekdays she walked to University Avenue where she caught the downtown bus, and when the weather was bad, Aaron took her or she carpooled with a fellow employee. Ricky stayed with Nell, a sprightly neighbor woman in her sixties, living on her deceased husband's railroad pension and glad for a little more pocket money.

Aaron felt like he was stuck in second gear. Each day, the waft of percolated coffee and the sound of sizzling bacon was his wakeup call, and the daily dread of Army days was replaced by the everydayness of a job. After breakfast, he was off to work behind the wheel of his car. This was his favorite part of the day, driving. There was something regal about gripping the steering wheel and holding dominion over a powerful machine, on the streets, in the driveway, or in the shop. This automobile worked because of him and controlled the roadway because of him. Aaron's. His passion for the car at times could be a disturbing obsession. Aaron was so well tuned to every sound and imperfection; he could often diagnose problems from the feel of the accelerator pedal.

Each day at noon, he took his black lunchbox to the back to sit among hundreds of used car parts, which hung from the ceiling and walls or lay in greasy, disorganized mounds. Neatly packed into his black lunchbox were a Wonder Bread Spam sandwich and Highland potato chips, with Snowballs or Twinkies as a treat. Hidden safely in the corner behind broken-down transmissions was a bottle of vodka or whiskey, which he drank in the shadows. After work, he'd stop at the bar, then head home, usually in time for dinner. Then bed, or camping in the chair or sofa, depending on how he felt. In the morning, the sound of sizzling bacon and the smell of coffee woke him.

* * *

Ricky was speeding forward, growing every day. At first, he was never far from his mother's loving arms and her sweet warm nuzzles, or at arm's length in a baby carriage. Then he went crawling on hardwood floors, and the shiny, slick, pale yellow surface of the kitchen and bathroom floors, and among a forest of table legs in the dining room. Most fascinating was a cold-air return grate in the floor with its square holes and deep blackness on the other side. When Ricky forced objects through the grate, they magically disappeared, and no amount of peering produced even a tiny glimpse; that is, until the magic was revealed one day when his father lifted the grate and reached into the darkness to retrieve a spoon and a trove of Cheerios lining the dusty bottom.

Later, on sunny, warm days, there were trips to the backyard where his babysitter, Nell, would set him on the ground as she hung clothes or beat rugs. Ricky entertained himself by bringing his fingers together to grasp tiny blades of grass and direct them into his mouth. When he learned to pull himself to his feet, he took his first proud steps into Nell's outstretched arms. Suddenly, the chairs and table legs looked different, and the mysterious black hole was forgotten as his world stretched out to more rooms and even outdoors, across new terrain to shrubs, trees, flowers, and the tall weeds that grew along the fence and garage.

By the end of his second summer, and his first full year of life, the lush, grassy terrain shrank under the hot Iowa sun into survival clumps living off the tiny reservoirs of moisture in the parched hard earth.

There came another Thanksgiving and another Christmas. Winter was cold, white, and dead. Early spring showers showed the promise of abundant life but also its imperfections: the sea of yellow dandelions turned into ugly stalks of puffy white globes, awaiting the wind's help to complete the cycle before it began once again, when the earth would become cracked and brown.

In the US, making goods and babies continued. It was boom time. The rewards of new homes, cars, appliances and wealth beyond anything imagined were the dreams of peace. But a new anxiety was reaching out its dark hand to many returning servicemen who, if they'd been lucky enough to find jobs, struggled to reconnect with loved ones. For Aaron and Mary, life was full of day smiles and night cuddles, but strained by worries about Aaron's drinking, and the nightmares that kept him sleeping on the living room sofa or chair.

* * *

Aaron loved the brotherhood of the brown bottle, loved a swallow or two in the spare parts back room, loved to stop at the Forest Tap. Once there, it was difficult to break away, and when duty called him home, there was a quart of beer for the drive. Every night, there was beer on his breath. When he cleared out the empty beer bottles and cans from his car on the weekends and sent them clanking and clinking into the trash barrel, he could see Mary shaking her head in silence.

Her silence only added to Aaron's burden. He hated seeing her long face when he showed up late for dinner or missed it entirely, or her angelic concerns when she said anything. He thought he was making progress—the home remedy was allowing him to sleep in bed with her more often than not, and she should be happy with that. Even then, though, he talked in his sleep, rolling from side to side and yelling out in the night.

Tonight, he was tossing and turning until after midnight when he rolled out of bed. Mary rolled over, tired from working and taking care of Ricky and the house. Feeling his way through the dark living room, leaning against the hall wall, he stumbled into the kitchen. He opened the refrigerator and jumped back, shielding his eyes against the bright white interior. After a few minutes of hanging on to the door, he reached for an open quart of milk and took a swig.

It was well over a hundred degrees that day and the Iowa humidity was like a wet blanket. Moonlight cast shadows on the kitchen cabinets. Looking out the window, he was startled to see there was something moving, darting in and out from behind an elm tree next to the garage and then behind the bushes along the property line. It was deathly silent; the only sound was of his breathing. There it was again. This time, he could see a rifle sticking out from behind the tree. Beads of sweat dampened his forehead, and a wet stain was growing on his T-shirt under his arms.

Minutes passed, then a half hour. He stood stiffly, unable to move. He reached for his rifle. It wasn't there. Frustrated he dropped to his knees and felt along the floor, then along the countertop. Peeking out the window, drenched with sweat, he began to feel dizzy, his breaths rapid and shallow. *Where is my rifle?* The drill sergeant said to never let it out of his sight. It was a matter of life and death. Aaron stood motionless, listened, and watched. There it was again. He slid a kitchen drawer open and retrieved an eight-inch meat carving knife.

"Aaron, what are you doing?" Mary called out in the darkness before switching on the kitchen light.

The kitchen light flooded the room and startled him. He dropped to his knees and shielded his eyes. "Turn the light off. Quick."

Mary could see that he was holding the knife at his side, pointed at her.

Flipping the lights off, she pleaded, "Aaron, what's going on? Is someone out there? Should I call the police?"

"Hold still." Aaron moved back to the kitchen window and looked out into the darkness.

Mary was unable to move from the doorway. After a few minutes, she whispered, "Do you see something?"

"I don't know," he answered wearily.

Mary moved to his side and looked out the window with him. "What is it?"

"Out there, next to the garage, behind the tree."

After a few minutes, Mary said, "I don't see anything." She could feel him trembling. "I don't think anything's there. Really, I don't see anything."

Mesmerized by the swishing back and forth of night shadows, Aaron took a deep breath.

Mary moved closer and put her arms on his shoulder then around him. He was soaking wet with sweat. She could feel his shoulders slump. The knife dropped to the floor. "Come on, let's go to bed." As if he were a small child, she took him by the hand and led him out of the kitchen to the bedroom.

14

AARON WAS USUALLY ever dutiful, rising early with military precision, grateful for daylight, and happy to put the night behind him, no matter how hungover he felt. When Aaron entered the kitchen, Mary watched anxiously, curiously. It was as if he brushed away the previous night like it never happened. Gobbling down his breakfast, still groggy and half-drunk, he was anxious to be up to his elbows in a greasy engine block or to slide beneath the jacked-up front end of a '40 Ford Coup, anything to avoid facing Mary. After he ate, he gulped the last coffee and bolted for the door.

Mary stopped him. "Aaron, wait. Do you remember what happened last night?"

He frowned. "Mary, you know I'd never hurt you."

Standing before him, she put her hands on his shoulders. "I know. I'm worried about you, not me. We have to talk. We need to find help."

He nodded, but said nothing, because there was nothing to do about it. It was just the way it was. "I'll be late." With a quick kiss, he headed out the door.

Driving to work, he shook his head, still haunted by the images of the night before, clinging to him like a fine mist. He recalled standing in the kitchen, the overhead light flashing in his eyes, the glint of steel from the yard, the terror in Mary's eyes. The nightmares were torturous, but the look on her face was worse. The harder he tried to forget, the more intense the nightmares, and alcohol was losing its effectiveness.

Suddenly the car veered off to the side and hit the curb. He jerked it back to the roadway. He took a deep breath and blinked his eyes several times, pinching himself. His head hurt, and his body ached. He must have drunk more last night then he remembered.

He thought about his boss, Barney. Lately, they weren't getting along. *I hope he's not a jerk today. He's always late; why can't I be?* He was so critical of Aaron, always finding something wrong with his work. Several unhappy customers had come back with unrepaired cars, and Barney blamed him. Barney no longer went to the Forest Tap at lunchtime and told Aaron to stop going as well.

Aaron worked the whole day with his head down, sullen and quiet, avoiding Barney. Ignoring Barney's glare, Aaron became friendly with the new guy Buddy, a smiling, scraggly, bearded second-generation Pole. Together, they went for beers after work. After Buddy insisted it was time to go, Aaron still wasn't ready to go home and face Mary. He knew how disappointed she was. Seeing her so unhappy was worse than the nightmares.

Aaron decided to go downtown to The Legends bar, a who's-who hangout with cheap Falstaff beer on tap. He had been there once before and enjoyed sitting alone at the long-polished mahogany and brass bar with the twinkling bottles and glasses arrayed on a shelf in front of a bar-length mirror. Throughout the bar, there were autographed black and white photos of famous people who had shared these barstools, from baseball players and well-known singers to movie stars and boxers. The last time Aaron was there, Gorgeous George, a professional wrestler, was surrounded by curious fans. Tonight, there was no one famous, but the beer was cold, and the bartender let him be, that is, until Aaron was thrown out for fighting.

It wasn't until after midnight that Mary heard the car drive in the driveway. Aaron stumbled into the kitchen. She flipped the hallway light switch on to see him leaning against the door jamb. He flung his hands up to shield his eyes from the light.

When she saw his face, something clicked inside her. It was as if he had just stepped off the bus from boot camp. His face was swollen and his right eye completely shut. There was caked blood on his eyebrow, and when he opened his mouth to speak, she could see blood and his front tooth chipped.

"Mary, you're up," he slurred his words.

"Up? I'm always up. What happened?"

Regaining his balance, he weaved his way through the kitchen and entered the living room. Leaning forward, he grabbed onto the green, overstuffed chair, fell backward and then slumped sideways. "What happened to me?" he asked, slowly drawing out his words.

"Yes, what happened?"

"Well, doll, I ran into a door," he said, chuckling to himself, leaning against the door jamb. The room was spinning. "Yep, I ran into a door."

Mary stood in the hall doorway, shaking her head wearily. "Where do you get such talk? I am not your doll. I'm your wife." Backing away, she began to say something and stopped. Instead, she said firmly, "I'm going to bed."

As she did, Aaron lurched from the chair. He caught his balance and reached out and grabbed her by the arm to stop her. "Hey, why so early?"

"Aaron, you're hurting me."

Aaron quickly released her arm, as if he had just touched a hot skillet. Dropping his head into his hands, he said, "Oh, my God. Mary, stay a minute."

"You're drunk."

"Yep. Again. I'm drunk. I wish I wasn't. I wish every time I drank I wasn't. It's like before I take a drink I say, 'Aaron, what's wrong with a drink or two?' Then one, two, three drinks, and I want to die. And then I have another."

The smell of alcohol and smoke from his clothing filled the dimly lit room. The hallway light reached out to reflect off Ricky's face standing outside the living room. "Ricky!" Mary blurted out.

Aaron turned and saw him, wide-eyed and shocked.

"Ricky, everything's okay." Mary hurried to him, swooped him up into her arms and held him tight. "Come on, let's go back to bed." Turning toward Aaron, she firmly commanded, "Go to bed."

He did as his wife had ordered, but the spinning room swirled out of control, and he spent the night on the bathroom floor. The next morning, again he was late rising, and Mary made no effort to wake him. He was going to be late for work—again.

Barney could see right away that Aaron was in no condition to work. He looked sick, and his face was swollen and bruised.

A decision had already been made anyway. Before Aaron could slip on his work overalls, Barney showed him the door.

"Aaron, you're a good mechanic, very good. But you're also a drunk. I'm putting our customers in danger letting you work on their cars. I have no choice. You're fired! For your own good, sober up."

Aaron didn't go far. After driving around for a while, he decided he couldn't go home, so mid-morning he was drinking at the Forest Tap. The bar was empty that early. Bart, who usually worked nights, was rubbing down the bar. He looked up curiously and nodded.

Bart was a portly, bulbous-nosed, clean-shaven career bartender. He'd sworn off drinking after years of sitting on Aaron's side of the bar. Bart. He thought being a good customer who didn't drink qualified him as a skilled bartender. He'd admitted when he got the job, it was the only thing he knew how to do. When Aaron was clear- eyed, Bart liked him. He knew Aaron loved his family and was always quick to talk about Mary and his son, and several times, Aaron had shared a well-worn, faded picture of her, the one he carried with him during the war. But Aaron never said a thing about his Army experience, and Bart knew not to pry.

The bar smelled of spilled beer and stale cigarettes. Setting his black lunchbox on the bar, Aaron ordered a glass of Schlitz, drank it in one gulp, and set the glass on the counter firmly enough to catch Bart's attention.

"Not working today?"

With a faint smile, Aaron held his glass out. "Barney fired me."

Bart studied Aaron as he refilled his glass. He could see his right eye was swollen and turning black, and his front tooth was chipped. He had seen this scene before. "Hey, Aaron, you got money to pay for those beers?"

"Sure, I got money." Reaching into his pocket, Aaron laid several crumpled dollar bills on the bar and a few quarters, nickels and pennies.

"This should be enough to get me through for a while."

Late at night, the bar thinned out: the regulars had gone home. Aaron had moved to the end of the bar and could barely hold his head up. Twice, he laid his head on the bar and Bart nudged him.

"Go home. Get out of here while you can walk." After several attempts to encourage him to leave, Bart went around the bar, put his arm around him, and guided him to a back table. "Aaron, you're going home. But first, you need to sober up." After setting him down, he brought him a cup of coffee. "Here, drink this. You gotta go home."

Aaron drank the coffee, and laid his head on the table and went to sleep. It wasn't until after midnight that Bart nudged him again. "You gotta leave. Go home. Go be with Mary."

"I need to get a job." Aaron slurred.

Bart wiped his hands on his stained white apron. A bar rag was hanging over his shoulder. "Don't get a bar job; you couldn't afford it."

"That's funny." Aaron tried to gain his balance. He glanced from side to side to determine where the exit was and suddenly turned the other way. "I gotta take a piss."

Knocking a chair and table to the side he found the back hall, stopped and leaned against the wall before he found the bathroom's entrance. When he came out, Bart could see the front of his pants were wet. Unsteadily, he leaned on Bart's shoulder and weaved his way back to the bar. Bart helped him with his coat.

Looking down to the loose change scattered on the table, in the dim light, Aaron began to pick up the coins, one at a time, studying each one as if he was looking for rare collectibles. Holding them out, he asked, "Are these mine? I need a job. I'm gonna start tomorrow. But tonight, I can't go home."

"You have to go home. Be with Mary," Bart admonished.

"I can't. I don't deserve her. She's a good woman. A great one. I'm just a bum. No job. A drunk. You know that. You've seen people like me."

"Sure, but they didn't have a Mary. Lot of guys wish they had someone to go home to. She loves you. Go to her. Don't screw that up."

"I already have."

"Tomorrow, you go get another job. No, tomorrow is Fourth of July. Go celebrate. Forget Barney. It's not worth it. Lot of guys get fired and move on. Move on."

"Fourth of July?" Aaron mumbled.

Bart helped Aaron outside. "You gonna be okay to drive?"

A gentle breeze slapped Aaron in the face like a blast of hot air from an oven door. "Hell, yes, I can drive. I gotta get home so I can be blessed by Pastor Woodruff tomorrow. You know her father is a pastor?"

"We could all use a little blessing."

Tomorrow, Aaron had planned to take Ricky to Riverview Park, to ride on the train and carousel, and to press a penny with Ricky's birthdate on it, like the "Lucky One" penny he had given to Mary. Once again Pastor Woodruff would gather up his congregation in the park and pray for the lost and wounded and give thanks for the returning heroes. Aaron could imagine the disappointment on Pastor Woodruff and Sarah's faces when he showed up. A Jew had stolen their daughter away. They would never get over it. Pastor Woodruff's prayer would be for God to show mercy, send His love to everyone, and open the hearts of the misguided, so they could accept Jesus as their savior. Mary would squeeze Aaron's hand in understanding, or maybe it was hope. She didn't understand. Heck, he didn't. Certainly, her parents couldn't. Bart guided Aaron to the door. Across the street was his precious Ford. "I see you got it running," Bart said. "Don't be crashing that gem of yours."

Aaron had bragged how recently a customer couldn't afford the repairs on a blue 1942 Ford Coupe, so Aaron had bought it from him and repaired it from junkyard parts. Aaron had already known someone who wanted to buy his '34 Chevy. Bart had been the one to point out how few 1942 autos had been made because of the war.

Aaron's mouth was dry and his tongue and lips thick as he tried to pull words out of the sticky fog inside his head. "Okay, I'm moving on. Here I go."

Aaron heard the bar's door shut behind him. Clinging to his black lunchbox like it was the only thing he owned, his head was spinning as he adjusted to the dark sky and blinding illumination of the street light a few feet away. He staggered momentarily, looked to the east and then west. Too drunk to drive, he just wanted to sleep. He ducked into the dark alley and arrived at the bar's backdoor alcove. He sat and, using his folded hands as a pillow, pulled his jacket over his head and stared into the night. The streetlight squared itself against the building across the alley, then began to sway back and forth. His eyelids grew heavy.

When sleep came, he imagined he was sitting in a dusty, overstuffed chair awash with midday sunlight. He could hear footsteps on the second floor, then creaking behind him. "Purdy," he yelled out. Aaron opened his eyes and blinked, trying to focus. Unable to keep his eyelids open, he laid his head back on his hands. Behind his closed eyelids, he saw the face of the German boy crying out for his mother. Aaron jerked his head and opened his eyes. They were sore and dry. When he closed them, Sarge was smiling at him as he slid a picture across the table of his two-year-old son wearing a sailor outfit. There was a knife sticking out of his chest.

Suddenly, he could feel something firmly poking him in the chest. When he opened his eyes, Aaron saw two policemen, one pressing his chest with a nightstick. "Hey, buddy, wake up."

Off to the side, the bright light of a flashlight glared into his eyes. "Get on your feet."

Aaron shielded his eyes and slowly sat up, gripping his lunchbox, he tried to push himself up from the doorway. On his third attempt, he leaned back toward the wall, which was further away than he judged, banged into it and fell back to the hard cement. The policemen grabbed him under the arm and pulled him to his feet. The light was still glaring in his eyes.

"Shall we haul him in?"

"No, he's probably a vet. Been seeing a lot of this lately," said the second cop.

The two officers checked Aaron's driver's license to get his address and then loaded him into the squad car. Vagrancy and public intoxication would be the charges, Aaron figured, and an overnight stay in the pokey the penalty. Or if he had a record, it might be a few days. Or the judge might send him to the County Farm, give him more time to dry out.

When Mary answered the door, Aaron was draped between two policemen, his head hanging low. The policemen explained where they found him. She could see he was drunk. Before leaving one of the policemen admonished her. "You'd better get your man under control, or we will. Did he fight in the war?" Mary nodded. "Then get him some help."

The minute Aaron's head hit the pillow, he was asleep. Mary lay stiffly staring into the abyss, wondering, listening to Aaron's heavy breathing next to her. Occasionally he jerked unexpectedly, shaking the bed as he had done so many nights before.

Mary was prayed out. God was not answering. She had left her youth for womanhood with a man she had loved and married, still loved, had carried his son while he soldiered in a far-off land and now was slogging along herself, like Aaron had in the French and German mud and snow, each step harder than the other. Lifeless auburn curls and early wrinkles around her eyes greeted her in the vanity. She would have preferred a friendly deception, but the mirror insisted on reality.

Aaron twisted and turned, dreaming, once again, of the German soldier on top of him, flashing his knife. He always vividly recalled the nightmare. The usual resolution was to wake up and go to the couch. He wondered if someday the dream would end differently. Would he make his escape, or would he battle back and win? Would the dream end with his death as was intended? Do people die in dreams? Was it true that his life would end if he did?

Tonight, the struggle was different. The knife was no longer in the German soldier's hand, and Aaron's hands had found his throat and were choking him. The German's face was turning red, and his eyes were bulging and on fire. The soldier's screams were garbled. The high pitch of his wailing surprised Aaron. He sounded more like a woman. There were tears in his eyes. Her eyes? In the faint light, he saw long hair and smoky eyes—the tears were Mary's.

Aaron jumped back and caught himself before he slid off the bed. Groping for her, he yelled out, "Mary! My God, Mary. Is that you?" He could hear her gasping for air.

Aaron rushed to the wall switch and flooded the room with light. Mary was curled in a ball, sobbing, her face swollen and red, the crimson bedspread half on the floor and half clutched in her hands. Aaron shrank into the corner and shielded his eyes from the overhead light, searing into his memory the never-to-be-forgotten scene. Aaron hopelessly watched her, trying to grasp what had happened. *Did I do that? I couldn't. Who am I? What am I?*

"Mary. My God. What have I done?"

Mary leaned up on one arm and tried to gain her composure. She tried to talk. "Aaron," she garbled in pain, grabbing her throat.

Aaron wanted to go to her, but his legs wobbled, and he slumped to the floor.

Mary laid her head back on the pillow and began to cry softly.

Aaron watched and moved his lips. "I was—"

The room was silent except for Mary's soft crying.

"He was . . . it was him again." Aaron stammered in such a low voice his words couldn't be heard. *What kind of monster am I?*

Mary wanted to speak and kept swallowing, trying to undo the knot in her throat, but it was difficult to find the words. She was unable to speak. She wanted to say she was okay, but she wasn't. She wanted to say she understood, but she didn't.

"This can't go on. We can't. I have to leave," Aaron declared.

* * *

Early morning seeped into the room through the parted curtains, adding a layer of contemptibility and, just as quickly, confirmation. Aaron watched Mary from the corner of the room. Her eyes were closed. When she opened them, he said, "Mary, I'm leaving. I'm going away."

Each time she tried to talk, she coughed, and it hurt more. She wanted to say, "We'll get help." But in her silence, he heard, *"Go!"*

When Aaron left the bedroom, still numb from the alcohol and what he had done, he stopped at Ricky's bedside. Ricky was sleeping peacefully, smiling in his own dream.

"Ricky, I love you, my boy. I want to be your father, but I don't. I don't know what I'm doing. I'm afraid I'll break you every time I pick you up. What can I do?"

Life was taking Aaron down an unintended path, to the final road sign that screamed, *You shouldn't be a father, shouldn't be a husband. Why am I even alive?* The war made some people stronger, and others simply died, fast or slow, but for Aaron, dying came in the slow merciless cuts of shame and regret, in memories that played inside his head over and over. *I'd be better off dead. Better off.*

"Ricky, I love you." Tears gushed as if a dam was breaking. "I drink too much, and I can't stop. I have nightmares I can't stop." He whispered, "I'm no father. No husband. What can I do? I'm better off dead. Staying, I might hurt her again. Or you. But leaving hurts us all. But I'm no good to you, no good to her."

When Mary finally came in, he went to the bedroom and closed the door. Fifteen minutes later, he appeared with his duffle bag slung over his shoulder, off to war again. Ricky was playing on the dining room floor. His gaze followed Aaron as he walked to the front door and dropped his duffle bag to the floor.

"Mary, I hope you know that wasn't me, that it hasn't been? But I guess it is . . . " Shaking his head, "I'm leaving. I've gotta go."

Mary burst into tears, startling Ricky. "Oh, Aaron, we'll get through this."

Aaron could see the red marks around her neck. He looked over at Ricky and dropped his head.

"Ever the angel. How? Can you tell me how? By praying? By hoping? What will solve this? I can't be a husband. Can't be a father. I won't take the chance of hurting you again. My leaving might turn out to the best thing a father can do. The best for your life."

Mary sat in stunned silence. "No!" She said hoarsely. "We'll get through this. I know we will. You won't do it again."

"I can't take the chance. If I ever harmed you, my life would be over. Leaving, my life is over. But not yours."

"I'll take my chances. Dad always says light always overcomes the dark. You are a good man. I'll take my chances."

"You're such an angel."

Mary began to cry again, louder. "Don't go. Please don't go." She rushed to him. He turned away. "Aaron, listen to me. You can't leave. We'll do something. Anything. But no running away!"

Aaron looked back to her. Tears formed in his eyes and he wiped them on the sleeve of his shirt. Her parents would be disappointed. His too. Nobody would understand. He wanted to reach out. Go to her. He wanted to tell her how much he loved her. But he couldn't. He knew he shouldn't.

"Tell them what happened. Tell them the truth. That's all there is. I took a hundred dollars from the savings can. That's all I need. I'm not sure where the car is. Probably at the Forest Tap. The other one is at Barney's. Sell one of them. You should get a hundred dollars for the Chevy." Turning toward the door, he wiped his eyes, then hoisted the bag over his shoulder. He looked back to Ricky playing in the dining room, and then to Mary on the ottoman, crying into her hands. "Mary, I'm so sorry. I wish I had never come home."

15

THE STREETS WERE quiet so early in the morning. Standing and waiting for the city bus, Aaron could see his house in the distance and heard the faint screech and rumble of a street car. A block away, he saw the trolley with its long arms reaching out for the overhead electric lines that snaked down the center of University Avenue.

He got off the bus at Seventh and Grand and walked south, through an alley, to the Trailways Bus Station on Locust Street. Inside, three people waited. A tall, thin, sleepy-eyed, balding man rested on his elbow on the ticket counter. Aaron stood before him and studied the schedule.

"No buses leaving till noon?" Aaron asked.

"Nope." The ticket agent studied him and, before Aaron could say anything, he added, "If you need to get out of town sooner, try Greyhound. They got a morning bus for Chicago." Looking back to the clock, he added, "Might have left. You best hurry."

Aaron turned and bolted for the door. If he didn't leave now, he might lose his nerve. Red, white, and blue banners hung from the lamp posts up and down Locust Avenue on both sides of the nearly vacant street. It was 7:30. Only a few cars were driving. As he raced up the road past the dark stores, smartly dressed mannequins in the Younkers store window stared out blankly. Turning north, he could see the RKO Orpheum Theater ahead, advertising The Big Steal, starring Robert Mitchum and Jan Greer. Turning east on Grand, the Des Moines Theater was just hanging the marquee for its new July 4th feature, *Calamity Jane and*

Sam Bass. The star's names were just being added, Yvonne DeCarlo and Howard Duff. Next to it, the Paramount Theater featured *Sorrowful Jones*, with Bob Hope and Lucille Ball. The Greyhound bus station was just beyond the theater.

There were only fifteen passengers waiting for the bus to Chicago when Aaron arrived. He quickly purchased a ticket and was the last to board. He selected a window seat as far back as possible, hoping to avoid eye contact with the current passengers and any new passengers who would board at one of the stops along the route. The cityscape quickly turned to fields of corn, dotted with farmhouses and clumps of protective trees, then smaller cities and more country, then more cities. The bright sunny day was a stark contrast to the pressure cooker brewing in Aaron as his emotions jiggled to the top, each mile to near overflowing. Sleep was hard to come by. Not having had a drink since last night and the lack of comfort thwarted any dreams but allowed for pounding dread.

They crossed over the Mississippi River into Illinois, making a stop. Aaron asked the driver if he could retrieve his duffle bag from storage, then tossed it in his seat, partly to lean on, partly to prevent anyone from sitting next to him. Along the way, they picked up fifteen new passengers, mostly men. Aaron wondered what their stories were. Were they traveling to or away from something, like him?

Two women took a seat two rows ahead and adjacent to his. They could have been sisters, and were certainly sisters of stature, both medium height with pillowy waistlines, wearing blue bandanas covering mixed brown and white hairs. The remaining ride to Chicago included listening to their never-ceasing, wide-ranging, loud conversations about their poor health—bad neck, bad feet, bad backs. "I don't abide by any doctor," one exclaimed. "Doctor wants to treat my sore, scratchy throat and I take a couple of shots of whiskey, and that does it."

The July plains-hot bus windows only opened partly, the whining strain of the bus motor and grinding gears as they rode up hills on thumping cupped tires distracted him from the mundane drivel of the complainers. As he watched the scenery pass, he reflected on his misery. Sometimes when the bus turned and the sun shifted overhead, he found himself peering at his own reflection in the window. Like a ghost of himself, the reflection seemed to ask if he was doing the right thing, where he was going, what was ahead. *Does it matter?*

When he arrived in Chicago, it was early evening. The Greyhound weaved between Fourth of July parade traffic in downtown, inching along Wabash Avenue. The long Midwest summer sun cast shadows made it feel like nightfall.

Greyhound shared the Chicago Union Bus terminal with several independent bus companies, including Indian Trails and the Indiana Motor Bus. Weaving his way out of the terminal, Aaron calculated how much money he had, and, in the back of his mind, how much thirst it would ease. A few beers would be good for figuring out his next steps. Ten blocks later, he was sitting in a bar called Shorty's, watching the head sizzle at the top of his second glass of beer.

Shorties was an everyday bar, a man's man place to sit up to the bar and drink alone, no pictures of celebrities like Johnny's, nobody famous bellying up near him, or anything to suggest a Fourth of July celebration. When he arrived, there were only two open stools and he took the one at the far end, away from the door. The bar was so thick with smoke, he couldn't see the faces of men at the other end of the bar.

The bartender had to be the proprietor of Shorty's. He was an angry five feet tall, if that, wearing a scowl that had formed permanent crevasses in the corners of his mouth. Aaron watched as he stretched up full length to pull the long shinny wood spigot to fill a glass of Falstaff, expertly running beer down the side of the glass, tipping it gently to release some of the head down over the top to ensure the customer got what he paid for.

Aaron emptied his pocket, laying a couple of crumpled dollars on the bar, sending notice to Shorty to keep 'em coming. Aaron could tell by the bartender's friendly growl at the regulars that the man sitting next to him was a stranger to the bar as well, and so the bartender would wait to be paid when he served him. The stranger was of medium build, with heavy eyebrows that curled at the ends, his hair the color of his tattered, dirty brown, newsboy-style hat resting on the bar next to his drink. When he raised his glass to take a drink, Aaron noticed he only had two fingers and a thumb on his right hand.

With a broad grin on his face, the man asked, "Where you from?" Looking down to Aaron's duffle bag on the floor next to him. "More important, where you headin'?"

"Out east." Aaron's answer came out without thinking. His easterly direction was more because the first bus out of Des Moines was heading that way. There was no thought of reversing directions.

"Me too."

In the uncomfortable silence between them, their attention was diverted to the end of the bar where two men were arguing, waving their hands in the air, swishing aside the smoke. Only bits and pieces of the loud exchange could be deciphered.

"Which way is the train station?" Aaron asked. "Train station? You want to buy a ticket?"

"Yeah, I guess. See what the schedule is. See what it costs." "You must be rich."

"Hah, I ain't rich, that's for sure."

"Well you ain't stupid either, so you ain't buying no train ticket." Aaron didn't know how to take the response. It sounded friendly enough. Aaron reached into his pocket for his Zippo lighter and flipped it open and closed several times.

"I'm going out east too, but I ain't buying no ticket." The man's bushy eyebrows did a lot of his talking.

Aaron set the lighter on the bar and looked at him, cocked his head, then looked over to Shorty, and with a nod of his head slid his glass to the edge of the bar.

"Gotta smoke?" the man asked.

Looking down to the lighter, then back to man the sitting next to him, Aaron said, "Don't smoke."

"They call me Three Fingers." He held up his right hand to make his point. "You Vanko?" *Vanko* was stenciled on Aaron's army green backpack. "Earl?" The man's gaze shifted to the name stitched above the pocket of his shirt.

Aaron looked down at his shirt pocket. He was wearing clean, gray, cotton garage work pants and a mechanic's shirt of a former employee of Barney's. "No. Somebody else's shirt. My name is Aaron. I'm from Iowa."

Smiling, Three Fingers exclaimed excitedly, "Hey, they say I was born in Iowa too, but I only remember Colorado." Looking down to Aaron's lighter, he strained to read the inscription.

Bernhard Ich liebe dich Lulu

"You don't smoke." Aaron followed his gaze that was locked on the lighter. "Why the lighter?"

"Just a souvenir, I guess." "You kill a guy for it?"

Aaron twisted his head around and pinched his eyebrows. Nobody but Mary had asked about the lighter.

"Nope. German left it. I picked it up." That was the same story he told Mary.

"I'm heading to Baltimore. To the Camdens. You ever been there?" *Baltimore. That's where Sarge was from. Somewhere nearby. Think it was called Brooklyn Park. Mike Talbot said something about Baltimore, too. Or a town near there.*

"Never been there, but had an army buddy who lived in the area.

He said he'd get me a job in the Potomac Yard. It's a train yard."

"I know the place. Got picked up by one of the yard bulls. He didn't haul me in, just showed me the best way to get out of there. Usually, they like to rough you up or take you to the judge. You want to go to Baltimore, I'll get you there for free. Good price, huh?"

Three Fingers explained that in a day or two, they'd hop a train. "Waitin' for a grainer," he said. "It's the best way to travel and see the country. Been my way of getting around for over ten years now. No trouble at all." Holding up his three-fingered hand, he added. "'cept this here."

"We gotta take a little hike first, to Blue Island. This is a rough side of town and walking at night can be a bit of a challenge, so we best get going. But if we leave now, we can be there in a few hours. Got a place for you to sleep." Looking down to Aaron's pack, he added, "You against a little walking?"

"Long as it's not muddy."

The farther they walked, the farther they moved from civilization. They passed through some rough neighborhoods quickly, with a careful view to potential trouble, but only encountered the curious stares of black men smoking cigarettes in small street gatherings. The streets sparked with shards of broken glass, and cigarettes glowed like fireflies from the rooftops.

The farther they walked, the brighter and more plentiful the stars. After an hour of silence between them, Three Fingers began talking, nonstop, and then, as if he was taking a long breath, there followed another period of silence. Silence wasn't much of a friend to Aaron; thoughts of Mary always filled the gaps, and over that ledge were worse thoughts. *What's she doing right now? Am I doing the right thing?* He always answered himself the same way. *I don't have a choice. It'll turn out for her, she'll know in the end.*

Aaron shook his head and focused on Three Fingers, who had moved out in front now by ten yards or so. "We got much more to go?" Aaron asked. They had been walking for over two hours.

"Gettin' close."

A quarter mile later, they were on the outskirts of nowhere, on a dirt road, hugged by thick brush and a forest of trees beyond it. The place reminded him of Miller's Bend, but there were no cottonwood trees here. Ahead they could see a flickering campfire. Three Fingers hollered out,

"Hello, fire!"

"Is that you, Three Fingers?" "One and only. Got a friend too."

Ahead, there were three men sitting in a circle around a roaring fire. The hot days had cooled some, close enough to feel the lake effect, but not necessarily to require heat. The fire was their light, kept the bugs away, and served as their cookstove. A large boiling pot was resting next to the fire on some rocks.

The three welcomed Three Fingers like a long-lost friend. New logs were thrown on the fire. Flames shot up into the moonless starry heavens and sparked a confabulation of catch-up stories of legends and friends still riding the rails, and the ones who had taken their last ride on the westbound train.

"Haven't seen you since Spokane. Last time—" The voice came from the older man sitting stooped over the fire, underneath a dark curly storm of dark brown hair.

"Yeah, been a lot of places since Spokane," Three Fingers reflected. "Spent some time in Southern Californ-i-ay. Place is filling up with crazy people. Never going back. Not even at gunpoint."

Three Fingers looked over to Aaron. "This here is Aaron. I call him Army."

Pulling two large cans of beans out of his pack and setting them next to the pot, Three Fingers exclaimed, "This here's for both of us." Looking back to Aaron, "This be Mulligan stew. Help yourself. Might turn out to be the best you ever tasted."

Out of the darkness, a voice called out from a sleeping bag, "But it might kill ya."

Three Fingers motioned to Aaron. "Never know what's in it; that's what makes it so good."

Campfire hospitality produced a pot, spoon, and bedding. Introductions circled the fire: Vicar, Callus, and Curly, whose hairline was halfway back on his head and what hair he had curled over his ears. Other names were called out, accompanied by pointing to men in sleeping bags off to the side. The conversation shifted to old rail- riding adventures.

"So Hurricane got it?" Three Fingers asked. "What happened?"

Vicar replied, "Got rolled by some kids. Clubbed to death." That sent shivers around the circle.

Suddenly, Curly jumped to his feet and rushed to the side, close to the darkness but still lit by the fire. He was larger than he had appeared when he was slouched in the circle.

"Smitty!" he shouted. "Zip it up. You know we don't abide that. You do that again, and you're out of camp forever. And word travels to other jungles." They prided themselves on a clean, uncluttered camp, and one of the rules was no urinating nearby.

When order returned and Curly returned to the fire, Three Fingers asked, "Have you seen Sassy Sally? Heard she got married."

"She got married all right, but she'll be back," Vicar explained. Curly added, "Unless her husband kills her first."

"Understand there's a B & O grainer leaving for Baltimore."

Callus answered, "Tomorrow. Midday we think. Three guys here are taking that one."

Vicar turned to Aaron, squinting across the fire through smoky eyes. Vicar was older than the others, his face wrinkled beyond his years. He seemed permanently plastered with a hard-luck smile. The sound of the cracking fire muffled his voice. "So, Army, what's in Baltimore?

With no destination in mind, it was the first place Aaron could think of. "My Sergeant's from there." No one questioned him further.

Curly stretched out and rose up, "I'm gonna catch some z's." Everyone looked on as he unrolled his bag and climbed in.

"Like I always say, remember, Jesus was a hobo," Vicar

proclaimed. With a wink and nod back to Aaron. "Out here and everywhere, it's just you and God."

Everyone knew Vicar, not just in the jungles, because his name was often riding the rails even when he wasn't. He was welcomed in any camp. He never preached to anyone, unless asked, but wisecracked around flickering fires, offering a font of information and prayer when needed. Legend was that he was a college graduate.

When Curly was settled and contemplations returned to the fire, more curiosity about Army broke the stillness.

"You married?"

Dread swept over Aaron. Looking down to his hands, searching for an answer, he noticed he was still wearing a wedding ring. Immediately his right hand went to it and began to work it up and down his finger. *Should I take it off? Mary. Never. I never will.*

"This?" Taking a deep breath, formulating a response, holding back, Aaron held his hand out. "Just a memory."

Aaron hoped they'd leave him alone, and they did, letting him listen and learn. Before long, his mind wandered back to only a few days ago when things had been okay. *Were they okay?* Night horrors flared out of the campfire, faces of soldiers, the eyes of the German trying to kill him. He instantly doused such thinking, but it was like putting out a house fire without a hose.

Next, Callus retrieved his bags and moved to the edge, where the dark met the firelight. Then Vicar said, "I need to get some shut- eye." And soon it was just sleepy-eyed Aaron, now Army, and Three Fingers, poking the fire.

"Tomorrow morning, we need to get you supplies for the train ride. There's a Sally not too far from here."

Aaron lifted his head. Three Fingers could see he wanted to ask a question. "Salvation Army. Sallys always have a good heart, not all preachy. We'll get you a bedroll. Water bottle, always gotta have water. Two or three cans of food will do. Don't get me wrong, I can go from here to Baltimore on a slice of bread. I tell you what. I used to be able to make it from Billings, Montana to Minneapolis on a pack of smokes, water, and beans. Gotta be prepared, though. Heard of guys being locked in boxcars. No matter what, bring water. Like to take a bottle or some beer. You don't need that much."

Aaron remained seated, mesmerized by the fire, as Three Fingers readied a flat spot and laid down on top of his bed roll. "Been doing this a long time?" Aaron asked.

As if he could read Aaron's mind with the question, Three Fingers grunted. "You might be getting the wrong idea about all this. Sure, I had some tough stretches, and like I said, Californ-i-ay was the worst. Ate out of garbage cans. Not so loving there. Kind of uppity about us hobos. When they do help, it's because they're so much better than we are. Helping out is more about telling their friends how good they are."

The fire was now a bed of coals. Lying flat, staring up to the stars, he continued in a sleepy voice. "You know we don't just hop trains? Oh, sure there are a few bums that just ride, but most of us work for a living. We just don't work steady. Just restless, I guess. Some running to, some running away. From whatever. Take me, I'm a damn good carpenter. I can always get a job. Got places that will always hire me back, 'cause I'm a good worker. How 'bout you? Do anything?"

"Mechanic."

"There you go, the world always needs mechanics. Thing is, we like riding trains. You'll see. It gets in your blood."

Aaron spent his first night in the jungle trying to make sense of what he'd heard. They could have been speaking a foreign language when they talked about couplers, crummies, high iron, rods, gunnels, bindle-stiffs and mission stiffs. Aaron laid out his bag as close to the dying embers as he dared. What little bit of light radiated from the coals was the only company he would have until morning.

* * *

It was a long, drawn-out morning, hiking into town to get outfitted and then hiking again and waiting, trading more tall tales. As they neared the tracks, the screeching and squealing of trains sounded like dinosaurs breaking through the brush. The earth shook. They stopped at the edge of the brush, out of sight.

"Wait here until the tracks clear." Three Fingers pointed. "Track Three. See those grain cars? Grainers are best this time of year. It's like traveling on your own front porch. This is gonna be simple. Pick the ones standing still if you can. Anytime you can catch a stationary train, do it."

"Boxcars are second on my list. Here's the thing about boxcars, get 'em when they're standing still. But if for any reason they're not waiting for ya—now listen to me carefully," he said, holding up his finger-short hand, "these are my lucky digits. I tried to get on a train that was moving too fast. Not as hard a lesson for me as some others." As trains moved back and forth on two of the tracks, Three Fingers continued his hobo schooling. "The door latch is always on the left side, and if you can't count the lug nuts on the side, don't even try. Grab on with both hands, always with your bare hands. Never use gloves. Gloves might slip. Make sure it's moving in the right direction, never the other way, because you've gotta swing in." Instructions kept coming faster and faster, like everything he knew was spilling out. Aaron was supposed to remember it all. "If there's one unit, then it's going to the yard, three or more, it's going all the way. Never catch a string of empty cars. They're hunters. The swaying back and forth will jar the teeth right out of your head." Three Fingers spotted their mark and motioned Aaron forward.

"Here we go. Just follow me."

They hopped on to a parked grainer, easy, and settled in, waiting for the train to take them east.

16

THE DAYTIME TRAIN trip east was everything Three Fingers had promised. A hundred thousand tons of steel gobbled up the landscape at sixty miles an hour, checking off the miles to clackety- clacked lullaby music. It was like riding a titanic, charging bull. Aaron was like a child watching the many personalities of Mother Nature pass by, one minute slapping the train angrily with the back of her hand, then open-armed and smiling. From their position on the back end of the grainer, a lean-to roof kept them out of the elements for the most part.

The farther east they traveled, the more frequently smaller towns dotted the landscape. The houses were sometimes so close to the tracks he could smell the white sheets hanging on the clothesline and see faces peering out back windows. As they traveled through the backyards of America, they saw the honest side of people, their true personalities showing in the rusting or lovingly painted swing sets, scraggly grass, makeshift storage, and lawn furniture arranged in odd groups.

The only adversity they faced were the occasional kids throwing dirt clogs or rocks at the trains, and riders when they could be seen. Easy to hit a train, even moving this fast, but it was pretty hard to hit a person. Sometimes they'd get waves from smiling school kids, yearning for a ride. Other times people stood beside their autos at crossings, just watching, like people do on the beach, feeling the power of the ocean.

Night time was when the booze made good its promise to be the elixir for the darkness. When Aaron looked over to Three Fingers, his head was resting on his pack, snoring, smiling dreamily. Clickety- clack by day was the groaning of the devil at night. Sometimes the bottle kept the devil at bay, but tonight, he was flashing on images of a cooing giggling Ricky. When Aaron had come home from the war, he had brought whispered promises and hopes, served up daily in whiskered belly nookies for his boy. Now those blessed images taunted him and filled him with remorse, made him question what he was doing.

When the train pulled into the Camden, like mice fleeing a sinking ship, men Aaron didn't even know were aboard went scurrying. They hastily made their way away from the Yard to a nearby hobo jungle. It was like a convention. Three Fingers was greeted like royalty. Feeling invisible, Aaron hung back and watched, then backed off. Before long, he was walking down a paved side street toward an unknown destination, a stranger in a town of strangers.

Soon he was in a business section, where there was a little grocery store, laundry mat, pharmacy, a five and dime, and a hardware store. His stomach was growling, so he headed toward the diner at the end of the street. He could feel what was left of the $100 he had stuffed in his front pocket was safe. A quick mental calculation determined there was enough money for lunch today.

Only steps away from the diner, a large man stepped into his path. He was wearing a navy blue, cotton work shirt, a larger-than- life Chevy emblem above the pocket. His hands were greasy and callused. A chew of tobacco stuffed into his mouth made his cheek bulge out and leaked brown juice over his lower lip. He spat brown on the sidewalk in front of Aaron's feet.

"Where do you think you're going?"

Pointing to the diner, he answered, "Get something to eat."

"Nope, you ain't. We don't allow no hobos beggin' on our streets. You turn around and go back to where you came from."

Aaron was in no mood to argue. He expected he wouldn't find much sympathy in bystanders either. Hesitating momentarily, wondering whether to turn and walk away, his first thought was to say he wasn't a beggar.

"You hear me?" The man shoved him backward so hard Aaron nearly lost his balance.

"I heard you. I'm leaving." Aaron turned to walk away.

The man followed close behind. "I ain't gonna see you again up here again, am I?

Aaron quickened his pace. "No, sir. I'm leaving."

For several miles, Aaron walked aimlessly, heading for what he thought was the Chesapeake Bay. According to Three Fingers, it was the largest inland bay he would ever see. For a while, he wandered in and out of trails and roads in a heavily wooded area that meandered along a river, his resolve tested with every step.

As dusk was closing down the day, up ahead, he saw a brick- faced building with a single Washington blue door lit overhead by a single sconce. There was one small window that flashed National Bohemian Beer. There were no parked cars within sight.

As his eyes adjusted to the dark inside, Aaron saw two dusty animal heads hanging high over a long bar—a moose and a buck deer. Across the sawdust-covered floor, he could see neatly stacked beer mugs glistening on the brightly lit ledge behind the bar. Beside the mugs was an American flag folded into a triangular shape and a big glass container filled with hard-boiled eggs.

The bartender was leaning on his elbows at the end of the bar, smoking a cigar and reading a newspaper. Pulling a mug from the ledge, the bartender held it up to Aaron. "Beer?" His black oily hair was combed straight back over his head. He wore thick eyeglasses that magnified his eyes in a way that made Aaron feel like he was staring.

Aaron laid a dollar out on the bar. "Where is everyone? Looking around at the empty bar.

"Dhey vill be 'ear." The bartender's accent was unrecognizable. Aaron had heard many different languages in the service, but nothing like this.

When the bartender returned to his cigarette and paper, Aaron reached into his pocket and pulled out the lighter, fingered the inscription, then set it on the bar. He reached back in his pocket and stacked quarters neatly beside it. *Should I call Mary to see if she's okay?* The distance between them added to the horrors, but also to what good memories were left.

Wanting so badly to hear her voice, his Army mind waged war against a heart adrift. Pouring beer over his boiling blood to cool it wasn't working at the moment. What was the price for his heart winning out? A call might give her hope, but it might weaken his resolve, too. He spread the quarters out, then stacked them again.

What will I say? Up to his neck in loneliness, he resolved again and again not to call her, not that he wouldn't like to hear her voice. She might beg him to come home, or ask him not to call again, either way a loss. But when the fever broke, he remembered he could never go home and why.

The bar filled up with men taking a break after work, hoisting beers to end the day—bus drivers, train yard workers, city street workers and garbage collectors. He tended to his beers, remained silent, and avoided eye contact with the bartender and patrons. Then as quickly as breathing in and out, the bar emptied, and just a few patrons remained. All night, in between flipping the lighter open and shut, stacking and restacking quarters, and downing beers, he'd beat back thoughts of calling Mary. Now he thought, *I'll write her a letter.* Well past the point of sobriety, in a fleeting sleight of hand moment, he asked the bartender for a pen and paper.

With the pen poised over the paper, Aaron struggled to form thoughts and keep his writing legible. Above the paper, he could see the barkeep's reflection off the bar top. When he wasn't resting on his elbows, smoking cigars and reading the newspaper, he was polishing the counter over and over. Aaron flicked the lighter, trying to think.

When he saw the bartender making his way toward him, he stuffed the lighter back onto his pocket, wanting to avoid any conversation about it, and crumpled up the unfinished letter and tossed it on the bar.

"Vhere you frum, Mack?" Aaron flinched when he saw his gaze lower to the name on his shirt pocket. "You name Earl, it is?"

"I'm from Iowa." In no mood for bartender conversation, especially a thickly accented one that required him to pay close attention, he answered with a dismissive wave of his hand. With a shrug of his shoulders, he thought, this was just like Bat'ko. Bat'ko and Maty sitting with him at the kitchen table when he was studying flashed before him.

"Iova. Long vays frum here. Ja? Don't take any much brain to see you lucked out?"

Aaron steadied his gaze on the bartender's face then pushed his empty glass toward him. When the bartender returned, he leaned on the bar, ready to talk again, pinching his words. "So, vie you here?"

His magnified eyes seemed to mix his thoughts and words together. "Just heading east and ended up here. Getting a job on the railroad." As an afterthought, he added, his words slurred, "My sergeant lived here. He was a genuine war hero. A schoolteacher in a place called Brooklyn Park. You know where that is?" Aaron shook his head and took a deep breath and sighed. "He was the best.

Sergeant Collier, the best damn sergeant you could ever have." "Collier. Ja. A hero? Just reading about Collier hero in newspaper, vas hero too. Maybe same guy, ja? He's new football coach of new high school. Arundel. Just read about in paper. Such a cu . . . incence, how do vou say? Ja."

Nah. It can't be. He doesn't know what he's talking about. Picking up his quarters from the bar, he muttered. "Different guy, has to be." Aaron staggered toward the door, stumbled and knocked a chair over. Catching his balance, he steadied himself and looked around for the front door. When he arrived, he leaned on the doorjamb and looked back. "Which way is that high school?"

"Arundel. Just go north three blocks. Cross Patapsco River Bridge. Straight. Few miles."

* * *

The next morning, after sleeping it off in the woods behind the bar, Aaron staggered to his feet. What he'd thought was a grassy spot in a park turned out to be bare ground. He tried to brush away the dirt covering his pants and shirt. The sun was bright. He estimated it to be mid-morning. As he was eating his last two slices of bread, he recalled bits and pieces of the conversation with the bartender.

What he heard seemed fuzzy, and he wasn't sure to believe it anyway. It couldn't be true. Sarge was dead. Nevertheless, he began to walk north, toward the bridge, trying to remember the directions. He headed east until he saw the school.

Standing outside a tall wire fence surrounding a football field, Aaron saw a man standing on the far side. *It can't be him.* But even from this distance, he was strangely familiar, an image of the past, perhaps because he wanted it to be. *The nurse said he was dead.* Pressing hard on his memory, he thought harder. *Maybe she said, "He probably didn't make it." Maybe Sarge is here.*

Aaron looked at his long, dirty fingernails. His baggy pants had a hole in them and were filthy from sleeping on the ground. *When was the last time I bathed?* He thought he probably smelled. Maybe he was used to it. His duffle bag was at his feet.

The man looked up and saw him and crossed the field. *Did he recognize me? He couldn't from this distance. It can't be him anyway.* There seemed to be no recognition from the man, just deliberate steps directly toward him. He wasn't smiling. The look on his face was earnest. When he arrived at the fence, though, he stood facing Aaron and smiled at last.

"You're not dead!" Aaron exclaimed.

"That's a fine way to greet your old sergeant." He reached out his hand, then pulled it back when he realized there was a fence was between them. "Hope not. Got a football season ahead. The boys are depending on me."

"You don't remember me, do you?" "VANKO? Aaron Vanko?"

Richard Collier's gaze studied him from head to toe but displayed no reaction to the ragged man standing before him.

Aaron took a step back and looked down at his feet. "Sorry, I. . ."

"Good to see you, Aaron." Pointing to the far side of the field

To the gate, he said, "Meet you there."

When he arrived at the gate, without hesitation, he reached out and gave Aaron a bear hug. "Good to see you," he said again. Coach Collier was stitched above his shirt pocket along with a symbol of a wildcat. The quiet sergeant was still a block of wood, but now his steel-gray eyes were smiling, not the serious ones he remembered.

Aaron's mouth was agape. "The last time I saw you, Sarge—" "No one calls me Sarge anymore. It's Dick. *Coach* to the boys."

Shaking his head, Aaron muttered, "Some of the boys and I came to see you, at least we tried to. Some nurse chased us away, said you were probably dead. We tried to find you."

"Don't worry about it. I was in rough shape. Wouldn't have known you were there. I wasn't there long. Probably Nurse Kratchet. That's what they called her. She was a bitter old maid. Think she hated soldiers, or just men. It took a while to get back on my feet, but here I am, alive and well." Waving his hand toward the football field, he stood even straighter. "The new coach of a brand new high school."

Hesitating, he could see Aaron was still processing what he was hearing. No doubt it was like talking to a ghost.

"You had breakfast? Well, I guess it's more lunchtime. How about some lunch? My car's over there." He picked up Aaron's bag, pre-empting any resistance from him. "Come on, let's go." He could see Aaron hesitate. Smiling, he added, "That's an order, soldier."

The diner was two blocks away. Sarge was greeted like a local royalty. They ordered meatloaf and mashed potatoes and gravy. Sneaking glances at the other patrons and to Sarge, he gobbled his food. Aaron couldn't remember eating so well. Lunch conversations kept drifting back to Army days. Finally, Aaron gathered the courage to ask, "Why did you put me in for the Distinguished Service Medal? I was no hero."

"Are you kidding? You are a hero."

"I don't even remember what happened. I was too scared."

"We all were. You did your job. You saved American lives. That's all that mattered."

Sarge's voice drifted into the background. Aaron could picture the Sarge with a knife sticking out of his chest, the German boy lying beside him. Just minutes before, he was probably trying to help the kid.

Sarge interrupted. "You know, a lot of guys thought you killed Purdy. Nobody would have blamed you. I knew you didn't. You told me you didn't. and that was good enough for me."

Aaron shivered at the reminder of what happened in the farmhouse. "No, he was killed by a German soldier, like I said."

Sarge studied him under furrowed eyebrows. "So what happened to the German? You said he ran off."

Aaron reached into his pocket and pulled the lighter out and handed it to the coach. "He left this behind. He could have killed me. I never reported that. He could have, easily."

Holding the lighter in his hand, his Sarge read the inscription. "Sure as hell doesn't matter what happened. Main thing is, he didn't, and here you are." Handing the lighter back to Aaron, he continued, "Why are you out here anyway?"

"I'm off to see Talbot. He told me he could get me a job on the railroad in the Potomac Yard."

"He's not there. He married some girl and moved to Georgia. But there's more to it, isn't there, Aaron? I remember you had a wife." Sarge looked at him curiously. "You were head over heels."

"We had a falling out." Sarge studied his old comrade, sensing Aaron's discomfort. "I've been pretty restless since I came home."

"Look, we all got demons. I remember when you joined the unit. You weren't all that excited about killing Germans. War is tough on soldiers like you. Remember when we talked in that muddy foxhole? I said you needed to make a choice. Suspect you're in the same spot. Making choices."

Sarge raised his eyebrows and smiled. "We have a team meeting tonight, an introduction of coaches and players, but tomorrow, I want you to come to the house. Meet the wife and kids. Get some chow."

Aaron peeked at his still-grimy hands. He tried to wash them in the washroom and wipe off his tattered and dirty clothes. "I can't come to your house looking like this. I'm sorry, I look so—"

"It doesn't matter one bit." Rising off the stool and laying several dollars on the counter, he put his hand on Aaron's shoulder. "I got an idea. Let's go." Aaron had no choice but to follow, since his bag was in his car. On the way out the door, Sergeant nodded to Aaron and said, "Hey I remember you had a kid too?"

"Yeah." Aaron swallowed hard. "Richard."

Shaking his head, Sarge grinned, "The hell you say."

Fifteen minutes later, Sarge checked Aaron into a nearby motel. "You get yourself cleaned up. Do some laundry. I'll pick you up at ten tomorrow morning." Handing him a ten-dollar bill, in his best commanding voice, "Take this. Be right here at ten tomorrow."

Aaron had never stayed in a motel. There was a bed, dented in the middle, covered by a tattered, red bedspread, adorned with bright orange steering-wheel-sized flowers, near a chest of drawers. He headed to the small bathroom with a small, white tub, a used, miniature bar of soap and two thin, white towels to clean up.

After he showered and shaved, washed his clothes, and sewed his pants with a borrowed needle and thread from the motel office, he fell asleep. Flashing lights on his closed window drapes and loud music woke him. *Dancing* and *Cocktails*. A crowd of people could be friends or enemies, nowadays, but he needed something to drink. When he entered, he settled on a bar stool at the far end of a long, sticky bar top, backed by a long, well-lit mirror fronted by shelves of hard liquor. As the night wore on, the smoke became so thick he couldn't see to the other side of the room. From his perch, he watched men dancing with their women, a few women with women, and listened to loud voices trying to talk above the jukebox. This bar was nothing like the beer halls in Germany, large cavernous buildings stuffed with American soldiers. This low, crowded, dark-ceiling, windowless bar was loud and smoky. The jukebox took nickels continuously, one after the other. There were even fights over who got to plug the machine next. It didn't take long to realize this was the America's Sweetheart bar. The Teresa Brewer song "Music, Music, Music" got nickeled six times in a row.

Put another nickel in In the nickelodeon
All I want is loving you and music, music, music . . .

In between, there were a couple of popular Doris Day slow dance songs, then a lively "Buttons and Bows." Then back to Teresa Brewer. Aaron stayed to himself. He avoided his reflection in the mirror and the patrons. Mostly he stared at his beer or the bottom of his glass. He had the fleeting feeling that he would belong here, all cleaned up, except for the mechanic shirt with Earl stitched above the pocket. He had meant to toss it out in favor of his backup, but somehow when he was following Three Fingers' packing directions, he had lost a few things.

He still had trouble believing Sarge was alive and a high school football coach. He had life made. *Funny how things worked out,* he thought.

It was well after midnight when he left. The crowd had thinned. Directly in the path to walk back to his room was a group of men leaning against the fender of a Chevy Coupe, bottles of beer in hand. They stopped talking as he neared them. He could feel their stares. One of the guys was larger than the others. There was a hint of recognition, but he dared not look closer.

When he drew even with them, the larger man blocked his path. Aaron recognized him from the other day by the Chevy emblem on his shirt. He was missing a front tooth, and his large flat nose reminded Aaron of the big Swede boxer in boot camp. The flashing neon sign behind him reflected in Aaron's bloodshot eyes. The man standing next to him was as round as he was short. The third man was zipper thin. He stayed in the big man's shadow.

The Chevy man stepped forward and poked Aaron in the chest. "What do you think we have here? I'll tell you. We got Earl. I know you, Earl." Turning to his audience, "You know what Earl is? He's a hobo, a bonafida hobo." Poking Aaron in the chest again, he growled, "You know how we feel about hobos in this town."

Next, the fat man stepped forward and pushed Aaron back. "You know there's a bounty on hobos in this town." Tilting his head and looking up at the big man, laughing. "What is it, we cut off an ear and take it in, and they give us a reward, right?"

The three accomplices joined in the laughter.

"So, Earl, you don't listen very well. Where you from? They all stupid there?"

Aaron turned and walked away, hoping they wouldn't follow or that he could break outside the circle and run off.

The fat man cut him off, "Gotta be from somewhere. Everybody is. Even bums like you." Pointing to the thin man, he said, "He's even from somewhere."

Aaron turned and began to walk away again. "Iowa. I'm from Iowa."

"Hey, a farm boy. Soo-ie, soo-ie, soo-ie! Is that how you talk? You a hog farmer?"

Aaron heard the rustle of footsteps behind him. On his right he saw a flash, then the thin man's fist struck him in the side of the face and knocked him nearly flat. As he tried to straighten, the fat guy punched him in the face and knocked him to the ground. Aaron rose to his knees. His right eye was closing and filling with blood.

The thin man cheered him on. "Whoa, Jimbo, you got him good." Aaron could see the thin man's fist coming toward him, but was helpless to avoid it. It hit him squarely in the face and knocked him backward to the ground.

"Guess you want to stick around after all," the thin man said.

The fat one kicked him in the ribs, then again, forcing a blast of air from his lungs.

"Hey, he got any money?" the fat man said.

Before Aaron could roll over to guard the front pocket that held all his money, the thin man kicked him in the stomach as casually as kicking a ball. The Chevy man was next. His kick landed on the side of his face, splitting open a wide gash in his check.

Clinging to consciousness, he felt hands trying to dig into his pocket, then another kick to the head. There was laughter, then everything went black. And silent.

* * *

Where was he? What day was it? What did it matter? Lately, Aaron never knew what day it was anyway. He'd lost track of war days too—marching, taking cover, digging foxholes, sentry duty, more marching, fighting. Never knew a day of the week. The last few days were like that, merely hours on a faceless clock. When he was young and asked Bat'ko what day it was, Bat'ko always answered, "What does it matter, you only have todays."

No dreams. No nightmares. Just a black hole—nothing to remember. Nothing to forget. Climbing out of the blackness was like the dawning of a new day on a cloud-covered winter morning, the edges of life first, then faint voices in the distance. He saw he was surrounded by a white curtain. He remembered riding on a train. Three Fingers. The smoky campfire. He saw Sarge. Was that real? I am supposed to meet him. Aaron's body jerked.

The voices behind the curtain were louder. There was an antiseptic smell. His head began to roar. Breathing was difficult and painful. Suddenly, he was aware of another person beside him, a smiling face, fuzzy at first, then slowly coming into focus. She was wearing a white hat. A nurse. He was in a hospital. The voices outside the curtain began to sharpen. His gaze drifted to his left toward his duffle bag, his shirt and pants draped over it.

The face beneath the white hat moved closer and stopped at the edge of the bed. She reached out and rested her hand on his shoulder. Her auburn curls and amber eyes were suddenly familiar. He gasped. "Mary! Oh, my God, Mary."

In a soothing voice, the nurse asked, "Hey there, John Doe, you got another name?"

Slowly the nurse's face came into sharp focus. "Aaron."

"I'm Dorothy." Her face was round, her cheeks sunburned, her lips full. She was wearing bright lipstick on a smile as genuine as sunrise and with as much promise. She placed her hand on his. "You know how you got here?"

Aaron's blank expression answered her question. "The police brought you in."

"Did I do something wrong?"

"Besides being a punching bag for a bunch of hooligans, not that I know of."

"I'm supposed to meet someone. He's picking me up." Grimacing, he leaned up on one elbow, then collapsed back into bed. "My Sergeant." Breathing in was as painful as breathing out. Even his soft-spoken words poked at him like knives. "Is it ten yet?' He tried to rise again.

Easing him back into the bed, the nurse asked, "What day are you supposed to meet him?"

"It's Saturday. Right?"

Smiling, the nurse placed her hand on his shoulder again. "No, it's Monday. You lost a couple of days."

"You aren't going anywhere yet. I'll call him for you." Aaron closed his eyes in resignation. "No."

"Let me call your friend for you."

Without opening his eyes, he answered again, "No."

"Doctor says the police want to know when you can be released."

Aaron knew the police wouldn't be friendly. He could end up in jail. "When is that?"

"I'm not sure. When you can walk, I guess. Tomorrow maybe." She gestured to his duffle. "You're an Army guy, right? You did good for us." She winked. "If I hear when they're coming, I'll let you know."

17

LOOKING OVER HIS shoulder all the way down the highway, Aaron felt like a hunted man. If luck was with him, the fastest way out of town was hitchhiking. The nurse had warned him before breakfast that the police were coming, so he was hungry, but he figured that was better than being full and in jail.

The duffle at his feet was a beacon to the Army veteran whom he caught a ride with almost immediately. He still hadn't seen the Chesapeake Bay, but he felt its breeze on his face. Maybe he'd get there after all.

The driver, a carrot-top string bean in a gray suit, jumped out of the car and reached out his hand. Aaron shook it awkwardly. "How far you going? I'm only going to Washington D.C."

With a wave of his hand and a shrug of his shoulder, Aaron pointed south. "As far as you can take me."

Carrot Top hesitated and steadied his gaze on Aaron's face. He could see Aaron had been in a fight. One look at his duffle, though, told another story. "I was with the 101st," Carrot Top said. Before Aaron could respond he threw the bag into the back of his truck. Good luck for Aaron, being picked up so quickly, but bad luck for his cracked ribs. The front seat of the brand-new Hawthorne-green 1950 Ford pickup was loaded down with newspaper bundles, so he had to ride in the back.

When the truck pulled away, the sun was slanting directly into his eyes. It was another hot and humid day, and the breeze in the back of the truck was welcome. He shifted side to side to find a comfortable position, grasping the side to steady himself, coughing over the bumps.

Decisions Aaron made while recovering in the hospital bounced around in the back of the truck with him. Seeing Sarge had lifted him up, ever so slightly. Sarge had helped him weave his way through hell. Maybe he could have helped him now, but he couldn't go see him looking like he did. He had to put that all behind him. Then there was Mary. He made it out of hell into her loving arms, and she got a drunk in return for her prayers. A street bum.

He'd thought about calling Mary the minute he'd come to in the hospital, for the millionth time. His resistance had been strong until now. He needed her to know. The events of the last two days had clarified things. He would call while he had the conviction. Perhaps if they talked again, things would be clear for both of them.

Carrot Top dropped him off on the northern edge of the district, at a gas station in Hyattsville, Maryland. Aaron gingerly climbed down from the back of the pickup and gained his balance, nauseous from not eating all day and the seesaw ride in the truck. As it drove away up Main Street, Aaron surveyed the town. In front of him was a small one-room gas station, barely a shack, large enough for two or three people and a single, rusty Texaco gas pump. Inside, he could see an old man resting his elbow on the counter. At the edge of the cracked asphalt was a phone booth.

Across the street was a landmark, ivy-covered, brick, two- story building that had been there longer than the town, a stop for highwaymen, soldiers, and area farmers, and probably once a way station for drinking ale and pre-revolutionary debates. The faded, dirty *Roadway Tavern* sign blew cockeyed in wait of a gusty wind. The second floor was abandoned, storage now, once sleeping rooms. As he looked back, the truck taillights disappeared.

He squinted to read the directions on the front of the black phone in dimming daylight, then deposited his nickel and pulled the 0 all the way back over the top of the rotary dial and released it. He swallowed hard, firm in his resolve that he was never going home again. He'd never see Mary again. But they had to talk. He instructed the operator he wanted to call Saylor, Iowa.

The operator responded in a pleasant voice, "Wait, please, I'll connect you with a long-distance operator."

As he listened to the various operators his call passed through, he could hear each breath, in and out, and feel his heart beating against his chest, "Pittsburgh operator," "Columbus, operator," then Indiana, Illinois, and finally Iowa. The Des Moines operator was the last voice to be heard, "Please deposit 50 cents for three minutes."

He didn't know what to expect. It didn't matter. Maybe she would be glad to hear from him. Maybe she would be mad. She would know it was him–she would know. But when she answered, she was just quiet. She didn't even say hello. He could hear Ricky playing in the background. Then she said, "Your mom died." His heart sank.

Aaron began to tremble. Had he heard her correctly? Maty was dead. *I should have been there.* "Mary. My maty?"

"She got pneumonia. She died Saturday night. I went to see your father. He left me standing there and went to the barn. He refuses to talk to anyone. Said he'd bury her."

That was Bat'ko, for sure. If Aaron had been there, he still would have waved his hand and walked away.

Before Aaron could talk, she asked, "When are you coming home?"

Was that relief in her voice? Forgiveness? Tears began to stream from his eyes. He swallowed hard, trying to hold them back, refusing to let her hear him crying. His voice cracked. "I want to. I'm so scared." Hearing his own words surprised him. This was not why he called. Not the commitment he made lying in the hospital and bouncing around in the back of the truck. "But that's not why I called."

"Where are you? Are you okay? Aaron, talk to me."

Wasn't that just like her? Even now, through long distance wires, she knew he wasn't okay. Damn her. *Hate me. Be mad at me. Please don't care. Torture me.* "Mary. No. I'm far away, too far to come home. I wanted you to know. To not hold out hope. I can't come home. Do you hear me? Never. Never, never! You must understand that."

She began to cry. "I don't believe you. You will come home. I know you. I know who we are. I know you feel lost right now. But I'm still so lucky to have you. The Lucky One. Remember?"

The voice of the operator interrupted. "Please deposit 50 cents." "Mary, I haven't got any more quarters," he lied. "I'm hanging up now. I love you with all my heart. You're a good woman. So much more . . . I can never come home. Please believe me."

"Aaron, I love—" The line went dead.

* * *

It was dark now. A single, ensconced light illuminated the *Roadway Tavern* sign across the roadway. When he entered, he took a seat at a back table. When the tavern closed at midnight, he was still its only customer. The bartender politely but coldly asked him to leave.

Aaron didn't go far. Across the street, the interior gas station lights were off. Only a single yellow light bulb lit up the gas station entrance. Crossing the sharp edge of the light into the dark yard of the station, he found two abandoned cars beneath a chestnut oak as wide as either one of the cars was long, with only a few remaining leaves clinging to sturdy branches shooting out from tangled trunks of several trees that had grown together.

Climbing in the back seat of a rusty '35 Pontiac, he pushed his duffle bag against the door and pulled a stiff, oily canvas tarp over him. Sleep was hard coming. *I wish I had stayed on the farm. Could I have done that?* The Army recruiter had said as much. If only wishes could turn back the clock. Maybe Maty would be alive.

The conversation with Mary hadn't gone the way he wanted. He wanted her to understand. He could never come home. It still weighed on him that he wasn't able to meet Sarge, even though there was no way he'd show up this way. He wanted his respect. He knew when he woke up in the hospital he could never earn that.

Finally, when his eyes went glassy and were peeking out of mere slits, he was jolted by the vision of the cold blue Aryan eyes of the German soldier holding the knife. Opening his eyes wide, he fought back, trying to stay awake and shift his thoughts away, but was unable to find a comfortable memory. In the war, Mary's smile had been a safe harbor he tried to call on, but now he had to push that aside. He pushed aside an image of Ricky on the floor flaying his arms, smiling up at him. He couldn't think about them. Maty was dead. He had nothing but a few dollars in his pocket and whatever he carried in his pack. In spite of what Vicar said, "Out here and everywhere, it's just you and God," he wondered where God was, and whose God would hear his prayers.

Now, as weariness was throwing punches he couldn't duck, he could no longer keep his eyelids from closing. He braced himself for steely blue eyes of the German death's-head soldier on the other side. But it wasn't the blue eyes that took control. He was jolted awake by the sound of Mary's voice. From a distance, he heard Mary's voice calling out his name. He could see the phone booth and the phone dangling down on the end of the line.

"Mary, hang up. You've got to hang up," Aaron called out, "Aaron, I'll never hang up!" she cried out.

"No, hang up. You must hang up."

He heard the rustle of footsteps and saw a beam of light bouncing in the dark from beneath the grimy, oily tarp.

A beam of light began searching the car interior. "Hey there. You get out of there."

Aaron kept his head buried. "You. Out."

Aaron pulled the tarp back and turned his face toward the light, and raised his hand to shield his eyes.

Aaron made a ghoulish picture: two black eyes, black stitches over one eye and on his cheek. Startled, like he was staring at death himself, the gas station owner took a step back. Gathering himself, the man shouted out, "Who do you think you are? You bum, get out of here. This is my property." As Aaron crawled out of the car, the man shoved him hard.

Aaron stumbled and fell to his knees, rose up, and began to walk away, turning his face from the light.

Throughout the night and the next morning, Aaron walked, until he found the Washington D.C. Salvation Army. He ate his first meal in two days and slept for two. He found a nearby liquor store, bought a bottle of whiskey, and spent a day and a night in a nearby park. There began an exhausting cycle, two days of binging and two days at the mission.

When he ran out of money, the Salvation Army found him a job washing dishes at the Commodore Hotel, a block from the Capitol. Every day but Sunday, he arrived at the back door and left the same way, and was allowed one meal. He was warned to never leave the kitchen area.

Aaron settled into a routine. He was able to earn enough for a weekly one-room rental, a mile and a half from his job, and two miles from the Sally. His one-room apartment had a cook stove, a twin bed, and a bathroom down the hall. It was a place to sleep when he wasn't sleeping in the park and a place to drink when he wasn't sneaking brain Novocain out of a paper bag. He felt pardoned by day and pursued by the hangman at night.

At the end of one day like all the rest, after finishing the dinner crowd dishes, he took the day's garbage out to the alley. This was his first relief after two hours of non-stop flurry. Even the pungent alley and the strong night breeze were welcome relief from the hot kitchen. The front page of the morning edition of the *Washington Star* drifted out of the dumpster, wriggled around at his feet, and wrapped around his leg. He shook it free and watched it twirl and paste itself against the wall. He picked it up and began to toss it in the dumpster.

A teaser headline announced a sports page story on the game Sunday between the Washington Redskins football team and the Chicago Cardinals. Below it was a picture of a man who was in town to give a speech. He looked vaguely familiar.

War Hero to Speak

Bernhard Klaus will be speaking at the Shoreham Hotel Saturday, September 24, 1949, before the annual conference of the Jewish Holocaust Alliance.

Aaron studied the picture.

Klaus was a member of the French resistance and is credited with rescuing thousands of Jews from Nazi Death Camps. He is an original signer of the Israeli declaration of independence and a member of the Knesset, the new legislative body of Israel, that proclaimed a state on 14 May 1948. He has been the recipient of numerous awards, including the French Croix de Guerre.

Aaron folded the paper and put it in his pocket and carried it with him to work the next day. He had agreed to sub for a co-worker at the Saturday morning breakfast, which would allow him to go to the Holocaust Alliance meeting that afternoon.

Days were still hot and humid, but the nights were cooler. The trees were showing the first signs of fall. As he made his way up Massachusetts Avenue through the downtown area, he saw his reflection in the shop windows. Barely recognizable to himself, Aaron saw the image of someone else, a man blighted by war and regret.

The conference was at the Shoreham Hotel, an old landmark, a three-and-a-half-mile trek up Massachusetts Avenue, past the Carnegie Library, the Daniel Webster Statue, around DuPont Circle, and through a familiar footpath, shortcut through Rock Creek Park. Flashes of memory jolted his nerves like exploding night-sky fireworks, unfolding brilliantly before they fizzled out and floated back to earth. Always at his side, each step along the way was filled with memories—the German soldier boy staring at him, Purdy's crooked yellow teeth smile, another boy dead at his feet, a tall knife protruding from Sarge's chest, Fritz and Tony fishing, the weight of the mysterious blue-eyed German and his knife at Aaron's chest. With each step, he could feel the Zippo lighter nudging him along. *Could it be the same man? What will I say?*

So intent on catching a glimpse of the man of his nightmares, Aaron forgot about hotel security. When he passed the hall where Klaus was supposed to be speaking, he caught his first glimpse of the man he came to see. There were a few men standing at the open double doors blocking his view. Shifting back and forth, in between heads, he finally got his first good look. *It's him.*

Standing at the lectern, the man of his nightmares was wearing round wire glasses, a gray, tweed sports coat, a white shirt and muted black tie. He wore a skullcap, too, and spoke quietly but very clearly in a thick accent. If Klaus was a French resistance fighter, why did he speak German and why had he worn a German uniform? Now he could pass for a New Yorker. The room was holding its breath in rapt attention.

Aaron felt exposed standing at the entrance. If hotel security saw him, he was sure to be thrown out, maybe even jailed. He noticed an open double swinging door on the far side of the ballroom, and catering staff kept flipping through or lingered as if waiting for the meeting to end so they could sweep in and clear the tables. Aaron backed away and slipped down a side hallway. His black pants and white shirt blended in with the service employees, including the stains from work.

"So, we have a country and a constitution, and we are even recognized by the United Nations, but not without a battle, a foreshadowing of the years ahead. The war will go on in an ever- changing world. Evil has only gone into hiding, the devil waiting for a new day. The war days ahead are not about land. Down through the ages, powerful people, who have been willing to do the devil's work, have wanted to wipe Jews off the face of the earth. Until mothers love their sons as much as they hate us, the war will go on.

"Friends have become enemies, and sometimes enemies have become friends. The United Kingdom has chosen to be our enemy. America has become our friend. Because we are surrounded by people who want to kill us, America's friendship is vital. We will have to fight to the last person."

Applause erupted, and people rose to their feet. Pausing. Smiling. Bernhard surveyed the room. Before continuing, he looked off to the side toward where Aaron was standing, and their gazes locked momentarily, one a glint of fleeting recognition and the other knowing a face he had seen so many times in his mind. It was as if a sudden breeze brushed the side of Bernhard's face.

"Thank you, America. I've been getting a lot of recognition lately for my part in the Nazi resistance movement. I'm sure glad I didn't get that sort of publicity five years ago." A smattering of polite snickers caused him to pause.

Bernhard continued, "People like me, and there are many, aren't the heroes. No one who has ever stood in my shoes felt like a hero. Often, we did things because we had no choice. Those whose choices turned out badly, those were the real heroes.

"Every day my own hero reminds me of what we are still fighting for. My hero is the woman I love, my wife. The woman who made a choice and sacrificed so much. In 1943, the Nazis gave my wife Lulu a choice to divorce me, to disavow me. You see, Lulu is not Jewish. She made her choice and was sent to a concentration camp in Czechoslovakia. When I heard this, I pledged with my life to rescue her. My help came from a surprising source, my friend Albert Goering." Bernhard paused and let the elongated hush fill the room until uncomfortable coughs broke the silence. "Most people recognize the name Goering as the devil's, and it is true, Hermann Goering inflicted the most horrific atrocities on humanity the world has ever known. Hermann Goering was the second in command to Adolph Hitler. But his brother Albert was a fierce opponent of the Nazis and dedicated himself to saving lives, Jewish lives. He was one of my contacts in Germany. Few men held as much hatred for what the Nazis stood for as did Albert. He is credited with rescuing thousands of Jews from death camps.

"Using the evil name to his advantage, he intimidated the death camp Obefuhrer into releasing hundreds of prisoners, including my wife. Until we reunited in France, I never knew she had been tortured and blinded." Bernhard hesitated and took a deep breath, and clenched his jaw, mustering the courage to finish. The audience leaned forward in their seats. Softly, he continued. "My inspiration now lives with me in Tel Aviv.

"On this special day of special days, Rosh Hashanah, our year of 5710, it is a time to renew our commitment to the Jewish state of Israel. For centuries, we have been persecuted and attempts made to wipe us off the face of the earth. Without Israel, we will not exist. We will be lost. Assimilated. Our customs lost. We must never let that happen. We have our own county. The world owes us that. Someday we will be a nation of Sabras, everyone an Israeli born.

"New Year's Day is also a time for personal commitment and renewal for each of us. This is a day we look into our own hearts. Lulu reminds me every day to not let the tragedies that befall us keep us from our God, from being what He wants us to be, and to do. She tells me, if you lived through a death camp, you know what it is like to be alive and to have purpose. She reminds me to ask you, how are your life tragedies affecting you? Was your tragedy living in a death camp, death and cruelty at your shoulder? Were your eyes put out?"

Aaron was transfixed. Once again, he was in the grip of a stranger who had held his life in his hands and once again he was powerless. Out of the corner of his eyes, he noticed a man in a black suit and black tie staring at him. He moved up beside Aaron and stood there like a shadow. He must have been hotel security, but Aaron ignored him and continued to focus on Bernhard Klaus, by the man of his nightmares. *Don't kick me out, not now. Please not now.*

Aaron turned slowly and looked at the man. Aaron's eyes were moist and burning. An unblinking standoff froze the moment, the entreated facing his inquisitor, hoping for a few precious moments with a man who once held his life at the point of a honed black carbon commando knife, who even now a few feet away had him tight in his grasp. With the feeling that he was interrupting a man in prayer, the hotel security officer blinked and his eyes softened in a heartfelt, mysterious moment.

Aaron looked back to Bernhard. "We all live with the sadness for the so many that were lost, who we keep alive in our memories. Daily we make choices, the choice to be thankful for all the blessings of our lives, or the choice to let ourselves be consumed by tragedies, and always, we must make the choice to never let this horror happen again. Lulu could have let her blindness lock away all the horrors to poison her, but instead every day she adorns our house with flowers she can't even see. So I bid you L'shanah tovah. Remember Israel in your prayers."

Aaron watched as the meeting concluded and attendees began to exit. Several men, mostly blacks, set about to clear the meeting room tables, moving back and forth, balancing large trays of stacked dirty dishes, twirling around each other like ballerinas. Careful not to get in their way, he eased beside the double doors and leaned against the wall and watched.

Bernhard was standing in front of the room, surrounded by three men wearing skullcaps with tassels under their black jackets. They reverently offered handshakes and appreciations, speaking quietly with great emotion. "My father and mother died in one of those camps. Bless you." At times they engaged in heated conversations as Bernhard listened intently.

Aaron looked on, studying the man who had spared his life. When he last saw him, he was wearing a German uniform. Now his blue eyes looked over a well-trimmed blond beard. He still had the build of a footballer, but his shoulders were rounded now.

The room thinned out until only a few remained in small clusters in the back of the room. The one man who was hanging on to Bernhard twice began to leave, only to turn back for one final comment. Aaron moved closer and stood an arm's length away, close enough to be noticed but not so close as to interrupt. When Bernhard was finally alone, urgency gripped Aaron, and he stepped up to him.

"Excuse me. You don't remember me?"

Bernhard lowered his eyebrows and peered out over the top of his spectacles.

Aaron's slumped. He had a pained expression, like a beaten child bracing for another whack.

"I'm sorry. Perhaps I should. My mind draws a blank. I always worry when I meet someone it is a face I am supposed to forget."

"My memory is good. Very good." Aaron pulled open his shirt to reveal a long scar on his neck. "I'll always have this to jog my memory. I could show you the scar on my chest too."

Bernhard was momentarily speechless. Then with a glint in his eye, he shook his head a little. "No, I don't. But this scar, maybe it is a blessing. You are alive, no? My reminder is Lulu. Did you hear me talk about her? My great blessing."

"You spared my life."

"So I should remember, huh? You're an American?"

"I was in the Army. It was somewhere near Kitchleimbolanden. We were in a farmhouse."

Bernhard raised his eyebrows in a spark of recognition; the picture was slowly coming into focus. "Yes. I remember. You made it." Aaron's voice cracked unexpectedly. "We fought there, and you gained the upper hand, but you didn't kill me." Shifting from side to side, he felt his heart began to race.

"You were the soldier. Yes, I remember."

Aaron held his hand out. "You left this behind."

Bernhard instantly recognized it and plucked the Zippo lighter from his hand, like he was picking up a baby bird. "I always wondered where I lost it." Turning it over in his hand, he rubbed the engraved words lovingly. "I always carried it. Then it was lost, and a small piece of Lulu had slipped away. I worried that perhaps it was an omen. I lost it right before she was rescued from the death camp."

"Is she here?" Aaron asked.

Bernhard shook his head and twisted his mouth. "She doesn't travel very well."

Both men paused, searching for words.

"Yes... I was . . ." Bernhard looked off to the side, searching his memory. When he looked back to Aaron, his blue eyes were filled with sad determination. "You were with a soldier. There was no way out of the house. It was unavoidable," Bernhard said. Snapping his fingers, "He would have killed me just like that."

"Yes, for sure he would have. He was no friend of mine. No friend of anyone's. He was an evil man. He hated Jews. He hated everybody. Purdy. His name was Purdy." A slight smile crept into the corner of his mouth. "My sergeant thought I killed him."

With a shrug of his shoulders, Bernhard said, *"C'est la guerre,* I guess. The French have a better way of saying some things, don't you think? The way of war." Suddenly, his face lit up. "Will you have dinner with me?"

Aaron searched for a response. "I am not very . . . I don't go to restaurants very often."

Bernhard had noticed that Aaron was thin, his hollowed-out cheeks reminded him a little of refugees from the war. He saw his clothes were stained. Smiling, he took Aaron's arm.

"I'm starved, and it looks like you could stand a good meal. Please have dinner with me?" He could tell Aaron was agreeable, "Meet me at eight. I will buy you a good Italian meal. Angelo's is but a few blocks from here," pointing off to the south, over to P street South on and 15th. "We will drink wine. Drink to our survival, hey?"

* * *

While Bernhard was in his room cleaning up for dinner, Aaron went to Rock Creek Park to wait, under the Lazan's Legion Bridge, a place familiar to him. The last time he sat in this very spot it was with a bottle. Now there was no bottle to comfort him, just thoughts of Bernhard and this strange surprise.

Bernhard was a different person than the one he battled in his head, sporting a tweed sport coat and a skullcap, not the gray German field uniform with the death's-head patch. In his nightmares, the image was of a ruthless killer, his executioner's blue eyes staring down at him. Bernhard of *Kitchleimbolanden* was a man who could singlehandedly wipe out a platoon of soldiers, who welcomed a hand-to-hand fight as an Olympic fighter would. All for Hitler, the evilest man ever. What was the truth? The hand-to-hand combat was real. Killing Purdy was real.

Aaron could still feel the knife point piercing his skin. Still, there was the scar. The man of his nightmares seemed more real than this Bernhard with the warm blue eyes and smile, the man who greeted him with a handshake.

Aaron could see ahead there was a small grocery and next to it Angelo's Restaurant. There he was, standing outside waiting for him. As he approached the man in the tweed sport coat his mind raced with conflicting thoughts. When he arrived, without hesitation, Bernhard reached out and wrapped his arms around him in a bear hug, like a long-lost friend. "I am so glad you made it."

When they entered the dark restaurant, they were greeted by a diminutive man with the puffy, red cheeks of a trumpeter, wearing a shiny blank waist jacket. "Bernhard." Angelo greeted him loudly with a broad smile. "I have been waiting for you. I have your special table in the back." They were seated at a private table, simply draped with a white linen. A candle in the center cast dancing shadowy patterns off the walls.

Angelo pulled the chair out for Aaron and they were seated. Quickly he swept away a carafe of red wine and returned shortly with a bottle of Chianti Classico. "For you, my best wine."

When Angelo rushed off to the kitchen for bread, Bernhard said, "I know this place is not kosher. When I come to Angelo's, I am a bad Jew. I like it here, though, because here I'm not famous." Rubbing his stomach, he added, "And the food."

Suddenly a woman burst out of the kitchen, wiping her hands on a marinara-stained apron, which could have been mistaken for a butcher's. She was the female version of Angelo, the same height, red-faced, round, and full bosomed. "Bernhard," she bellowed out, smiling broadly, and wrapping her arms around him, kissing both cheeks. "You are our most famous customer."

Bernhard put his fingers to his lips. "Shhh. I am not famous. I am only a most privileged guest." Looking over to Aaron, he rolled his eyes.

"I have a special just for you. I know you like my veal. I have been preparing it all day just for you. I will serve it, but there is a delay. Let me bring you a plate of my fettuccini alfredo. You will like that. Then the veal."

"Of course, Maria. I love all of your cooking." Angelo appeared beside her beaming. "This is my friend Aaron. We were in the war together." Bernhard winked at Aaron. "And Sophia? She is a woman now?"

Angelo's expression turned into frown. "Ha. Of course, she thinks she's a woman. And she has a boyfriend." Shaking his head. "He thinks he is a man. Today's youth, they know it all. They don't know anything."

Bernhard held his glass up to Angelo in thanks and then toward Aaron in a toast. Aaron lifted his glass, "L'Chaim." Aaron clinked his glass with Bernhard, but instead of taking a drink, he paused, studied it, and set it on the table.

"You live in Israel?" Aaron asked.

"After the war, I had no home to go to. Like so many other Jews. Our homes, our possessions all destroyed or stolen. So we turned to Palestine, refugees lost to the winds of war and homeless for thousands of years, seeking a new home. Now we are a country, and in twenty years, we will be a country of sabras. I come here often to beg for money. I am a beggar now for my nation. We have many needs."

Bernhard closed his eyes as if he was watching a video history of Jewish expulsions, genocides. "Maybe the world finds peace only when the people in our part of the world find peace. Not until then. When we have found humanity's soul, when politicians are not as important as people, when people are in charge of politicians, not the other way around. When people are not led like cows. We have a saying, 'We will have peace when mothers love their sons more than the hate.'"

Aaron reflected on what he said. *Here is a man who has more courage than a hundred men, yet he calls himself a beggar. A man who was never afraid of the dark, could spot evil and stare it down. What is wrong with me?*

"You are famous. I saw the article." Aaron pulled the wrinkled article out of his pocket and showed him. "I thought, all these years, you were a German soldier."

Bernhard brushed it aside with a wave of his hand. *Bat'ko does that.* Smiling, he responded. "Me, a German soldier. Oh, for sure, there were Jewish German soldiers, yes. Not me. I was in the French resistance. I was raised in a little town, Saint-Avold, fifteen miles southwest of the German border. *Mon père* was a beet farmer. *Mère* was French and Père German.

"I had three brothers." Bernhard, up to now, had been brimming with joy, but for the first time, he grew serious. "They all died in the war. All were resistance fighters. Two were captured and killed. I don't know what happened. Maybe a pistol shot to the head. My youngest brother died right after the war ended. It was as if he was awaiting the end of the war so that death could put him out of his misery. If you aren't killed with a bullet, sometimes your own kind of bullets kill you."

Bernhard had seen enough death, but Aaron could tell his story was more than about death as he continued. "There is more to be afraid of now. The war is just beginning. No Hitler, but the whole world wants to control us. Now I fight for the future, the forever future of Israel. While the devil may have slipped away, he is regrouping and on the prowl for new hearts to infect. More Hitlers. Then it starts again. And the world cannot be counted on to rescue us again. The price is steep."

Just as quickly as his smile drifted off into the flickering candlelight, he sat up in his chair and with a wave of his hand he changed the subject. "Where are you from?"

"Iowa. A small town in Iowa."

"Yes, I know Iowa. Corn. Pigs and cows, yes?" Aaron nodded.

"We need farmers in Israel. Farmers are turning the desert into crops and have planted trees. Turned the desert from brown to green trees and grass. If you come, you may never want to leave. You will live under constant threat, yes, but Israel will creep inside your very soul. It will start as just a nudge and end up a lump in your throat."

"I was a better mechanic than a farmer."

"We need mechanics, too."

Angelo interrupted the conversation when he filled Bernhard's wine glass. He turned to Aaron and could see he hadn't drunk any. "You don't like the wine?" Bernhard could see Aaron was uncomfortable and caught Angelo's gaze and with a nod and a wave Angelo set the bottle down and walked away.

Aaron began to tap his fingers on the table ever so softly. For a minute the air was filled with contemplations and quick glances before Aaron spoke up. "You spared my life. Why?"

"I think I knew you were not my enemy. I could see you were not a killer. You just wanted to live. In the war, I learned there were two kinds of soldiers, the ones who can kill and the ones who can't. You were not a killer."

Aaron stopped tapping his fingers. "Funny, my best friend told me that before the war. He didn't make it."

"Would you have killed me?" Bernhard asked. "Hand to hand is a different kind of killing. Pilots drop bombs on faceless enemies. I'm talking about looking me in the eye and killing me."

"I was fighting for my life."

"No. You would not have. You would have hesitated, and you would be dead."

Aaron's response was detached. "My last thought, with your knife at my chest, was sitting in the car with Mary at Millers Bend. Mary is my wife. Was. It's a special place. I was going to die. I just wanted to see her." Aaron stared out into the dark restaurant. An older man and woman had taken a table not too far from them. Swallowing hard, Aaron continued, "I did kill. He was a boy. I wish—"

"All kills haunt you. It is only the cold-blooded who sleep well." The food arrived, and the men sat quietly, enjoying their meal. All the while Bernhard's words echoed in Aaron's head. *All kills haunt you. Even Bernhard? Cold-blooded killers sleep well?*

For several minutes, knives and forks tinkled against the ceramic plates, cut food, and moved it from plate to mouth. Gazing across the table, Aaron watched as Bernhard cut his veal with the precision of an assassin. There was loud chewing and smacking and groans of satisfaction.

Aaron had never eaten so well, not at home and certainly not in the Army, although when his unit was relieved and moved back to Spa, at the time, he had felt his first hot meal was the best he'd tasted. Here, again, he wished he could keep eating, but quickly he felt bloated, and he had to stop.

He watched Bernhard's delight. He was a man happy to be alive—to still be fighting.

There was nothing to his appearance that suggested he had any remorse about his life. He'd made a choice when the war broke out, or choices were made for him. Nonetheless he accepted his choices and moved forward—unwavering. He didn't appear to be a man who wavered on anything.

Bernhard's chewing slowed. He looked through the flickering candle-light, and said, "You asked me why I didn't kill you, and I know you're still wondering. Here is the answer. I did not kill you because I saw you were Jewish. You were not a killer."

Aaron looked puzzled, setting down his fork.

Bernhard continued, "In that farmhouse, when I saw your tags, I saw you were Jewish. I hesitated. It was in that moment I decided you were not a killer. That is what happened. Then I thought how good it would be to talk to an American. I love Americans."

"Yeah, that is what my tags said." "You are not Jewish?"

"Oh, yes, I'm Jewish. On the night before I left to join in the fight, my maty told me I was Jewish. I never knew until then. I have never been to a synagogue. My friends were Christian, and I had been to their churches. Didn't know what a Jew was. I still don't, really."

"However, this came to be, you are Jewish. Once a Jew, always. It is in our blood."

Aaron continued. "My father was driven out of Ukraine by the Russians. They slaughtered his family and took his brother into the army. He was just a boy."

"That is what we have been fighting for thousands of years. Negroes have been persecuted for 200 years, no? We have been for thousands. Except we can hide because of our skin color. We can say we are Christians, if we are willing to lose who we are as a people."

"Why? What have we done?"

"We have been in the way of ignorance, or they want our land, people trying to exert control for some gain. It's never one thing. It used to be about Jesus, like God versus Jesus. But I say God is God. God of all religions. Does any religion claim their God is better? No, they claim their words are better, their prophets.

"Do you know where your name comes from?" Not waiting for Aaron to respond, Bernhard continued. "It is a good Jewish name. But it is a good Muslim name too. The Quran, the Muslim bible, refers to Aaron as a prophet of God. And a good Christian name. Aaron was the brother of Moses, a high priest and his right hand. It is written that God spoke to Aaron as well as Moses.

"Some would make this a holy war in the name of Jesus or Muhammad. Jesus was a Jew. If he was standing here today, he would say he was a Jew. He would never have denied it. His father was a Jew, his mother Mary was a Jew. A strong woman. They were all Jews. The last supper was a Seder. Men decided Jesus was the savior and Jews didn't think so. So men are always right, no? And they fight over being right.

"Aaron, Israel is not a religious state. We are for home. Others fight for religion. We are Jews with a constitution that says nothing about religion. Just the Rock of Israel."

Bernhard stopped stroking his goatee and eased back in his chair, sighing deeply. "I am passionate, no? But there is a reason! What if you come to Israel and see? You can farm or be a mechanic. We will give you land if you want to farm."

Aaron was staring across the table with his mouth open, still struggling to see Bernhard as a Jew, not a German soldier. Seeing Bernhard was still confusing—hard to get used to. *So he is a Jew, a famous one with a seat in Heaven already picked out. And he talks about a God for all people.*

"My wife is a Christian. Her father is a pastor." "My Lulu is Christian," Bernhard countered.

The conversation stopped awkwardly looking for a new starting place. Bernhard leaned forward in his chair. All night, he had wondered about Aaron. He had thought about him before now, wondered if this good man survived the war when so many were trying to kill him, in so many ways, and so many expecting him to kill his way out of it. Only a special person like that could survive.

And maybe he didn't survive. He noticed the first time he saw him at the hotel he was down on his luck, seemed lost. Every word he spoke seemed apologetic. *Apologetic for what? That he wasn't a killer? That he did kill? That he lived?* A lot of soldiers feel that way. Something had a grip on him. *Why is it that good men like him can suffer more than evil ones? And he, so far from home.*

Bernhard began to stroke his goatee again, as if rubbing his whiskers coaxed the right words over his lips. "Why are you so far from home?"

Aaron should have known the question would be asked. It was as obvious as the stains on his white shirt. He was surprised the questions hadn't come sooner. He knew it was hard to lie to this man. *This man didn't kill me and I think I can fool him?* "I have nightmares about you."

"I have nightmares about me, too." Bernhard tried to lighten the moment. He could see Aaron was struggling with how to answer his question. "Yes, we all have nightmares. I saw things and did things. We all did."

"I'm still back in that farmhouse waiting to die." Aaron felt tears on his face. He looked around trying hard to hold back, but they kept coming. "I wish I had. I wish you had ended it then."

Bernhard's eyes moistened, and the silence between them swelled. The air was stifling.

Aaron began to tap his fingers on the table again. Aaron was used to silence, but in his usual silence, he had only to answer to himself. Silence with Bernhard was frightening, and he couldn't let the silence linger. He needed to fill it. Aaron ever so cautiously stole a furtive glance at the other patrons.

Bernhard stared at Aaron across the flickering candle light. His gaze was steady and steadfast, studying his soul. Since that day in the farmhouse, they had been moving toward this moment, both unaware it was coming. Time was working to arrange this moment, so many obstacles had to be cleared, so many times it seemed impossible, not the merest glint of possibility, each corner that veered off, each wrong road, but fate was ever persistent in wanting this to happen. "I am glad I didn't end your life. There must be a reason why I didn't. A reason that neither of us understands. There I was, prepared to kill you, not a doubt in my mind, and then, as if somebody whispered in my ear, I heard, 'He is not your enemy. He is the enemy of everything wrong in this crazy world.' That thought didn't come from me. Don't you ever wonder where thoughts like that come from?"

"I love my Mary. I don't want to live without her."

"So why are you not with her?"

"In one of my nightmare battles with you, we were in bed, Mary and I, and I almost killed her. I thought she was you. I would rather die than hurt her."

"Of course, you would. As I would Lulu." A slight upturn of Bernhard's mouth hinted at a smile. "So, a man who can't kill is worried about hurting the woman he loves? My friend, I would stake my own life that could never happen. Under any circumstances. You are no killer. Aaron, your war is over. She is safe with you. You couldn't have killed me, so why do you think you could hurt her? You don't think what I saw bothered me? That I have my own nightmares? You don't know how many nights I wept in Lulu's arms. She taught me to let go. It appears you have a choice to make. That is how we live, by making good choices. Let Mary help you."

Aaron had heard that before. "Sarge said that too." Aaron, the boy who couldn't kill, who once did, was suddenly very tired, but not afraid to sleep.

* * *

It was late when they parted, and dark outside the restaurant. When Bernhard said goodbye, there seemed more to it. Reaching out, he pulled Aaron into his arms. "The war is over for you." Nudging him back with a chuckle, he added, "Unless you want to come to Israel."

Aaron wanted to say thank you, but the words tripped over his tongue and ended up being just goodbye. All the while they both wondered if they would ever see each other again.

Aaron made his way back to Massachusetts Avenue. The street was especially quiet. Apartment buildings and stores were dark, leaving only street lights to guide him. In the first two miles, he saw only one person and an occasional car.

On his way home, twice he looked back toward the restaurant to find it was well beyond his sight. Their time had come and gone. Now, ever so slowly, their meeting was slipping into memory until just fragments would survive. Beginnings and endings, most lost, a few you know and never forget. *Will we ever see each other again?* he wondered. *Does life work that way?*

Along the traveled roads, streets and highways, dirt ones and paved ones, side roads and dead ends, two lives intersected in a farmhouse in Kitchleimbolanden, and Aaron spotted a fallen skater and rescued the love of his life. Life changes that fast.

In the distance, a beacon of light caught his eye, just a twinkle, like a lighthouse warning of danger or lighting the way. As the distance closed, the twinkling light grew brighter and more colorful. With all his concentration, he watched it as if it was a guiding star, like the North Star to a wilderness hiker.

A block from the light, he saw it was a flashing neon Gunther Beer sign. He arrived outside the tavern. So easily could his experienced feet have taken him inside. So easily could he have plunked some money on the bar and felt the cold beer in the back of his throat, and the first few minutes of its rescue. But his gaze was drawn to another light on the corner, a telephone booth just a few steps away. Sarge said he had a choice to make. So did Bernhard. Was it as simple as that?

Standing by the phone, as he felt around in his pocket for change, he began to read the instructions. Still searching for change, he flipped open the coin return and ran his fingers around inside. He smiled at his surprise to find a nickel inside. When the operator came on, he asked to make a collect call to Mary Vanko, Des Moines, Iowa. As he listened to the different operators from cities and states between Washington D.C. and Iowa, he thought of their last conversation.

A bead of sweat dripped down from his forehead. His first thought was to hope she was home, but then he worried what he could say. He had been so emphatic that they could never be together. Before the operator could ask if she would accept the charges for a phone call from Aaron Vanko, Aaron blurted out, "Mary."

The operator repeated the question.

Mary hesitated, and Aaron's heart sank. He wouldn't blame her.

After a long pause, Mary answered cautiously, "Yes. Aaron, are you okay?"

"Mary, I'm okay." His heart was racing. "Mary, I met the German. Well, he's really French. The man of my nightmares, he's famous. You know who I'm talking about?"

"I guess so."

"The man who spared my life. Remember my telling you how I couldn't close my eyes without seeing the killer's eyes? He could have killed me with a flick of his wrist, but didn't. Do you know why?"

"Aaron, what is this about?" Mary's voice seemed so close by, but so distant too.

"He didn't kill me, because he was not a killer. He wasn't a German at all. He pretended to be German to save lives. He saved thousands. He says I could never hurt you. He knew that at the time, and he knows that now. I know that now. He's so right. I could never hurt you. Not ever. I know that now."

The phone went silent. At first he wondered if she was still on the phone. His heart sank.

"Mary, can I come home?"

Aaron held his breath. The silence was worse than words. Mary began to cry.

"Mary, will you still have me?"

His journey had finally arrived at this moment. *How did this all happen? Bernhard said, "There must have been a reason why I didn't kill you. A reason that neither of us understands."* The seed Bernhard planted was growing into a tree. Destiny had conspired to bring Aaron to this moment. Are humans ever supposed to see the conspiracy that shapes their lives? Along the way, fate enlisted the help of accomplices to keep him safe and on the path—Shorty the scowling bartender, the friendly Norwegian who knew about Sarge, Three Fingers, the wise Vicar, and the carrot-topped man who delivered him to Washington. The Chevy mechanic wasn't supposed to be there, but Dorothy the hospital angel put him back on his path. And there was the wayward wind that wrapped the newspaper trash article about Bernhard around his feet.

"Aaron." She sniffled and cleared her throat. "I've been down on my knees praying for you. For us. I always knew you would come back. Of course. It's the answer to my prayers. "I always told you how lucky I was to have you as my husband." Softly fighting back tears, she added, "I told you to always remember I'm the Lucky One and you're Lucky Two."